TRUMP
OF THE
DEAD
A ZOMBIE NOVEL

Author's Note: Despite the navigational locations and highways in this book being real, I've take a few fictional liberties.
So if you want to try and find them, use GPS, not this book as a map.

Trump of the Dead: A Zombie Novel

Copyright © 2021 Anthony Giangregorio

ISBN Softcover ISBN 13: 978-1-61199-103-1
ISBN 10: 1611991-03X

All rights reserved.
No part of this book may be reproduced or transmitted in any form or by any means, electronic or mechanical, including photocopying, recording, or by any information storage and retrieval system, without permission in writing from the copyright owner.

This is a work of fiction. Names, characters, places and incidents either are the product of the author's imagination or are used fictitiously, and any resemblance to any actual persons, living or dead, events, or locales is entirely coincidental.

This book was printed in the United States of America.

A Living Dead Press book

TRUMP OF THE DEAD
A ZOMBIE NOVEL

ANTHONY GIANGREGORIO

OTHER WORKS OF FICTION BY THE AUTHOR

Anthologies Edited by the author

Book of Horror Volumes 1-2   / Headshots: A Zombie Anthology
Dead History: A Zombie Anthology Volumes 1-2
Dead Worlds: Undead Stories Volumes 1-6
Eternal Night: A Vampire Anthology / Book of the Dead Volumes 1-6
Clowns of Terror: An Evil Anthology   / Rat War: A Horror Anthology
Children of the Dead: A Zombie Anthology
Night of the Wolf: A Werewolf Anthology
Twisted Fish: An Aquatic Anthology
Superheroes VS Zombies: A Zombie Anthology
End of Days: An Apocalyptic Anthology Vol 1-5
Earth's End: An Apocalyptic Anthology
Love is Dead: A Zombie Anthology   /   The Book of Cannibals Vol 1-2
Emails of the Dead: A Zombie Anthology
Zombie Erotica: An Undead Anthology About Sex
Tales of Bigfoot   /   The Book of Horror
Tales of the Dead: A Zombie Anthology
Time of Death   /   Monster Party
Mutant Apocalypse   /   Horror Carnival
Zombie Tales (with Vincenzo Bilof)
Zombies and Fairy Tales: A Zombie Anthology
House of Terrors: An Anthology of Fear
An Undead Christmas: A Zombie Anthology
A Very Dead Christmas: A Zombie Anthology
Christmas is Dead: A Zombie Anthology
Christmas is Dead…Again: A Zombie Anthology
Dead Christmas: A Zombie Anthology
Gnomes of the Dead: A Zombie Anthology
Zombie Buffet: A Zombie Anthology
Creature Feature: A Monster Anthology
Just Before Night (w/ Joe Tonzelli) (Prequel to Night of the Living Dead)

Young Adult Anthologies

Ghostly Tales of Terror / Halloween: Tales of Terror

Kids Books and Young Adult

Zombies Are People Too / The Lonely Zombie
Ten Silly Monkeys Jumping on the Bed
Ten Silly Monkeys Jumping on the Bed: Coloring Book
Children of the Void / Zombies Are Cool
The Zombie in the Basement
The Haunted Theatre / The Junkyard
Only the Young Survive: An Apocalyptic Tale

Novels by the Author

Rats / Victory of the Dead: A Zombie Novel
Deadfreeze: A Zombie Novel / Dead End: A Zombie Novel
Adventures of the Cowl: A Superhero Novel
Comedy of the Dead: A Zombie Novel
Dead Mourning: A Zombie Novel
Rise of the Dead: A Zombie Novel
Last Stop / Clan of the Bigfoot
Curse of the Beetle (with Richard Marsh)
Kingdom of the Dead: A Zombie Novel
Sunset of the Dead: A Zombie Novel (Sequel to Day of the Dead film)
The Monster Under the Bed / The Dark
Visions of the Dead: A Zombie Novel (with Joseph Giangregorio)
Human Harvest: Alien Abduction (with Keith Luethke)
Dead Fall: A Zombie Novel / Souleater
Revolution of the Dead: A Zombie Novel
Road Kill: A Zombie Novel / The Bottom of the 9th

Short Story Collections by the Author

Dead Tales: Short Stories to Die For
Christmas of the Dead / Dead Things / Dark Places
Dead Offerings: Collected Work (Hardcover)

Editor

Living Dead Press Presents: Spring & Summer Magazines

Book Series by the Author

The Dead Rage Series

Dead Rage   Book 1
Blood Rage   Book 2

The Warriors of the Apocalypse Series

Warriors of the Apocalypse: Book 1
Warriors of the Apocalypse: Dark Holocaust Book 2

The Deadwater Series Books 1-13

Deadwater   / Deadwater: Expanded Edition
Dead Rain   / Dead City
Dead Wave   / Dead Harvest
Dead Union   / Dead Valley
Dead Town/Homeward Bound
Dead Grave
Dead Salvation / Dead Army
Dead Invasion   / Dead Incursion
Dead Terminal

Opinion

Reviews of the Dead: 25 Zombie Movies to Die For (with Tony Schaab)

Chapter 1

"Mr. President, there's an emergency; you're needed, Sir," the aide said softly as he pushed open the large door to the bedroom within the White House, where President Donald J. Trump, the 45th President of the United States, was sleeping.

The bedroom was completely pitch black, the darkness so thick the aide couldn't see the hand he raised before him, as he slowly stepped inside the room. Slowly, he eased the door open some more. Now at least the wan light from the hallway helped him to see a little better, though it was six a.m in the morning, and all the lights in the White House were still set for night.

Trump stirred in his bed, mumbling something about Fake news. As the aide drew closer to the president, who snored loudly, he leaned over and touched Trump's hand, patting it gently.

The snoring suddenly stopped, but Trump's eyes remained closed. "Melania? Is that you? Is it my birthday again already?" He began lovingly caressing the aide's hand. "That's perfect. I am feeling a little frisky." He puckered his lips and leaned in to kiss the back of the slightly embarrassed aide's hand. This was nothing; he'd seen and experienced far worse working for this president—unfortunately.

"Ah, no, Sir, it's Fred," the aide said quickly, then yanked his hand back like it had been on a chopping block with the cleaver falling. "Melania is in her own bedroom on the other side of the White House."

Trump's eyes popped open and he looked up at Fred, his aide for the past three and a half years in office. Fred was loyal, and so far had been very good about keeping his mouth shut about the goings on in the White House. As Trump's personal aide, the man knew everything about Donald J. Trump.

Too much, Fred would agree, if anyone had ever asked, which they didn't.

"Fred, what's wrong, why are you waking me up? I just got to bed a little while ago, after watching Fox news all night. Those guys love me, you know. Carlson, Hannity and Ingraham, they're my peeps."

"Your 'peeps,' Sir?"

Trump slowly sat up and yawned, then waved his hand dismissively at Fred. "Never mind, something I heard from Kanye." He rubbed his face with the palms of his hands. "So, what do you want?"

"There's been a…well, development with some of the most promising vaccines for Covid-19, Sir. It isn't good."

"Covid, Covid, Covid. I'm so sick of hearing about the damn China virus," Trump whined. "So help me, if this plague causes me to lose a second term. Without it I would have won by a lot, a landslide even but now, it's up in the air." He glared at Fred. "So what's the development? What's the matter?"

Fred didn't respond, but merely stood before his boss.

"Well? Speak goddamn it."

"I think you should wait and be briefed by the Task Force, Sir. They can tell you better than I can."

Trump glared at his aide for another ten seconds, then his shoulders sagged. "Fine. So we're doing this right now?"

"Yes, Sir, in the Situation Room. They're all waiting for you there now."

Trump stood up, wearing nothing but a wife beater t-shirt and boxer shorts, black socks on his feet.

Fred averted his gaze slightly, not too much to be noticed, but some. Seeing Trump in his underwear was almost as bad as seeing him naked, which Fred had had the displeasure of being exposed to multiple times. The president's body was shaped like a wrinkled pear.

Well, if a piece of fruit had arms and legs, that is.

Though the president wore tailored suits that hid a lot of his out-of-shape physique, they still didn't hide it all.

"Will Pence be there?" Trump asked as he slid into a white robe, his favorite one, and a pair of brown leather slippers. He would often wear this ensemble as he roamed the halls of the White House in the early hours of the morning. He didn't sleep much. His brain was always working, you see, trying to come up with his next plan.

Since he was a young man, he'd strived to be in the limelight, to have people talking about him. He always had a scheme to make this so.

One such scheme had netted him the presidency.

That hadn't been planned, however. He had run for president in the hopes of getting his name, his brand, out there more, so people would remember he *was* still out there, in the world. It was to be the biggest ad campaign ever to get him noticed like never before. The greatest commercial ever, his run for political office.

But he hadn't planned on running against Hillary Clinton, someone so disliked it had made his being elected almost a shoe-in. It was like the Democrats had handed him the office of the President of the United States on a silver platter.

Democrats; their incompetence knew no bounds.

Trump had already decided that Republicans were like the jocks at school, who ruled it all with an iron fist, while the Democrats were more like the nerds, taking what scraps they could, and when things didn't go their way, they could sit around and whine and complain till the cows came home.

But they could never do shit about any of it. They had to eat shit served to them on a plate, and shovel in as much as the Republicans wanted to spoon feed them. Not that Trump was a true Republican. He was nothing in his heart, NPA (No Party Affiliation) his allegiance only going to the party that could do more for him. At the moment, that was the Republicans. Hell, in the past he'd even given campaign donations to Democrats.

"Is Mike going to be there?" Trump asked again.

"Yes, Sir, Vice President Pence is already waiting."

"Good old Mike, he's like the dog I never wanted, you know. So loyal and obedient. I swear, Fred, I could tell that man to get on his knees and blow me, and he would drop down and his mouth would pop open like a whore in a back alley who'd gotten a twenty for a ten dollar blowjob."

"Yes, Sir," Fred said. There was nothing more to say, and he never would. Trump was just talking out loud, which was something he often did. Sometimes he did it during a press conference. His boss had the bad habit of saying his inner thoughts out loud.

Trump waddled over to the master bathroom set off to the side of the room, peeing with the door open. He wasn't shy about his bodily functions, or he didn't think enough of Fred to be modest around him.

Fred frowned slightly, but not enough for the president to see, when Trump left the bathroom without washing his hands, or flushing.

He'd heard stories from the maids about the presents they'd found in the bowl, upon cleaning after Trump had been in the bathroom.

"Okay, let's go," Trump said.

"Uh, Sir, aren't you going to change?"

Trump looked at Fred as if he was an idiot. "What the hell for? I'm the fucking president. Who's gonna complain?"

"Yes, Sir."

With Fred leading the way, Trump exited the bedroom, walking through the section of the White House he called home, but only just, and made his way to the Situation Room.

He passed a few Secret Servicemen on the way, the men nodding politely. No masks were worn to protect from the coronavirus, which was rampant throughout the United States and the rest of the world. A Global Pandemic, the news said, the liberal media that is. Fake news, all of it. Fake science, was what it was, and masks were foolish. His own people all agreed with him, as well.

It was known throughout his administration to ignore the virus. Just like he said at his rallies. The country was turning the corner, and soon, the virus would be gone, like it had never been there at all. It better; he was gambling his re-election on that premise.

Which was why he ignored the virus, and let it spread wild and free across the United States.

The plan was a simple one, in his eyes. He wasn't as confident about his re-election as he let on, so he needed an edge to beat that old fart Joe Biden. So a little after the first case of the virus appeared in America, Trump decided to let it run free. Of course, he couldn't stop Democratic State Governors from doing their best to stop the contagion, but many governors were Republican, and they knew who would allow them to continue their rise in politics if they towed the line and fell into step.

Once the virus was in full swing, he knew in a few months, when it was time for the American people to begin voting, that if it wasn't safe they would have to resort to voting by mail.

Now, Trump knew his supporters well; once he told them not to fear the virus, that it was a Democratic hoax, they would do as he commanded, and so mostly only the Democrats would vote by mail, fearing the virus.

With that set up, he quickly got to work having his Republican lawyers do anything they could to stop the mail in voting from succeeding. Such as limiting how many ballot boxes per county, and that no mail-in ballots could be counted until after midnight on election night, or at least not until voting closed for in-personal voting. But his best idea was to install his own man as the postmaster for the postal service, who then began to disassemble machines that processed ballot mail, thus slowing it all down to a crawl. Next was to fight so that November third was the cutoff to receive those ballots by mail, even if thousands of ballots came in the next day. And finally, he planned on stacking the Supreme Court with his own people, so if he did actually lose the election, he could scream that it was all rigged, that mail-in voting was rife with cheating, and the case could go before the Supreme Court.

Ruth Bader Ginsberg was going to die any day now from what he'd been told. The old woman had been battling cancer and was well into her late eighties. Any day now she'd go. And before her body was cold and in the ground, he would have a replacement ready to go. His party controlled the Senate, so it would be more than easy to get the new nomination rushed and have he or she on the bench before the election.

Though Trump almost never cared about anyone but himself, he was slightly sad to see the old bird go. She was a tough broad with a distinguished career.

The double doors to the Situation Room were open when he arrived. Fred stood to the side and with a nod from Trump, the man went on his way, back to the residences, his job finished.

Trump entered the room, blinking slightly from the brightness and the noise. There were more than a dozen people inside the room, all sitting at a massive oak, oblong table.

At one end, the chair was empty, as that was where Trump always sat; to the right of it good-old loyal Vice President Mike

Pence sat, his white hair looking even whiter in the fluorescent lighting.

On the opposite side of Pence, was Trump's Chief of Staff Mark Meadows, with his arms crossed before him. Both men were talking with one another.

Also at the table were Jared Kushner, Trump's son-in-law and his Senior Advisor, and Four-star Admiral Brett Giroir, Assistant Secretary for Health. The others were aides and assistants, not worth mentioning. Hell, Trump didn't even know their names, nor did he care to learn them.

"Looks like the gang's all here," Trump said upon entering the room. Immediately, everyone stopped talking and stood up, showing their respect. It always got Trump a little hard when they did this. He loved power, found it a tangible thing, and everything he did in his life was in the pursuit of accumulating more.

"Sit down, everyone, no need for that," he said, every single one of them knowing he was lying, that they'd regret it if they didn't show him the respect he felt he deserved.

He went to the head chair, or what he felt was the head chair, as with an oblong table there was no 'true' head of it, and sat down heavily. Christ, it felt good to get off his feet. He was slightly winded as well. Being in his mid-seventies and topping the scales at almost 250, he wasn't going to be running any marathons anytime soon.

He winced slightly as he felt a rise of indigestion. Nothing serious but it annoyed him. He hadn't said anything to anyone about it, not wanting to appear weak, and to Trump, any form of sickness showed weakness.

Once he was seated, the others as well, he placed his hands on the table before him, his gaze falling on Pence first. "Okay, so what's so goddamn important that I need to be here at six in the morning?"

Pence cleared his throat, not wanting to tell the president the bad news. So he decided to pawn off the chore on Admiral Giroir, who though intimidated by the president, would tell it like it is, despite receiving the president's ire. "I think Admiral Giroir should explain, Sir, he knows the most about the issue at hand."

"Fine, then he can tell me." Trump shifted his gaze to Admiral Giroir. "Well, Brett? What's so serious?"

Admiral Giroir shifted in his seat, but he bullied forward. "It's about the vaccines, Sir, more than half of them won't be ready in time for the election."

"What?" Trump roared. "It's two months to the election, and I was promised they'd be ready! That's why I threw so much money at those eggheads! It's the one thing that can guarantee me a second term!" He slammed his right hand, palm down, onto the table. "Without it, that fucking Biden could actually beat me? Him? That old fossil!"

"Actually, he's only two years older than you," Admiral Giroir said under his breath. "You're pretty much the same age."

Trump didn't hear the doctor, too tied up with his tirade. "I gave those labs millions of dollars, for them to deliver! If not, then why the hell did I bother?"

"You bothered to save the American people from the virus, Sir," Mark Meadows said softly.

Trump ignored Meadows. That was the furthest reason there was for him to be rushing the vaccines to market. He stood up, his face turning red under the spray tan. There was a large bulge of a vein on his forehead. "I don't care what has to be done, but I want those vaccines ready. Lean on whoever you have to, threaten whoever you have to, but it better get done." He pointed accusingly at Giroir. "And if you ever mention one word of this meeting outside this room, so help me, you'll pay. You hear me, Admiral?"

Giroir only nodded slowly, understanding completely. In the past, he had gone rogue as far as the president was concerned, contradicting Trump and telling the American people on National TV that the virus was serious and would only get worse before it got better, despite Trump saying the exact opposite at multiple press conferences and rallies.

"Mr. President," Mike pleaded, "Maybe you should sit down, Sir, you're not looking so good."

"I'm fine, Mike, never been better actually." His breathing was growing heavier and his left arm had a stabbing pain going up and down its length. His chest hurt, too. He began to waver on his feet and all at once, the table and people around it began to blur. "I feel…I feel…"

"Mr. President?" Pence asked again.

Trump's body slumped face first onto the table, then rolled off it to settle on the floor on his back. A smear of spray tan was left behind on the table's mirrored surface.

Trump peered up at the ornate ceiling, not understanding what was happening. Faces hovered over him, leering in and out of his vision. He caught bits and pieces of words, but all of it was drowned out by the roaring in his head, as if his heart was stuffed into his skull and was beating crazily.

"Call the medic!" someone cried.

"Admiral Giroir, help him for fuck's sake!" someone else shouted.

"I'm a pediatrician, not a general practitioner," Giroir snapped back. "You help him."

"What's wrong with him?" Meadows demanded, his face close to Trump's as the man looked into the president's eyes, which were rolled up into his head.

"If I had to guess, I'd say he's having a heart attack," Giroir suggested calmly. "All that fried chicken and greasy food is finally catching up to him."

Even in Trump's fugue state, he made a note to remember that. Giroir would regret speaking about him that way. He slid into darkness, as the cacophony of voices continued around him.

An indeterminate amount of time passed. Trump thought it was probably only minutes, he had no real idea, as his eyes flickered open briefly. He heard the thumping of rotor blades and knew he had to be on Marine One. He couldn't turn his head, it was strapped to a gurney, and he saw an IV swaying above him with the movement of the aircraft.

"The test came up positive, he's got Covid," a voice stated. "It's probably what brought on the heart attack."

"No shit?" a second voice said. "Well, hell it took long enough for him to get it, considering the way he was running around everywhere to all his rallies and shit, never wearing masks or even taking basic precautions."

"That's who he is, man. He's Number 45, the fucking President of these U. S. of A's. Nothing scares this guy, even a goddamn global pandemic."

"How long to Walter Reed?" he heard another voice say from somewhere nearby, but just barely within his limited field of hearing.

"ETA, five minutes," the first voice responded. "There's a team of doctors waiting on him. I tell ya, he got lucky. If there wasn't a medic always on standby at the White House, he'd have been a goner."

"He should have been, the way he's so damn reckless," the third voice commented.

"Oh, please, nothing will take this guy out, he's like Teflon," the first voice replied. "He was impeached and he got away scot-free. And I bet not even the threat of dying can stop him."

Trump tried to speak but nothing came out; he slipped back into oblivion.

He woke up slowly, the white room he was in telling him he must be in a hospital, Walter Reed probably. Everything was out of focus. There was an oxygen tube under his nose and multiple bags of liquid connected to his left and right arms.

He was not happy, not one bit. A man who was always used to being in control, helpless in a hospital bed was one of the worst things that could happen to him.

His heart began to beat faster as he struggled to sit up, his breath rasping in his throat. A machine began to beep, loud and clear, and an instant later, three doctors and two nurses came charging into the room.

The doctors began talking over one another as they checked readouts and computer monitors hooked up to his body. He caught snippets of their conversations, such as "Suffered a mild heart attack." "No one knew he had Covid-19." And "He's on a cocktail of steroids and antibodies, but it might not be enough. We still might lose him."

That last one got his heart pounding like a triphammer, and weak from the virus, he succumbed to another heart attack.

The doctors and nurses went into action immediately.

"He's going into cardiac arrest!" a voice yelled. "Get the crash cart!"

His hospital gown was yanked down to his lower abdomen, exposing his bare chest to the air. Masked faces hovered over him like wraiths. He tried to talk to them, tell them to save him or it would be their careers, and their asses, but he couldn't talk.

One doctor leered over him, a set of defibrillator paddles in his hands.

Trump heard the man call out, or he assumed it was him, as the mask didn't allow him to see the man speaking.

The doctor yelled, "Clear!" just before the paddles came down.

Trump found his body filled with lightning from head to toe; his body jerked on the mattress and his brain sizzled in his skull.

Once more he fell into peaceful oblivion.

Chapter 2

Donald J. Trump opened his eyes, once more gazing up at the white ceiling tiles of his hospital room. This time his vision came into focus almost immediately.

Turning his head slightly to the left, he saw a row of flowers and wreathes, all with well wishes such as, Get Well Soon! and Hope You're Feeling Better! Not fully aware of what he was seeing, he didn't notice that the flowers were wilted, many of the pedals lying on the floor around the arrangements.

Shifting his gaze down by his feet, he saw that the only door to the room was closed. Nothing seemed amiss.

Shifting his head to the right, he looked out the only window in the room. It was daylight, and according to the clock on the wall it was five-thirty, the hands not telling him if it was a.m. or p.m. He turned his head away, not noticing that the minute hand on the clock wasn't moving. Nor did he realize the overhead florescent lights weren't on, and that the machines, such as an EEG monitor he was connected to, were silent. Not even one of them made a boop or a beep or a boop-beep.

It was silent in his room.

Eerily silent.

Gazing down at his body, the first thing he saw were the IV lines connected to his arms. Following the clear tubes, he saw them connected to multiple bags of IV nutrients. They had been jury-rigged together so that when one ran out, the next one in waiting would begin the IV drip. They were all empty now, the last one having only the minutest amount left. By the way it was all connected, there was no way it was authorized by the hospital.

Someone had hastily done it.

But why?

There was a nurse's call button on the side table and he grabbed it, pressing it repeatedly. He waited for more than a minute for someone to arrive, and when there was no activity, he pressed it again, holding it down and not letting up. He waited another minute, and when no one came, decided to give up.

The fact he was alone with no one coming to his aid filled him with anger. There would be many heads on the chopping block when he was finished with them.

Walter Reed was a well-renowned hospital, and to think this was the kind of care he was receiving was unthinkable. Unbelievable!

He decided if there was no one to help him, he was on his own, so he might as well deal with the situation at hand, and later, he would see how many people he could get fired in a single day.

His abdomen was smaller than he remembered, though it was slightly bloated. Peering over the side of the bed, he discovered a bag filled with yellow liquid. It was so full it was overflowing onto the floor, a wide puddle forming. Recalling older family members, he knew at once what it was. Covered with a sheet, he yanked it off him. Pulling up his hospital gown, he winced at the sight that greeted him. His lower region was lying on a wet and dry pool of brown. From the odor wafting up to him, it was his own body waste he was laying in. There was a tube coming out of the tip of his penis. He cringed. Reaching for it, he grabbed the tip of the tube, where there was a larger portion, round, like a balloon. In one smooth motion, he removed the catheter, the tube sliding out of his penis causing him blinding pain. Trump gasped as he removed it, and staring at the tube that had been inside his manhood, he tossed it away from him as if it was a live snake. It took him a few minutes to recover from that. The trauma being more mental than physical.

The next thing to do was to get off the bed. The rails on the bed were up, so he slid down to the bottom, his legs sliding over the edge. The floor was cold when he touched it, even though he wore a pair of light blue socks on his feet. Other than the socks and gown, he was naked.

Trump dragged a trail of brown with him as he slid off the bed, and once standing, needed to lean on the frame to hold himself up. He almost thought he would be okay, and smiled, admiring his strong constitution, when all of a sudden small flashes of light flickered before his eyes and he felt lightheaded. Without realizing he was doing so, he toppled onto his side, landing hard on the floor. His breath left him in a rush, and he gasped heavily and sucked in more air. One of the IV stands was pulled over with him, the other, with a longer tube, remained upright.

He rolled onto his back and remained supine for more than five minutes as he slowly regained his strength. Once he was feeling confident he was better, he sat up, his ass cheeks sticking to the floor, thanks to them covered in a slippery mess of bodily waste. He frowned, deciding he needed to do something about that ASAP. Using the bed as support, he got to his feet again, this time more wary of falling. Once standing, he grabbed a part of the sheet that was unsoiled and did his best to clean himself. Once finished, Trump tossed the sheet to the side, the soiled linen forgotten.

Now standing tall, he had a different perspective of the room. To the side of the bed there was a small wastebasket. It was filled with empty cans of Ensure, along with spent feeding tubes. There had to be two dozen cans there by the brief count he made with a cursory glance. Someone had been taking care of him; that was not in doubt. But where were they now? Where was the staff of ten or more that should have been doting over him day and night?

He removed the IVs in his arms next, tossing them away when he was finished. Realizing how thirsty he was, he took a few tentative steps forward, and when he didn't fall, he shuffled faster over to the private bathroom connected to the room. It was windowless, but was half the size of the large room his bed was in. He was the president of the United States, after all. He had a wing all to himself. His room wasn't a simple one any commoner would end up in. The bathroom had a large sink, shower and tub combo, and a small sitting area as well. Leaning over the sink, he turned on the water, using his hand to quickly gulp in handfuls. As soon as he finished, his stomach roiled inside him, unused to anything entering it physically for some time. He didn't last two minutes before he was throwing up all over the floor, the clear liquid splashing the pristine white tiles. When the dry heaves had ceased, and the spots before his eyes vanished, he rinsed his mouth out and drank again, this time sparingly. When it appeared like it would stay down, he turned off the water and for the first time since waking, gazed at his face in the vanity mirror over the sink.

He didn't recognize the visage before him for the first few seconds. Nor should he have. He looked very different from the last time he had his reflection peering back at him.

His trademark orange tan or makeup was gone, his face pale, his eyes sunken into his face. A mostly-white beard covered the lower half of his face as well, something he had never allowed to happen in his entire adult life.

But the most shocking thing in the reflection was that his hair was gone. He was bald! His flowing golden locks, the ones he'd paid so much for, were nonexistent. He was so floored by this he almost fell over, but only by gripping the sides of the sink allowed him to remain upright.

"My beautiful hair!" he cried out hoarsely, though it came out as barely a whisper.

He stared at his altered visage for a full minute, not believing what he was seeing. Finally, he pulled himself away from the mirror, realizing that no matter how long he stared, the face looking back at him wasn't going to change.

A few towels hung from a rack beside the sink and he used one to wash his lower regions, soaking the cloth and then rubbing it across his pale skin. When finished, he tossed the towel onto the floor, along with the soiled hospital gown.

Leaving the bathroom, he went to the only closet, wanting to dress in something more appropriate, but all he found were more gowns on a lower shelf. Not wanting to be naked, he had no choice but to don another gown. The rear of it remained untied, and his ass felt cold, but he was too preoccupied with his next move to care.

He went to the phone on the side table beside the bed. Picking it up, he discovered there was no dial tone. Trump pressed the lever a few times, like every actor in every movie ever made before the invention of cell phones, but still nothing happened. The line was dead.

Dropping the phone to let it clatter on the floor, his attention shifted to the door leading out of the room. It was time to leave the room and rip someone a new asshole for their incompetence for leaving him in such an atrocious state.

The door opened inward.

His eyes went wide in surprise at what was waiting for him in the hallway.

There were three bodies lying before the door, almost as if they had been stacked there to barricade the door from the outside. All three bodies were dressed in black suits, and when Trump leaned over to inspect one of the faces, he pulled back quickly. He knew the man. Even in death, he recognized Jerry, one of his bodyguards from the Secret Service.

Each body was wounded in a different way. One or two had arms chewed into by the looks of it, and one had a terrible wound in his neck. But all three did have one thing in common. Each had a large-sized hole in the back of their skulls from a bullet wound, the entrance hole much, much smaller. A large pool of blood surrounded the bodies, but it was coagulated and mostly dry. All three corpses had added to the pool by the looks of it.

So someone had shot the men in the head and then piled them before his door.

Interesting, but strangely unsettling. It wasn't a thing to do in a normal world, and the reason the bodies were there could not be a good thing.

He had to shove the uppermost corpse off the pile before he could get over them. Then he held onto the doorframe as he climbed over the corpses, his sock-covered feet slapping the cold linoleum tiles in the hallway. He got some blood on the socks and he left dark red footprints as he walked, but just the barest outline as the pool wasn't very moist and not much had soaked into the material.

There was no sound at all in the hospital wing, which seemed unusual. A hospital, any hospital, during the time of Covid-19 was always busy, even if this particular ward wasn't delegated for the virus.

Though most people would think the first thing to do would be to call out, to ask if anyone was around, and if they could help, that assumption would be wrong. When a place seemed so empty, so abandoned, the last thing a person would want to do is call out and draw attention to where they were.

Trump felt terribly uncomfortable, entirely out if his element. He didn't feel in control at all, and it wasn't a sensation he was enjoying. A cool wind came down the hallway, blowing his gown open at the back, his ass cheeks getting goosebumps from the chill. Something drew him in that direction, and he began shuffling down the empty corridor, his mind trying to take in everything he'd seen, from the dead Secret Service men to the scattered body parts strewn across the floor. Blood splatter covered the walls on both sides, but the owners of the blood were nowhere to be seen.

"Hello?" he said, his voice hoarse from non-use, deciding there was nothing to lose by calling out. "Is anyone there?"

A few doors down from his room, there was a small alcove, where a heater was located, directly below a large window, a heavy wooden bench painted white before it. The window was shattered, the wind coming from the opening. There was a white sheet tied to the bottom of the bench, where one of the legs was prominent from the rest of the piece of furniture. The sheet was now more like a thick rope, and the line that went up and out the window was taut, signifying there was something on the end that was still hanging from it.

From gazing outside, Trump could see he was on the third floor, so whatever was hanging obviously hadn't reached the ground, which was what he assumed would have been the reason for the setup in the first place. Unless it had been like a prison escape and someone had used tied sheets to shimmy down and escape the building. Both guesses were equally good, but he knew there would be only one way to discover the answer to the mystery.

Getting close to the opening, Trump peered out and down, the window looking out onto a small courtyard landscaped with grass, small trees and flowers, where patients and staff would go to relax and enjoy nature in its serenity.

It didn't look that now, however. There were multiple bodies strewn about the tall grass, from Trump's height looking more like dolls a young girl had left lying on the ground than former human bodies. He couldn't make out much about the bodies other than they were dead and covered in blood. They looked as if they'd been attacked by wild animals, the bodies devoured and torn apart in many places. One body didn't have a head attached to the torso.

A gust of wind blew across his face and something banged against the side of the hospital below him. He looked straight down, following the sheet to its natural end. He'd been distracted upon first peering out the window, but now he was completely focused on what was below him.

A body hung from the sheet, the makeshift noose wrapped around its neck. The corpse swung back and forth gently in the wind. By the white coat, scrubs for pants, and stethoscope the corpse wore, Trump was pretty confident the body was of a doctor or a male nurse. The feet were bare of shoes, both having been kicked off in the struggle with the noose. He looked past the body onto the grass below and saw the pair of Dockers lying alone amidst the high grass, which looked as if it hadn't been cut in weeks.

While leaning out the window, Trump dislodged some of the safety glass that had made up the window. The shards fell off the frame to land on top of the corpse's head.

To his utter shock, the pale face, upon the glass striking it, looked up at him, the mouth opening and closing, while making animal-like gargling noises. The man sure didn't seem alive, with sunken in eyes and teeth that stood out prominently as the lips receded from around the gums.

Not understanding how the man was still alive, Trump stumbled away from the window. Helping the man was the furthest thing from the president's mind. The first rule of being Donald J.

Trump was that you only looked out for one person, namely Donald J. Trump.

Trying to wrap his head around what he'd just seen, along with everything else, he made his way to a set of swinging double doors just a few feet away from the alcove.

Through the small rectangular window set in each door, he was able to see the hallway beyond. What he saw in the center of the floor, about fifteen feet from where he stood, was the half-eaten body of a nurse.

Her exposed bones glistened in the sunlight filtering in through a side window, and that was about all there was of her from the neck down; from there she was nothing but crimson bones covered in gore. It looked as if a pack of wolves had gotten to her, tearing into her torso but sparing the head. Only about half of her skeletal frame remained. Most of her ribcage was missing, the internal organs within ripped out of her and dragged away by the red smears covering the floor in all directions. Her head was positioned so that it looked as if she was lying on her back, gazing up at the ceiling in silent repose. Her eyes were closed, as if in sleep, and other than a few splotches of red on her cheeks and a pale complexion from loss of blood, her face was beautiful and serene. She couldn't have been a day over twenty-five years of age if even that.

Trump stared, mouth agape, not believing what was before him. He brushed the door with his knee, causing it to shake for a moment. Not loud normally, in the silent corridor the noise of the moving door carried easily.

It was as he stared at the half-devoured corpse that the head began to slowly turn to face him. The milky eyes opened and locked onto him, and the mouth sagged open. Upper and lower teeth clacked together, so hard the sound filtered to him on the far side of the closed doors.

With no usable body, the head could only move from side to side, the mouth parting, closing, parting and closing. Trump's gaze locked onto that of the dead nurse and he saw something in those milky-white eyes. He didn't know what it was but it made him feel unsettled.

He decided he didn't want to go that way after all, and he stepped away from the doors, choosing a new direction. He desperately wanted to remove himself from this house of horrors, get outside and find transportation back to the White House.

Moving down the hallway, he passed the nurses' station. The clock on the wall wasn't running, the hands stuck on 5:30, the same time as the clock in his room.

Leaning over the desk, he tried the landline phone, but once more was greeted to silence. There were scattered items on the desk. A pair of scissors caught his attention and he grabbed them, holding them tightly in his right hand. It was a feeble weapon but better than nothing. A disposable lighter, writing utensils, and a few clipboards with medical files were also there, but he ignored them.

There was a corpse lying on the floor behind the desk, a letter opener sticking out of her left ear, a small amount of blood seeping around the makeshift weapon. Female, without a doubt. Wearing green scrubs, the shirt had been torn open, and even with huge chunks of flesh missing, he could see the nurse had a great rack, even with one nipple bitten clean off. He would have banged her if given the chance. Though she wasn't as good looking as a few of the porn stars he'd fucked, she would have been good in a pinch.

He moved away from the desk and continued down the hallway, this side more messy than the hallway going in the opposite direction. But he kept moving, wanting to explore a little more and find a way to get outside. He was already growing numb to the blood splatter and loose body parts scattered across this side of the hallway. It was easy for him actually. He'd never had much empathy in his life for others, even his wives and children. It wasn't because he was evil; it was just the way he was made. Some people were naturally nice, others were not. Trump was a survivor, and that drive made him stand or crawl over anyone who prevented that from happening. It was just the way he was. It was his nature, much like the fable of the scorpion and the frog.

There was another set of double doors at the end of the hallway, metal with no windows, a heavy chain and lock loosely wrapped around the crossbars. He ignored the arterial spray covering the white ceiling before the doors, signifying someone or multiple someones had died hard here.

Words were written across the door in blood. It was messy and hastily scrawled, but it said **Danger Inside, Don't Open!**

Trump walked up to the doors, and slowly placed an ear on the cool metal. He closed his eyes to listen, to try and decipher what the danger might be. He leaned too close, pressing on the door. It shifted slightly, causing the chain across it to jingle a little.

It didn't take more than a few seconds before the door bucked under him, causing him to stumble backwards. The loose chain allowed the doors to part in the center four or five inches, and the instant they separated, a bloody hand shot out and grabbed Trump by his wrist. It felt like a vise had locked onto his arm.

Snarling, groaning sounds came from the opposite side of the doors, and faces appeared, noses jutting out of the crevice of the opening, mouths clacking as teeth opened and closed.

One nose slid off a face it was attached to, landing on the floor, nostrils up. Bits of gristle were on the side from where it had been attached to the face.

More bloody hands slid out to reach for the warm body. Only the chain stopped the tide of living dead from exiting and swarming over a beleaguered Trump.

Panicking, Trump fought to pry the hand off him but it was firmly wrapped around his wrist. Still weak from waking from his coma, he had no strength to resist.

The arm the hand was part of began to retract, pulling Trump closer to the grasping hands and snapping mouths of the hungry dead.

Chapter 3

Fighting not to be pulled into the parted doors, Trump fought as hard as he could, but the hand on his wrist wouldn't let go.

That was when he realized he was still holding the scissors taken from the nurses' station in the same hand. Transferring the scissors to his free hand, he began hacking at the offending appendage.

Bits of flesh flew off to splatter the door and floor. He didn't stop until he could see bone, and then he jammed the bloody tip of the scissors between the radius and ulna and twisted, the two bones snapping apart like a chicken wishbone. The arm separated from the hand, but the limb continued waving up and down, droplets of a gooey substance that was the blood of an animated corpse spraying into the air. Trump backed away and tripped on his own feet, falling heavily onto the floor. The hand was still clamped onto his wrist, but it wasn't hard to pry the fingers apart and toss the hand away from him.

"What the hell is going on around here?" he gasped as he scuttled away from the double doors. The doors swayed back and forth as the tide of bodies pressed against it, only the chain keeping them at bay. The skin on the body parts he could see were mottled and gray, looking more dead than alive, like the doctor hanging from the sheet outside the hallway window.

Trump didn't want to tangle with what was on the other side of those doors. Getting to his feet, he made his way down the corridor, and upon seeing a fire door, went to it.

Pushing on the bar, the door opened inward, but he didn't enter. The darkness within the stairwell was obsidian, not a hint of illumination other than from when he opened the door. Once that door was closed as he made his way down the stairs, he would be in complete darkness.

His mind raced with what to do. He recalled the disposable lighter he'd seen on the nurses' desk. Retreating from the stairwell, he went and retrieved the lighter and some paper, then returned to his original position at the fire door.

Wrapping the paper into a tight roll, he lit it, then stepped back onto the stairwell landing. At least now the darkness was banished slightly. He walked to the edge of the stairs, peering down, seeing nothing but inky blackness. With a hand on the railing, he dropped the paper, watching it flutter downwards. It flared brighter as it dropped, the wind of its descent fanning the flame, until it blazed out, the dark returning.

Trump frowned. That didn't give him much help at all.

He would need something that burned longer, and brighter if he was lucky.

Once more he returned to the nurses' desk and gathered as much burnable material as he could carry, then went back to the fire door. When he was on the landing again, he made a pile of the combustibles on the edge of the stairs and then lit it. A nice little fire began, growing larger by the second.

He didn't wait to see it burn at its peak, however. He began his climb down the stairwell, hoping the fire would be enough to have him reach the bottom. He only had a few flights to traverse after all. In his hands he carried the lighter and the scissors, one in each.

He was slower than he would have liked as he made his way down the stairs, and it took so long, between frequent rests due to his fatigue from being in a coma, that by the time he made it to the next floor's landing the light above had all but gone out, its feeble glow barely enough to see by. He gripped the bloody scissors and the cigarette lighter tighter.

When his right foot stepped onto the next landing, he was exhausted, breathing heavily and feeling like he might faint. The light above had finally gone out, the paper and other assorted combustibles he'd gathered burning bright but not long. He reached for the fire door's handle by feel alone, and pulled, wanting to get out of the stairwell, but the door wouldn't open. There was no latch on his side, just a solid handle.

He stood alone in the Stygian blackness, only the disposable lighter able to banish the darkness.

There was no sound within the stairwell, not even the dripping of water.

On the move since first waking in the hospital bed, a wave of fatigue washed over him, causing him to lean against the fire door and sit down. The objects in his hands were placed on either side of him, his arms already limp with exhaustion. He spread his legs open so he wouldn't fall over, in the shape of an inverted V. Feeling relatively safe for the moment, it took only seconds for him to drift off into a restless sleep.

Trump came to with a start, and at first thought he was blind.

Eyes wide, but no light within the stairwell, it was like he was sitting inside a black hole.

A dull thump from the door he was leaning against quickly explained what had awakened him; he still felt exhausted and wanted to rest some more.

Someone was on the opposite side of the fire door.

Getting to his feet after feeling around for the lighter and scissors, he picked up both. It took two tries to get the disposable lighter going, a small light flickering to life, causing him to see spots for a moment. Lowering the lighter to the side of the door, he studied the handle in more detail; there was definitely no way to unlock it from his side. Fire doors only allowed access from the hospital hallways, and once someone was in a fire stairwell, they had no choice but to go all the way to the ground floor to exit. Smokers would sometimes use the stairwells, but they always made sure to prop the door open in some way, or else risk being locked out of their floor.

He let up on the lighter, as it was getting hot on his thumb, blackness descending yet again. A disposable lighter wasn't meant to be kept on for a long period of time and would quickly become too hot to hold with the light still burning.

Another thump came to his ears, soft, muted by the metal door. Curious as to whom it might be, and if that someone could help him, he placed an ear against the cool metal, listening with his eyes closed.

It sounded like panting or growling, or both. From everything he'd already experienced, he was pretty confident it wasn't an animal. Maybe it was a good thing he hadn't been able to open the door.

But what if what was there pressed on the roll bar and the door was forced open? He didn't like the thought of that, and was already preparing to leave the landing when the exact thing he'd considered happened.

With a clack the door popped open, light from the hallway spilling into the landing. At least he could see now, Trump figured. He stepped away from the door, his feet teetering on the edge of the landing, the long and winding stairs below him lost in shadow.

A zombie stumbled though the open doorway and onto the landing.

The illumination coming from the hallway showed its face to Trump, but not completely, who could only stare in shock. He felt so vulnerable, so exposed that it was insane! The close-cropped black curly hair and dark complexion told him the zombie was a Black man. The uniform said the animated corpse was a security guard for the hospital.

Trump was a man who always took control of where ever he was, whether on a debate stage, a press conference or in a boardroom. He always dominated his foes. That was his mantra and had been since he was a child.

But this…this *thing* before him was a whole new level of crazy.

As the zombie stumbled out of the doorway and onto the landing, the door, on a spring, snapped closed behind it, the landing instantly becoming pitch black.

Just before the door snapped closed, the zombie spotted Trump, and as the light went out, Trump found himself being grabbed by the zombie, its hands gripping his hospital gown, tearing it off him, thanks to him not bothering to tie the straps. Naked, alone in the dark with a hungry monster, it was all he could do to stop himself from screaming.

He shifted his body so he wasn't hovering over the precipice of the stairs, his back slamming up against the metal railing. The zombie, not pleased with only getting Trump's hospital gown, came at him again, hands reaching out to grasp old, white-man flesh.

Trump didn't think, only acted, his left hand going up to block the zombie from getting too close, the scissors still clutched in his hand going straight out. The zombie came forward, the scissors sliding into its torso, Trump's hand disappearing within the cold chest of the creature. Vapid air that reminded him of rotting garbage, sitting on a New York street in July came to his nostrils, and he fought the urge to gag. Teeth clacked inches from his cheek as the zombie tried to bite him. Trump shoved the scissors deeper into the zombie's body, the blades slicing and dicing the organs within. The zombie felt nothing.

"Please," Trump begged. "Stop. Don't you know who I am? I've done more for your people than Abe Lincoln. I love Black people."

If Trump's words registered with the zombie, it gave no sign, not changing its attack on him. Trump's hand, stuck inside the zombie, felt squishy and wet, but cold, not warm like it should be if it was inside a human body.

The two struggled, dancing back and forth on the landing in total darkness. It was only sheer luck that had Trump pushing the zombie so that it ended up precariously at the top of the stairs, neither the zombie nor Trump knowing this as they struggled, entwined in the Stygian darkness.

Then one of the zombie's feet slid back but only landed on air. The zombie began to fall backwards, its arms flailing as it went, not understanding. With a sickening, sucking sound, Trump's hand popped out of the zombie's chest, but the scissors were left behind after becoming jammed up between a few ribs. He'd the forethought to let go of the scissors, and not be pulled along with the zombie.

Trump grabbed the railing as if his life depended on it, which it did, and instead of being pulled down with the zombie, it legs swinging outward as it began to fall into an empty void, the creature went tumbling down the stairs alone. Meaty thwacks filled the stairwell for a time, until only Trump's rasping breath could be heard. His heart was pounding a mile a minute and he wondered if he was going to have another heart attack. If he did, he knew he was finished. There would be no team of doctors to save him this time, no experimental drugs to keep him alive after getting Covid. But eventually, with the danger over, he began to calm down, his heart not doing a drum solo anymore.

He idly wondered if he should have worn a mask at rallies and when meeting people, after all, to prevent getting Covid. Maybe he shouldn't have been so reckless all the time, and should have acted like it was as serious as he knew it was, but decided not to pretend it wasn't.

He gave this errant thought another full microsecond of consideration before deciding.

Nah, he was right to do what he did and say that masks sucked.

After all, he was still alive and no one else was, or seemed to be, so it had all worked out okay for him from what he'd seen.

Last man standing and all that.

And thanks to the virus and his coma, his belly fat was gone. He looked like he did when he was in his forties. Unfortunately, his hair had fallen out, a side effect of having Covid, from what he'd heard. He recalled his doctors discussing the potential side effects of the virus, how some people, though they survived, had long-lasting medical issues to contend with, weeks and even months after recovering. He hadn't really believed any of that, assuming the doctors were over-inflating it all.

Standing in the dark, he realized he'd lost the disposable lighter in the scuffle with the zombie. Leaning over carefully, not wanting to fall over and pitch head first down the stairs, he felt around for it, but found nothing, the floor smooth. He ignored the wetness he ran his fingers through, the residue of the battle with the zombie.

With limited options, he had no choice but to descend the stairs without illumination. If he didn't, he would remain trapped inside the stairwell until he succumbed to starvation, dehydration or another unlucky attack that he wasn't fortunate enough to escape from.

Holding the railing tightly with his left hand, he began making his way downward, his stocking feet cautiously touching down onto each step, before he moved to the next one. His socks squished with each step he took so he decided they were worthless and took them off. Besides, being naked was bad enough, but just wearing socks seemed somehow foolish. At least it wasn't cold inside the stairwell, the temperature moderate.

His hearing was razor-focused on what was below him. He had no idea if the zombie was still active down there, patiently waiting for him to reach it. He'd never know when it would happen, either. One moment he would be placing a foot onto the next step, and the next he would feel the cold hands of the zombie grab him, followed by the pressure of its teeth sinking into his flesh, before turning into blinding pain.

He shivered from head to toe in expectation of that happening, and there was nothing he could do but continue downward.

His skin had goosebumps everywhere, the tension of waiting for the attack unbearable. He wanted to yell out, demand a response, but he knew to do that would be tantamount to suicide.

One step after another, he made slow progress, but never stopped.

His breathing was growing heavy as he reached the first floor landing. Recalling how high it had been from the third to second level, he was fairly confident he was almost to the ground floor. His hearing was so heightened that if he'd heard a pin drop, he would have jumped ten feet into the air. Trump ascended what he was mostly confident was the last set of stairs to the ground floor. So far there'd been no sign of the undead security guard, so if something was going to happen, it would be soon.

He was counting the stairs in his head, but he hadn't gotten an exact number earlier, only an idea, when his foot hovered out to come down onto the next step, but instead of that happening, his foot sank into something very, very squishy, cold and wet. His foot was surrounded by this sensation, as if it was being wrapped in a wet rag soaked in slime and mayonnaise.

Immediately, he stopped moving, not knowing what to do. Though he'd stepped in something that resembled an enveloping wet sponge of cold gravy, nothing grabbed him, nor tried to bite him. Not wanting to make more noise than needed, he paused, even his breath held in his chest.

He waited for a full ten seconds, then had to exhale, a great whoosh escaping his lips. Still, all remained silent.

Lifting his foot cautiously, a loud squelching sound emitting as he retracted it out of its predicament, he could feel what felt like slime rolling off his foot to drip back into what he'd stepped in. His imagination was going wild, as there was no way to know what it was his foot had sunk into. Like a game at Halloween, where the guests were blindfolded and had to figure out what they were touching, such as jello for brains and peeled grapes for eyeballs or spaghetti for worms, he could only assume by the sensations he felt.

But he did have more to go by. The stench of decomposing meat, blood and feces filled the air around him. He had a vision of being inside a slaughterhouse, one where no one had bothered to clean up any of the gore for weeks, if not months, but just let it rot where it fell.

The odor quickly became too much and he leaned over and vomited, his stomach heaving but nothing coming up. His stomach was empty and had been for some time, only the IV allowing him to survive to wake up from his coma.

With his abdomen muscles on fire, he forced himself to move, to step over whatever was at his feet and to escape the darkness surrounding him, seeming to suffocate him in its embrace.

His foot came down on the far side of the lumpy wetness, and on the floor he found the stairs were gone, that he had reached the bottom landing. He had a pretty good idea what he'd stepped in now that he knew where he was relative to the stairwell, but he tried not to think about it. He almost began to dry heave again, but he forced his mind to think of something else. Anything to take his thoughts off the sickly-sweet aroma of death.

The noxious aroma of rotting meat was so bad Trump could barely breathe, and without waiting a second longer, he crossed the small landing and reached out until he touched the fire door's roll bar. Not waiting a moment longer, he pressed the bar on the door, the door opening wide. It struck the wall with a loud slam, and though it was close to dusk, Trump having spent almost the entire day inside the stairwell, lost in absolute darkness, the wan light left in the day blasted his eyes as if he was staring into a spotlight.

Blinded, he stumbled backwards and fell over something. He landed on his back and his eyes closed from the impact and from the blinding.

When he opened his eyes again, his head was touching the floor still, and as he turned his head to the side, he found he was staring into the still moving milky-white eyes of the zombie he'd just stepped in.

Chapter 4

The undead security guard's mouth snapped, teeth clacking loudly within the stairwell. Trump rolled away, ashamed to admit he was terrified.

The zombie's spine had snapped in the fall down the stairs, but its head remained active. But unless Trump wanted to stick one of his limbs into its mouth, the head was pretty much harmless.

He realized that almost immediately, when the security guard didn't rise up, the body remaining limp, like a discarded rag doll.

The fire door slowly closed due to its spring on the hinges, casting the stairwell into darkness once more. But he did see there was a small bit of light seeping in from under the door.

Slowly, he raised himself to a standing position, and with his eyes more adjusted to the light, he pushed open the door once more and stumbled outside, naked as the day he was born.

As he walked onto the outer landing, he went too far and the door closed behind him before he realized it. Turning, he tried the handle but of course it was locked. No access from outside, just like the doors to the floors had been.

He felt exposed now, with nowhere to go if danger was waiting for him. He'd done a stupid thing just now. But he never looked back, it wasn't something he did. Only forward. The door was closed, it was done. He would just have to find someplace else to hole up for the night. He also needed clothing. He didn't have to go far with his white ass and dick hanging out for all to see. At the bottom of the six cement stairs, there was an old cloth tarp that had blown into the corner, where the steps met the building. He also regretted not taking the dead guard's shoes, but once again, too late now.

There were other forms of detritus as well, from old soda cans, dry leaves to wrinkled and faded newspapers. The tarp was filthy, covered in a hundred stains, from oil to what might have been blood. But the tarp was a form of clothing, and though it wasn't terribly cold outside, there was still a slight chill now that the sun was just starting to go down.

Dusk was falling quickly upon the land, and he realized the clocks on the hospital walls must have stopped long before that morning, perhaps in the evening whenever the power grid had gone out, leaving the hospital and everything else within eye sight without power.

He didn't know this for sure, but with darkness descending around him, and no street lights coming on, he simply assumed this was so.

He began walking, not knowing where he was going, but wanting to keep moving, to at least be active. He had always been a man of action, not words, though in the past years as president, he had to admit he'd been more wordy than a man of action. He'd talked so much shit on Twitter, if his words had been water he could've filled a million swimming pools.

He made no apologies. That was how the game was played. He had always attacked first to gain the upper hand, and not many of his adversaries had been able to stand it for long, usually relenting when he never ceased his assaults. Banks had foregone loans, deciding to forgive said loans, rather than fight him. Besides, when he claimed bankruptcy, they would only get pennies on the dollar, if even that, as they would have to come at him with lawyers who no doubt weren't cheap. Even his ex-wives had had no choice but to accept what he gave them, with NDAs to ensure they remained silent about any indiscretions they knew about. In his years playing a politician, not one ex-wife had come out against him. If they wanted to keep getting paid, they knew better.

He thought of Melania then, and wondered if she was alive or dead. She was a tough broad, no question. If there was a way for her to survive, she would have taken it.

He found himself in a parking lot, surrounded on all sides by what were once refrigerated semi-containers and shipping containers from Port Authority. But with no power they were simply containers. That was a big distinction, he could tell, because as he moved closer to some of the containers, the stench of rotting meat filled the air, along with a loud roar of buzzing flies.

One container door was wide open and he shuffled over to it, his right hand holding the tarp around his shoulders, his legs covered in zombie blood, one foot in particular coated with dark mucous, his bald head scratched from his recent adventures. He looked pitiful, and far from the presidential figure who once roamed the halls of the White House at four in the morning.

Breathing through his mouth to fight the urge to heave, and waving flies away from his face with his free hand, he peered into the container. In the wan light of the setting sun, he saw row upon row of body bags inside, and also bodies wrapped in simple garbage bags, probably when legitimate body bags had run out.

There had to be over a hundred corpses within the container. Moving away, he went to another one, also partially open. Pulling the door wider, he saw the same, row after row of corpses.

Stepping away, he spit to get the foul taste of rotting human meat from his mouth, and then continued onward. There sure as hell was nothing to see here. Nothing but death, by the thousands, if all the containers were filled.

Night was falling too fast for his liking. By the way the light was fading, he had thirty minutes at best before it was completely dark. With no streetlamps, it would be difficult to see, and with only the stars and whatever part of the moon would be out tonight, it would be tough going on foot.

He needed to find someplace to hole up.

Pulling the tarp around him more tightly, he began to move around the containers, weaving though the parking lot.

At the end of the lot, he had to climb over a small fence, and then step around some derelict vehicles. As he rounded a large van, he found himself gazing out at an open area filled with an assortment of military vehicles and caved-in tents. Some sort of emergency base camp had been set up at one time.

Black crows floated overhead, many more on the ground. Even here flies abounded, a constant nuisance. They would crawl all over his naked body, the tarp useless against them. He continually slapped them away to no avail.

A large helicopter lay on its side at the perimeter of the camp. He recognized it immediately. It was Marine One, a Sikorsky UH-60 Black Hawk. It lay on its side, its four-bladed rotor snapped off. The 21 million dollar aircraft resembled a hunk of junk, barely any part of it not damaged. It had either crashed or had tried to take off and had suffered a serious malfunction.

Seeing the familiar aircraft gave Trump hope and he shuffled over to it, wondering if perhaps he could use it to hole up for the night, before moving on the next morning.

Going to the rear of the copter, he didn't see a way in. Lying on its side, he would have to climb onto it to get inside. He went to the front canopy next, thinking he could break one of the plexiglass windshields to gain entrance.

But no sooner did he reach the windshields, than a zombie inside the aircraft slapped at the tempered plastic, smearing blood and gore across the semi-transparent window.

Startled, Trump prepared to run, or attempt to run, but before he turned to escape, he realized the zombie wasn't a danger to him. Not only was it inside the solid canopy, but it was still strapped down in its seat by the flight harness.

The undead pilot even had on his Aviators, still. Trump stayed and stared at the zombie, for the first time really getting a good look at one without fear of being attacked.

He realized he knew the pilot. It was Lt. Rogers. The pilot had flown Trump in Marine One countless times. That was all he knew about the pilot, however, never having cared enough to ask about the man's personal life.

There must have been a fire in the cockpit as the zombie's face was burned on one side, the flesh charred and flaking. The eye on the damaged side was bone white, resembling a hard-boiled egg. The orb had been cooked inside its socket. The lips on that side of the face were gone, too, as was the hair. The undead pilot looked like Two-face from Batman.

Trump had seen enough, and wanted to get away, accepting that the downed helicopter wouldn't be a place to hole up, even if the zombie was strapped into its seat.

Feeling terribly lonely, he decided to risk calling out in the hopes someone might be nearby. If there was anyone remaining within the camp area, he assumed they would be under his command as the Commander-in-Chief.

"Hello, is anyone here? Hello? Is anyone here?" It was more of a whisper than a shout, but that was okay with him. Seeing the undead pilot in the helicopter told him that the undead weren't just relegated to the hospital, that there could be more wandering around. A chill went down his spine at the thought.

He spotted movement to his right, near a news van. He frowned when he read the logo on the side of the vehicle. It was CNN. Christ, he hated them. All they ever did was talk shit about him. Even when he was trying to do good, they criticized him. The network's self-righteous pundits spent hours each day trashing him to the American people.

Upon reaching the van, he peered around its front bumper to see a woman crouched down low to the ground, trying to stay out of sight. She wasn't doing a very good job of it apparently, and she was lucky he wasn't a zombie—or else she'd have been dead meat.

He got a quick look at her upon first seeing her. She wore a knee-length skirt, now filthy and ripped at the edges, a white blouse that was covered in dirt, and hair that was tied in a pony tail, but hung down her back almost to her ass, which from first inspection seemed well-formed.

She was in her late twenties to early thirties, and the first thought he had of her was that he'd fuck her without hesitation. Her body was athletic, legs shapely, and perky breasts. Her face had the features of a porcelain doll, with a thin nose and high cheekbones. Even in his current state of undress and dishevelment, he felt his dick twitch ever so slightly beneath the tarp. He might have been in his mid-seventies, but he had no issues getting it up when needed. Of course, a certain blue little pill never hurt either.

She nearly jumped out of her skin when she heard Trump at the front of the van, his bare foot stepping on some gravel that crunched under his heel.

She jumped up, prepared to run, a tire iron in her hands, clutched so tightly her knuckles were bone white.

"Wait, I won't hurt you," he said, not wanting her to run away. "Please, I need help."

She paused slightly, crowbar raised, but she didn't run. Taking in Trump's disheveled condition, and seeing he was well past sixty, she hesitated from leaving; she was glad to see another living person, no matter how he looked.

Then her eyes opened wider when she got a better look at him. Her mind raced with what she was seeing, thinking back to the man she would see at the press podium at the White House giving a speech, and comparing that man to the one before her now.

"Holy shit, Mr. President, is that really you?" she said, her posture relaxing even more. She didn't need an answer, she already knew she was correct.

"In the flesh," he said, managing a small grin. "Of course, I've looked a hell of a lot better."

She stepped closer to him. "Last I heard you were in a coma brought on from getting Covid and having a stroke."

"Yes, well, as you can see, I'm fine now." Then he got a better look at her, past the grime covering her beautiful face. He realized he recognized her as well. "Wait I know you, don't I?"

She nodded. "Yes, Sir. I would hope so, given that I've been at every White House Press Briefing you've had since you were elected in '16."

He only nodded. "You're name is Catherine, isn't it?"

She frowned. "No, Sir, I'm Carrie Collins from CNN."

He made an annoyed face. "Oh yes, now I remember you." He stood a little taller, towering over her five-six petite frame. "You work for the left, telling lies about me all the time."

"No, Sir, that's not how it is at all."

"I bet you didn't vote for me either."

"Well, Sir, I...I don't see how my party affiliation is relevant, given our present circumstances."

"You're a Democrat, right?"

"I...yes, Sir, I am, as a matter of fact."

"Right, so you weren't going to vote for me in the 2020 election in a few months, either, I assume."

"No, probably not." She stood taller as well, getting some of her spirit back now that she wasn't so scared. "Truth is, I think you're a horrible president and I was looking forward to seeing you lose to Biden"

He scowled deeply. "I bet you were." He turned and began walking away.

"Wait, where are you going?"

"Away from you. I don't need to pool my luck with a filthy Democrat. You're all weak to me, worthless."

She followed him, despite his treatment of her. "Please, Sir, let me come with you. It doesn't matter who I voted for now. It's all gone to hell. None of that matters anymore."

He stopped walking, and was about fifteen feet from her. He hadn't been moving very fast, despite the way he acted like he wanted to leave her behind. Deep down, he wanted to be with her, too. She was the first living human being he'd come across since waking up, and though she was a Democrat, she was hot, and four eyes were better than two for watching his back. He decided he could still use her, and if she followed orders, even better.

"None of it matters, Sir," she repeated.

"It does to me," he said under his breath so she couldn't hear, but then gestured for her to join him. "Fine, it doesn't matter. Come on if you're coming."

She smiled and trotted over to his side, closing the gap quickly.

"Just don't forget who's in charge here," he said and began walking again. For a man wearing nothing but a tarp, he held his head high, walking for all the world like he was wearing a tailor-made suit and expensive Italian shoes.

It wasn't the clothes that made the man, it was the Man who made the man. He didn't know where he was going, but by moving, it seemed as if he was in control, and had a destination in mind.

"Yes, Sir," she said meekly.

Chapter 5

"All the people I worked with are dead," Carrie explained. "My family and friends, too."

"You mean all those talking head assholes on TV that used to say shit about me daily are all dead?" Trump asked as he walked around a pile of gore and gristle, mostly dried but covered with feeding insects.

She only nodded.

Trump smiled, happy for the first time since he'd regained consciousness. "Good, fuck them all."

"It happened so fast," she continued. "It spread like wildfire. We thought Covid was bad, but this was a million times worse. All around the world, the dead just…just…woke up and began to walk again. It was like some bad horror movie. And worse, if you get bit, it passes on some kind of infection that kills the host within days. Then, if the body isn't destroyed, they too get up and walk around, repeating the cycle."

He laughed. "No shit? I guess wearing a fucking mask didn't help, huh?"

"Are you seriously making jokes?" she asked, aghast with his insensitivity. But then she remembered who she was talking to and remained silent.

"I guess Pence took over for me," Trump said after a few minutes.

"Yes, he was sworn in after you went into your coma."

Trump raised his hands to signify all that was around him and beyond. "I guess he wasn't that great of a president if all this went down."

"He was better than you ever were," she quipped, but when Trump stopped walking and turned to glare at her, she looked away, cowed.

He resumed walking.

They both remained silent for another minute, only concentrating on placing their feet in places that wasn't covered with gore or detritus. They had minutes before it was full-on night. Overhead, the stars were already coming out, a thousand twinkling emeralds.

"You never asked about your family," Carrie offered when enough time had elapsed that she felt comfortable resuming speaking.

"No, I didn't," Trump said flatly, his tone telling her the discussion was over before it began.

They walked for another ten minutes until they reached the edge of the Walter Reed Facility. They were near the back of the sprawling grounds.

Wood Road was mostly empty, but there were a few vehicles scattered around the street.

"We need to find a safe place for the night," Carrie said. "It's not safe out here."

"Yeah, I kind of figured that out already," he said, not turning to look at her. "Why are you out here by yourself anyway?"

"People I was with got attacked by the dead. I managed to get away."

He didn't prompt more information from her. In truth, he didn't really care one way or another how she'd been where she was found by him.

At the end of the street, where it would run into Palmer Road, there were multiple military vehicles blocking the road in a blockade, all silent and dark, but none looking damaged in any way.

Trump began moving that way, the military a sign of hope for him.

"Hello, is anyone there? This is your president. I need help. Hello?"

"What the hell are you doing?" Carrie hissed, whispering more than speaking normally. "Be quiet. You'll lead them right to us."

"Who?" he tossed over his shoulder as he walked closer to the blockade.

"The dead, you idiot."

He ignored her, not understanding what she was talking about and not really caring. So far he'd seen no sign of zombies, and he was starting to think there were none on the grounds and surrounding it. She was a woman after all, inferior in every way to him. She was good for fucking and raising his children, that was it. He'd tolerated women his entire life, having to act like he at least thought they deserved respect, but there were no cameras or witnesses around at the moment, and he didn't see a reason why he had to keep feigning interest in the weaker sex.

"I think you need to shut the fuck up now," he hissed back at her. "I'm done listening to you."

"But, Sir," she began but he cut her off, pointing a finger accusingly at her. Even wearing nothing but a tarp, bald and naked beneath it, there was something dominating there.

"I said shut up. I don't have to listen to you anymore; those days seem to be over. You may be a piece of ass but you're nasty, too. Opinionated, like Hillary. I've dealt with your kind my whole life." Venom filled his voice, and she stood stock still, shocked. "Your just Fake news." He grinned, his white teeth showing easily in the falling darkness. He thought he'd put her in her place and he felt good about that. Dominating people was what he did well.

But then he realized she wasn't completely looking at him in her shock, but was looking *past* him, at the blockade.

Slowly but not fully understanding, he turned back to face the military vehicles; a few Hummers, a small APC and sandbags lining each side of the road.

People were coming out from around the vehicles and sandbags, and in the dim shadows of the falling night, he saw they all wore Army uniforms, as well as National Guard. Greens and camo were the colors of the day it seemed.

"We need to get out of here," she said, turning and running away. "Does that look like Fake news to you!" she called over her shoulder.

Trump hesitated longer, still not fully understanding what was happening.

But when the leading soldier's face became clearer in the dwindling gloom, he quickly understood the situation.

The soldier's face was nothing but exposed muscle, the flesh having been peeled off the face; the nose was gone, soupy phlegm dripping out of the open orifice. There was a massive chunk of the soldier's throat missing as well, dark blood seeping out of the jagged whole. Teeth marks were apparent. Trump's first thought was an animal attack but when he recalled everything he'd witnessed and what Carrie told him only moments ago, he knew that wasn't so.

Following behind the lead undead soldier were a dozen more, all in equal signs of distress. A few were missing limbs, or only had one eye, and two had no eyes, seeming to stumble around by hearing alone. Many still carried their weapons slung over their shoulders. One zombie had a large hole in its throat; its tongue had then been swallowed in death and down into the throat and out the hole. The tip of the muscle waved back and forth, like a slug peering out of a hole in a log.

Trump's jaw dropped, but only for a few heartbeats. He wasn't a stupid man, though many tried to say he was. He realized his predicament immediately, and turned and followed Carrie down the road. She already had a good lead on him, and he rushed to close the gap, hobbling more than running due to his bare feet and still fatigued from his coma.

But it was apparent almost immediately he wouldn't be doing such a thing as catching up to her. She was in good health and very fit, and though Trump had lost his belly fat, after being in a coma, his muscles were stiff, and he was barely able to make a decent shuffle, let alone a jogging gaunt.

"Carrie, please wait, I need your help!" he shouted, as he continued down the road. As soon as his shout left his mouth, more zombies appeared from the surrounding area, most of them looking like civilians, faces and exposed body parts ripped away, blood and gore covering them from head to toe.

Many had **DUMP TRUMP!** signs still hanging around their necks and other negative signs that were against him. Other signs were of rainbows and Black Lives Matter sayings also. It was all the people who hated him, all together once more. There must have been a protest here when he was in his coma, and the protesters had been caught and attacked by the walking dead. A smile came to his lips when he thought of all the people who didn't support him being torn to shreds by the living dead.

"At least there's some kind of an upside to all this happening," he mumbled and laughed.

But his merriment was short-lived, as the soldiers behind and the protesters to the sides, came closer.

"Carrie, I'm still your president! Help me, please? I'm begging you! Don't let me die like this!"

Carrie had a good lead on Trump and if she kept going, she would easily outdistance the zombie horde, but when she heard Trump calling for help, she slowed and finally stopped running.

She was in the clear where she stood, and she gazed back to the center of the road, most of it hidden in shadows now that night had fallen, only a minute of waning light remaining, if that. But she didn't see Donald J. Trump, the obnoxious blowhard who hated women and Black and Brown people, and cared for nothing and no one but himself.

What she saw was a frail old man, a human being, pleading for help, to be saved. Someone who didn't want to die, but wanted to live another day. And each day lived was a new day to change, when a person could become someone better than they were the previous day. She truly believed that. Perhaps it was her time in Berkley that made her think everyone had potential, that there were no truly evil people in the world, only misunderstood ones.

Something in her heart softened, and though she'd never cared for Trump, witnessing firsthand some of the horrible things he'd said while at the podium during a press briefing, her parents had raised her to be kind, to show love even when attacked with hate.

Shaking her head, and wondering what the hell she thought she was doing, that she had to be crazy, she began running back to Trump.

"Here, put your arm around my shoulder," she ordered him upon reaching his side.

"Oh, thank God, thank you, Carrie. I don't know what to say."

"Then shut up and get moving," she snapped, seeing the undead protesters closing in fast.

The odd couple began moving down the road, the zombies closing the distance with each step Trump and she made. For every step they took, the zombies completed two steps. It was painfully clear there would be no way to escape the horde if they were on foot.

Trump's breath rattled in his throat as he tried to keep moving, Carrie forcing him to walk at a pace he couldn't hold for much longer. He knew this and accepted it as fact, knowing his survival depended on him changing the rules of the game.

"It's no use," he said. "I don't have the energy to keep going this fast. They're going to catch up to us." He paused before suggesting, "We need something to occupy them for a while. A distraction."

Hunched over, doing her damndest to carry Trump, she barely heard him. She did catch the end of his suggestion, however. "A distraction?" she asked innocently.

Trump stopped walking then, and stood tall, towering over the petite woman. "Yup," he said coldly, and grabbed her by her arm and spun her so that she was standing before him.

Before she could do or say anything, Trump punched her in the side of the face with his right fist, the blow sending her reeling to the ground. He might have been in his seventies, but he still had a decent right hook, and Carrie was no match for him.

She hit the ground hard, dazed, agony shooting across her face. Spitting blood, she felt a tooth fall out with her tongue. For a few seconds she was unable to focus her thoughts, only the pain of her jaw and her brain trying to gather itself occupying everything. But if she thought the blow to the face hurt, when Trump raised his right foot and brought it down on her ankle as hard as he could, in essence hobbling her, she realized the pain in her jaw was nothing compared to her ankle.

Blinding white light filled her head and it seemed as if night had turned to day. She screamed in agony, the ankle feeling like it had been dipped in acid.

In her own world of suffering for a few precious seconds of time, she forgot about the danger creeping upon her. She rolled to her side, cupping her leg to her chest, as if by this simple act she could make the pain go away.

Trump was already shuffling down the street, his tarp billowing out around him like a cape. His bare feet made no noise on the asphalt.

When Carrie's vision cleared enough for her to see him leaving her behind, her head spun around like a top, seeing the zombies surrounding her.

"No, oh God no!" she screamed. "Trump, what are you doing? Help me. I came back for you! I came back for you!"

She tried to get to her feet, but the instant she put weight on her bad ankle she collapsed. Trying to crawl, Carrie was tackled before she could travel more than a few feet. Forced to the ground, she fought the attackers, punching and kicking, but when teeth sank into her exposed legs she shrieked in agony and terror. More zombies surrounded her, each fighting one another to get at her. When her arms were torn off she was still screaming, and when her head was removed from her torso after dual zombies chewed onto both sides until another grabbed her head and pulled, stretching tendons and trachea until they snapped free, she was all but done caring, already dead and feeling no pain.

Trump glanced over his shoulder once to see nothing but a crowd of bodies congregated in the center of the street. Once in a while the glistening of fresh blood was reflected in the moonlight. Seeing he was in the clear, he paused and watched for a few moments.

"Better you than me, honey," he said casually, as if he was watching a mother duck and her babies crossing the road, instead of a woman who had showed him mercy being devoured alive. "Say hello to Cooper and Lemon for me when you get to Hell."

When he'd seen enough, he turned and began moving down the street once more, his escape now assured.

As for Carrie Collins, she was already forgotten.

After all, it wasn't like she had voted for him.

Chapter 6

In the darkness of the night, it felt as if there were ghouls everywhere, just waiting to reach out and grab him. Trump expected gnarled fingers to pierce his soft flesh, tear into his limbs and torso to pull out the warm red meat within.

But though the unknown was a constant threat, there was an actual danger following him doggedly.

Trump glanced over his shoulder for the hundredth time that hour.

They were still there, of course, trailing him, getting closer with every passing minute.

His lead on the zombie horde had been shrinking almost immediately after he'd sacrificed Carrie.

Poor, sweet, naïve Carrie. She should have known better than to trust him. He only looked out for number one. Everyone else was expendable.

His distraction had almost worked perfectly, if not for a minor hiccup. A few zombies at the outer area of where Carrie was being devoured had spotted Trump before he'd managed to get far enough down the road to get out of sight. They had turned and followed him, others doing the same, until a decent amount were on his tail.

Others had joined in on the undead parade, and now there had to be close to sixty of the bastards tracking him. What had been more than a little chilling was how many were carrying pieces of Carrie. Four each held a limb, and were gnawing on the arm or leg like it was a giant turkey leg, while another carried her severed head. A few were munching on fingers, the white of knuckle bones poking out of the cracked lips. And another dozen each held a glistening organ, liver, spleen, heart and pancreas, all were on display, more than one chewing with what seemed like pure gusto. All of the zombies had turned poor hapless Carrie into take-out, carrying the food and eating on the go, their eyes now on the main course, namely Trump. Carrie had been but the appetizer to tonight's feast.

It had been almost two hours since he'd left Wood Road, and he didn't think he was going to be able to go much farther. He was at the end of his rope, exhaustion about to become so complete he was going to just fall over right there on the road he was walking down. He had no idea of his location, not knowing Bethesda, Maryland at all. Other than going to Walter Reed, he'd never bothered visiting the state.

He was barely moving faster than the lead zombie. Was it odd to think he knew that zombie? He thought he did. Wearing a dark suit and sunglasses, Trump could have sworn it was George, one of his Secret Servicemen who had traveled with him. It was hard to be sure, given George looked to have had half his scalp torn off along with a quarter of his face. The sunglasses hung askew, barely hanging on.

Trump was so slow; he knew there was no chance of trying to slip off the road and find somewhere to hide, to let the horde pass him by. In many ways, he felt like one of the walking dead himself. He was tired, filthy, and hungry, and the thirst gnawing at him was almost overwhelming. He'd consumed nothing after awakening from his coma, and before that he didn't know how long the IVs had been working and nourishing him, along with keeping him hydrated. He was probably dehydrated and malnourished, which explained his missing belly flab. His body had been cannibalizing itself for a while, no doubt.

But he was never one to quit. He was a winner and hated to lose, too much actually. Losing was something his mind simply couldn't comprehend. Even if all was lost, he would persevere, never stopping. He was in a fight to survive, the win being his survival, and being so competitive, he accepted the challenge—the fact that he didn't have a choice was irrelevant.

But battling lawsuits was one thing, his own physical stamina was quite another.

He managed another thirty minutes of a sluggish walk that was hardly better than the zombies' pathetic shuffle. The lead zombie of the horde had shortened the gap and was no more than fifteen feet away, and closing with each shambling step it took. The moans of the dead carried to him over the wind, sending a chill down his spine.

Deep down he realized it was almost over. Donald J. Trump was about to die.

It was hard to fathom, and harder to accept. A world without Trump didn't seem to be a world worthy of surviving—to the survivors of course, as he would be dead and it wouldn't matter too much to him.

Coming up on his right, a large SUV was parked against the curb, looking as if the driver had left it for the night and would be back in the morning. There was no damage to it at all. Windows were intact, tires inflated. Even the black paint was shiny, reflecting what moonlight there was. Other than a layer of dust, it was as the owner had left it.

The roof was high off the ground, and the hood was angled so it wasn't easy to scale unless a person was coordinated, which the zombies most definitely were not. Desperate and out of options, Trump moved a little faster, though his legs and feet screamed in protest.

His feet were bleeding as well, too much walking with no shoes. Plus, he was never a man who had walked very far, and when golfing used an electric cart. So, much like Homer Simpson, Trump didn't like to walk very much and went out of his way not to.

Upon reaching the giant SUV, an Escalade if he was correct, Trump began climbing up the hood, his feet scrabbling across the bumper, bloody smears scarring the pristine finish. He didn't get very far. He had to let go of the tarp to use both hands, and naked as the day he was born, he tried again, a corner of the tarp clamped in his teeth—he wasn't about to abandon his only source of clothing. With both hands free, it actually made it easier to climb the hood, his skin sort of catching on the paint, not letting him slide off. His body made weird noises as he ascended the hood, sliding across the black paint, like the sound an inflated balloon made when it was squeezed.

With the last of his strength, and ready to pass out from the exertion, Donald J. Trump, the 45th President of the United States, pulled himself up the hood and onto the windshield. His exposed dick and balls slid across the glass, and if there had been someone inside the SUV in the driver's seat, they would have gotten one hell of a show.

With his feet on the hood, his torso on the windshield, and careful not to slide off, his bloody feet making it slippery, he pulled himself the last few feet onto the roof, then tucked the tarp under his body so it was as close to him as humanly possible.

A heartbeat after doing so, the first zombie reached the SUV and tried to follow him up. But not as capable of climbing, and its clothes only polishing the front of the hood, all it did was scrabble with its hands like it was swimming in the air.

More of the undead horde arrived moments later, surrounding the SUV on all sides. Curled, gnarled hands reached up at him, many slapping the side windows and leaving bloody palm prints. Low moans filled the night as Trump sat in the center of the roof, his legs pulled up close, his arms wrapped around them. He hadn't sat in that position since he'd been twelve or so, but here he was, over half a century later, doing it again, despite the pain it caused him; he was far from flexible. But the only way to stay out of the zombies' reach was to remain in the exact center of the roof. If not for the height of the Escalade, they would have already gotten him, dragging him off the roof kicking and screaming; he would already have been turned into zombie chow.

In the wan gloom that was the night, he gazed out over the heads of the undead horde as they fought to reach him. He could see nothing around him but the silhouettes of a few homes, all dark, no signs of life at all.

Sorrow welled up within him and he could feel the urge to cry taking over. Any normal man would have given in to the sensation, already, and no one would have chided him for it.

Alone, in the middle of the night after the Fall of Man, surrounded and trapped by a horde of the living dead, one wrong move and you're dying painfully, torn apart like something from the Middle ages. It was a scenario no rational mind could imagine as a realistic event.

No one would fault a man who succumbed to the tension and terror of what Trump was experiencing.

But he was Donald J. Trump. The fucking President of the Untied States. He would never give in to such a base emotion as sorrow.

Somehow, while sitting in a fetal position, he managed to sit taller, his bald head held high. Not even his dick and balls sticking out between his crossed and raised legs could diminish his attempt at looking presidential.

He would never submit; as long as he breathed, he would continue the struggle. Not even a horde of walking dead cannibals would defeat him, nor would the threat of being dismembered and devoured could make him falter in his resolve.

But if anyone had been there with him, and had thought he was a man to be admired given his present crisis, they would have quickly given pause to such admiration.

For if somehow that person had been able to hear Trump's thoughts, said person would have fast realized that their admiration was being falsely given.

Because as Trump sat there on the roof of the SUV, surrounded on all sides, one thing that kept going through the president's mind was that he wished Carrie Collins, the goddamned left-wing news reporter, and her in itself a representation of the entire liberal media, was still with him.

At least then, he could have thrown her to the zombies yet again for a little entertainment to occupy his thoughts for a while.

Chapter 7

Huddled in a ball in the center of the SUV's roof, the night was agonizingly long, Trump managing to catch only a little rest as the clawing hands continuously reached for him. He was exhausted after the harrowing day he'd experienced.

Still weak from awakening from the coma, fighting and running for his life, and also weak from hunger and thirst, fatigue had overwhelmed him completely. He needed to really sleep, not just doze off for a minute at a time, but it was impossible given his present circumstances.

Flies buzzed around him incessantly, an unavoidable annoyance it seemed. Wherever the dead were, insects and rodents were sure to be along for the ride.

He mostly had to kneel on the roof, to ensure he was in the exact center of the Escalade. Even then, pale hands came close to grabbing him and pulling him off the vehicle. When he'd dozed off for the first time late into the night, shivering from the cold, a hand managed to grab a corner of the tarp. Jerked awake, Trump barely was able to keep from toppling into the horde. He'd ended up at the edge of the roof, barely hanging on, the grasping hands so close he could feel the wind of their passing. It was only luck that allowed him to inch back to the center of the roof and yank back the tarp. The irony was that if he'd still had his blonde locks, he would have been grabbed by his hair and pulled off the SUV. Being bald had prevented that and saved his life.

His heart pounded so fast he wondered if it was going to pop clear out of his chest. He was petrified, and he didn't like the feeling. He glared at the pale, dead faces in the night, wishing he could kill them all with a snap of his fingers.

After that he made sure to wrap the tarp as tightly around him as possible, like he had upon first getting onto the roof, and tucking the ends under his bare ass.

It grew colder with the passing of time, and with no actual clothing, his bones soon began to clatter inside his body, or so it felt. His teeth clicked together as he shivered, his body attempting to keep him warm, but all he was doing was expending more energy he sorely needed. Each time a gentle wind blew across his exposed flesh he winced. It was only sixty degrees out, and with clothing and a light jacket on it would have been a beautiful night, but when all you had to keep yourself warm was an old tarp, well, he had to guess it was all about a person's perspective.

Trump soon fell into a fugue state, half-awake, half-dozing. The moans of the zombies seemed to come from far away, as if he was at the end of a long tunnel and they were at the opposite, calling out for him.

His eyes half-closed, he tried to imagine the moans and groans were actually cheers, such as when he was at one of his rallies, and his acolytes were calling his name, chanting it over and over, their love filling him, making him stronger.

"Lock her up!"

"Build that wall!"

"Four more years!"

All his tag lines reverberated inside Trump's head. All the wonderful chants he had his people come up with. See, he knew that the average American citizen was a moron. Try and explain too much to them, like how he was going to balance the economy or fight Covid, would only go right over most people's heads. He knew anything he said had to be simple, such as three word chants to promoted ideas. Anything longer would get lost in translation.

Oh yes, most people were very stupid and preferred to be told what to do and would never bother to think for themselves or validate anything he said. They would simply believe it blindfolded, and take whatever he proposed at face value.

It had been the cornerstone of his 2016 election, and it would have been the same in his 2020 election, if not for what appeared to be a zombie apocalypse.

He had to chuckle at that. His administration barely gave Covid the attention it deserved, as if it would have done any better with the dead walking.

Maybe it was a good thing he'd fallen into a coma, that way no one could blame him for the fall of humanity. Not that he would have taken or accepted responsibility anyway.

"It's always someone else's fault." Words to live by and for him, how he managed to get elected to the highest office in America.

When it was near dawn, he found he couldn't sleep anymore, his hunger so great it was maddening. The low rumbling in his gut belayed the noises of the zombies moaning around him, and he admitted to himself that if there had been food somewhere nearby and he'd known about it, he might have considered jumping into the horde and making a run for it, he was so damn hungry.

He began to hallucinate as the sun rose in the east. He imagined he was sitting at the Resolute desk, and Nancy Pelosi was on her knees under it so that when he sat up straight behind the desk, she was hidden from view.

He was giving a speech to the Nation, and all the while, Nancy was on her knees, her face in his lap, his pants unzipped, going to town on him.

As he sat on the roof, eyes half closed, a smile creased his cracked lips. Just imagining that scenario filled him with pleasure and even caused him to become hard. It wasn't that he found her attractive, hell no, she was eighty years old, for Christ's sake, it was a power thing to him. He wanted to dominate her, ever since she insulted him for the first time, and in doing so, he would dominate the Democrats.

But then a zombie slapped the roof with its bloody hand and he was snapped back to reality, such as it was.

The sun eventually rose, but nothing changed for Trump. Stuck on the roof of the SUV, all he could do was stare at the zombies. He imagined what their lives had been like before they had died and returned.

No doubt their lives had all been pathetic.

Work, home, then work again, followed by a commute home. Day after day, week after week, month to month, and then year to year. The same grind every day, with nothing to look forward to but a week off per year, dragging the wife and sniveling kids to the lake for more trivial pursuits.

Never getting ahead, the same drudge over and over, interspersed with boring sex with the wife or husband once in a while.

So pathetic and sad.

Not like his life.

Since he was a young man, he'd strived to be in the limelight, to have people talking about him. And that had happened full fold upon him becoming the forty-fifth president of the United States. Now, all the media did was talk about him, every day and every night.

All he had to do was send out a tweet and they would discuss it for days. They couldn't help themselves. They were fascinated by him. Even when they said they covered him too much, they would continue, and thus by saying it was all too much, they kept going.

And that was just in America. He'd barely even begun to recognize all the media attention he'd received globally. On every corner of the planet, every country, rich or poor, unless someone was literally living in a cave, they knew the name Donald J. Trump. He was the most famous man in history! He would never be forgotten!

But as he knelt on the roof of the SUV, looking pitiful and slovenly, he couldn't help but wonder if the story of Donald J. Trump was finally over.

The early morning hours turned into afternoon, then evening. Somehow, he didn't know how he managed it, he remained immobile, never moving, a statue on the roof of the SUV.

But he was at the end of his stamina. Trump knew he would not make it through the coming night. Sleep wasn't the problem, but simply losing consciousness from hunger and fatigue was. He wouldn't know it had occurred until he snapped awake when the first set of teeth sank into his flesh. By then it would be too late to try and stay on the roof. By then he would be nothing but food for the dead.

So when hours later, the sun began its descent into the west, he had to accept that his time left alive on the earth was numbered in minutes.

Already, his eyes felt heavy, and all he wanted to do was close them, to just sleep for a few minutes. His upper body swayed back and forth as he fought to stay awake. His hunger was a non-issue at the moment, the need to stay conscious taking priority.

A voice in his head asked him what the point was. Why continue suffering, when the end result would be the same.

He shook his head to clear it, to snap himself awake, refusing to succumb to that inner voice.

He'd never backed down from a challenge in his life and he wouldn't stop now.

As the sun finally set, and he marked a full day on the roof of the SUV, with darkness enveloping him once more, he struggled to remain awake…and alive.

His mind dazed and confused from hunger and exhaustion, he managed to stay awake for the entire night. The few times he was going to pass out were prevented by his pinching his thigh so hard that he left a bright red bruise each time. But as the sun rose in the morning, bathing the street in its warm glow, he was done, finished, there was nothing left in the gas tank.

His legs were so stiff from not moving it was a miracle they held him up. Which was probably why they did. Locked in the same position for so long, it would have been a chore to move them even if he wanted to.

His eyes were so blurry he could barely see the zombies below him, their never-ending moaning and grasping for him becoming background noise.

But no man could go on longer than Trump had in the condition he'd been in before climbing onto the roof. His iron will had gotten as far as humanly possible.

His eyes closed, and he snapped them back open, forcing them to obey his will. But as soon as they opened, they were drooping again, and this time, though he tried to force them open, they ignored his plea, closing for good.

He wavered on the rooftop, already asleep, only his legs, locked in the kneeling position, allowing him to remain upright.

But then his head sagged, his chin touching his chest, and the added weight began to make him slump forward. Before he realized he was falling, he dropped face first onto the roof, his face slapping against the windshield. Only falling that way saved him from instant death, for he was mostly still in the center of the roof, his feet tucked under his butt, his body straight, like a hood ornament only he was on the roof, not the hood.

Two things happened simultaneously, one good, the other very bad. His eyes snapped open upon impact, and he ignored the bloody nose he got from hitting the glass. The other was that his tarp had spread out on both sides of his body when his ass had been raised into the air, and as soon as this happened, the zombies were grabbing the material, pulling and yanking at it.

A tug of war ensued, with Trump in the center, the meticulously wrapped tarp now detriment to his health. His legs became spread outwards as he attempted to keep his balance.

One side of the tarp tore, causing him to be pulled in the opposite direction. Before he could try and get up, to recover his position, he felt a cold hand clamp down on his right ankle, the weight pulling him across the roof.

He shouted for help, all sense of decorum forgotten in his need to prevent what was about to happen.

He kicked his leg out, and hit the zombie in the face, crushing its nose and making it loosen its grip for a second, which seemed odd given that if zombies didn't feel pain, then the blow to the nose should have done nothing to deter it from grabbing him. But semantics aside as to why the grip loosened, he withdrew his leg from its clutches, only to have another zombie's hand lock onto his right arm, which was hanging down across the windshield, and once more the tug of war renewed.

There was no way to stop the zombie as it used Trump's arm to haul itself up onto the hood, using him as a human rope ladder.

Slapping the hood with its free hand, the other clamped onto Trump, the zombie got so close to Trump that he could smell its fetid odor, even over the foul aroma of all the other undead bodies. Flies buzzed around Trump's head and landed on his face and scalp, but he'd learned to live with them more than a day ago, when first climbing onto the roof. The insects fed on the blood and sweat covering Trump's skin, the constant itching they made maddening.

Struggling though he might, there was no escaping the zombie holding his arm in what was basically a dead man's grip, its gnashing teeth only inches from Trump's hand.

He had no strength left to resist, and as the disease-ridden mouth opened and the yellow teeth parted, Trump could only stare in horror as the zombie's head came forward to sink its jaws into his arm.

Chapter 8

As the tug of war with his arm continued, Trump saw out of the corner of his eye the tarp he'd been using disappear into the crowd of undead. He couldn't help but watch it go with a wistful longing. That tattered and filthy piece of material in many ways had become his only friend over the past day and a half. It had kept him warm, surrounded him with security, and had protected him from the sun.

An item that before the coma he wouldn't have given even a microsecond of thought to. Just a piece of trash left in a parking lot.

Completely naked, he felt exposed and vulnerable, the thin material giving him a false sense of security. Now it was gone, as was all hope.

So tired he could barely resist, the zombie pulled his arm closer, its teeth barely an inch from his wrist.

He wanted to shut his eyes and accept what was going to happen, but he couldn't, so he only stared as the teeth got so close to his arm, that the hairs stood on end due to his terror. It was as if the dried lips of the ghoul were caressing his skin.

So imagine Trump's surprise at what happened next. Instead of feeling the coldness when the zombie sank its teeth into his arm, the head simply disappeared in an explosion of bone and brain matter. He closed his eyes on instinct, squeezing them tightly, as he was peppered with skull shrapnel, blood and gobbets of brain.

The hand around his wrist loosened slightly but did not let go, but Trump, seeing his chance to escape, pried the fingers apart with his free hand. Finger bones cracked and snapped as he removed each digit from around his wrist, the hand and the arm it was attached to eventually falling away to be lost in the undead horde.

Sliding back to the center of the roof, he opened his eyes to see zombie heads popping like over-inflated water balloons. One, two, three, they continued erupting, blood geysering out of neck stumps to rain down on the crowd. It was some kind of bizarre Woodstock celebration, with blood falling like rain as the crowd danced and gyrated in pleasure.

Dazed and not understanding what was happening, it took a few heartbeats for the reports of gunfire to filter past his fuzziness and sink into his mind.

Someone was shooting the dead, taking them down one at a time.

More heads popped around him, one after another.

Pop, pop, pop, splat!

It felt like forever but in fact was less than half a minute. In that short elapse of time, all the zombies had been put down, until the Escalade sat alone in a circle of prone corpses.

Trump could only stare, not fully comprehending that he was out of imminent danger.

The sound of an engine floated on the wind, and a few seconds later a large Ford pickup truck rolled up. There were two men in the cab and two more in the rear bed. The ones in the bed carried M16s. All wore camo clothing and gear, with large hunting knives strapped to their legs. They didn't look like military, as in U.S. armed forces, they looked like para-military. Men and women who liked to play war. The kind that thought one day they would have to rise up and start a civil war in America.

Trump looked up from the roof of the Escalade, his hand reaching out in a plea for help, then he lowered it back down. It was as if something inside him said it was all right to rest, that he could finally sleep. The danger was over, he would be okay.

As he slipped into a light unconsciousness, he heard the men as they gathered around the Escalade, ignoring the fallen zombies at their feet.

"Is he dead?" one man asked.

"Nah, just looks wiped out, is all," another replied. "What I want to know is why the fuck he's naked."

Trump, barely conscious, felt his body being removed from the roof. Even if he wanted to protest, he wouldn't have been able to so much as twitch a finger.

"Who knows why?" the first voice said. "Why are we taking him with us? He seems too old to do much work."

"He can work till he can't," a third voice said. This man had a deep voice, one that commanded attention just by the sound. "Besides, every living person matters right now. It's Us against Them, make no mistake."

"Well, the old fuck needs to work for a while to pay us back for all the bullets we just wasted saving his white ass." The voice sounded like it was a Black man, with a country twang to it. "It'll be nice to see another white old bastard working for us for a change."

Trump felt himself being laid down after being carried a short distance. Placed in the rear of the bed, he moaned in his fugue state.

Then one of the men gasped and exclaimed, "Holy shit, I think I know this guy! Yeah, it is, it is him?"

"Who? Who is he?"

"It's Number 45!" The surprise in the voice was apparent to anyone listening. "It's the fucking President!"

"What the hell are you talking about, Thames?" the voice carried authority, the leader of the group by the sound of the way the others deferred to him.

"Guys, it's Donald Trump. We didn't save some old man, we saved the goddamn President of the United States."

"What? Let me see," the leader said.

Trump sensed more than saw the sunlight on his face become blocked out as the leader of the men leaned over him, peering into the rear bed of the Ford.

"Shit, you're right. This is Trump."

"I thought he was dead?" the first man asked.

"No one ever said he died, they said he was at the hospital," the leader said.

"Why's he got no hair?" Thames asked.

"Who knows?" the leader replied. "We'll ask him back at camp when he comes to. He doesn't look like he's wounded, just looks exhausted. For now, let's get him back." There was hesitation. "Goddamn it, fellas, we found Trump. Maybe there's hope for this country after all."

If there was more of the conversation, Trump didn't hear it, as he'd finally succumbed to fatigue and was truly unconscious.

Chapter 9

For the third time in as many days, or so it seemed, Donald Trump slowly came awake, not knowing where he was, and feeling as if he'd been run over by a truck. But then said truck had backed up, rolled over him again, before pulling forward and bouncing over him one last time before driving off.

Cracking his eyes a little, he saw a canvas ceiling, which rippled in the wind that seemed to shake the building he was in.

He parted his eyes a little more and realized he was inside a large military tent.

A voice from beside him said, "Here, Sir, drink this."

A jug was placed to his lips and cool water ran into his mouth and down his chin to pool on his chest. He drank deeply, and was angry when the water jug was taken away.

"Not too much, Sir. A little at a time or you'll only throw it up."

"Who the hell are you?" he asked, his voice barely more than a whisper.

"I'm your nurse," she said and then reached up and checked the saline drip he was on, before walking away, as if the matter had been settled.

He tried to ask her more questions but he only managed a few croaking words that were illegible.

Looking down at his left arm, once more he saw an IV line in his wrist. Déjà vu filled him and made him shiver, despite the wool blanket covering him.

With his right hand under the blanket he touched his leg and chest, relieved to feel clothing. They were thin and soft—pajamas or something similar if he had to guess.

The nurse walked back to him, after leaving a desk ten feet away. She picked up his right arm and touched his wrist, feeling his pulse and timing it while looking at her wristwatch. The tent was large, over twenty by thirty feet in diameter. Other beds were alongside his, but all were empty. He'd watched enough MASH as a boy to know what a medical tent looked like.

"Where am I?"

The nurse ignored him, still counting. Upon finishing, she placed his arm back on the bed and wrote something on a clipboard.

"You're in Maryland."

"Can you be more specific?" he asked.

She shook her head. "Captain Morrigan will tell you everything. He wanted to know the moment you came to." She spun around and returned to the desk, where she picked up a two-way radio. She spoke into it, her voice low and clipped.

Trump didn't hear what she said. Not that it mattered; the moment he tried to sit up, the tent began to swim around him, and he slumped back onto the bed. He felt himself slipping into unconsciousness again. He raised a hand to call the nurse over but she didn't notice. The hand, barely raised more than an inch off the bed, flopped back down, the owner already sleeping again.

The transfer from unconscious to conscious was much smoother this time. Opening his eyes, Trump was alert almost instantly, and his body was devoid of most of the aching it had suffered upon his last waking moments.

There was no jolt of wondering where he was. He remained in the medical tent, in bed, covered up to his chin with a gray wool blanket. The IV was also still attached, dripping saline automatically. An empty bedpan sat on the floor near the bed.

"Good to see you're awake, Sir," a strong and authoritive voice said from a few feet away at the foot of the bed.

Trump recognized it immediately, from when he'd been saved from being devoured by the dead, and his eyes followed the voice. "I know you. You saved me from those creatures."

"Yes, Sir, I did." Morrigan stood up and went rigid, as if at attention. "Captain Thomas Morrigan at your service." He then snapped a salute and held it.

Trump studied the man before him. Wearing camo from head to toe, he appeared to be in his late twenties to early thirties. He was a child compared to Trump's age, but the president had learned years ago that young didn't mean incompetent, and had taken many youthful disciples under his wing.

The man's brown hair was cut short on the sides, military style, what he'd heard called a 'high and tight.' His hairline was receding early for a man his age. His eyebrows were thick, close to a unibrow, and the nose was long and birdlike, the chin slightly pointed. He had the look of a rat, truth be told, but Trump wasn't about to say that, if ever, and certainly not until he knew more about his predicament.

"At ease, son. I guess I have to thank you," Trump said.

Morrigan relaxed slightly and dropped his salute. "Not at all, Sir. You're the President of the United States and it was my honor to rescue you." He bowed slightly. "I'm at your disposal, as are my men. We're MAGA all the way. Not one Democrat. Only red-blooded, American Republicans."

"How long have I been out?" Trump asked, nodding at the man's words and inwardly pleased.

"About half a day since the last time you woke up, Mr. President," Morrigan explained. "Nurse Tammy called me, but by the time I arrived you were out again. I don't blame you one bit, Sir. The state you were in. It's amazing you're already awake now." He smiled. "It must be that tough constitution you've always had."

Ignoring the compliment, not knowing if the man was being genuine or not, Trump sat up a little in bed, Morrigan moving so that he pulled Trump's pillow up higher so the president could recline more easily.

"Yes, I've always been fast to recover if I ever got sick." He paused then added, "Which was almost never. Healthy as a horse, always have been." It was a blatant lie. Trump had been sick often as a child, either with the flu or a cold. It was just one more thing he frequently lied about.

"Of course, Mr. President," Morrigan agreed, nodding emphatically.

Trump studied the man for a few seconds, reading the captain's body language. He sure seemed to believe what he was saying. Which was excellent news for Trump. "So you're a Captain? In what branch of service?"

Morrigan went to the chair and dragged it closer to the bed, then sat down again. "I'm not a real Captain, Sir. That is, I'm not in the actual military. But we use their rank signs anyway. After all, serving in the military is for losers, right? That's what you said, you know, before the dead began to run around like illegal immigrants." He sat taller and added, "I'm the leader of a group that calls itself the Lost Sons of Freedom, Sir. We're a paramilitary group. MAGA is our mantra and we fought hard to make it so. For almost four years we've been doing our best to help you do God's work, and even now we still fight." He shook his head. "It was a terrible blow to the country when you went to Walter Reed from a heart attack brought on from Covid, but we figured that was a lie, the Fake news trying to discredit you. They said you were in a coma, then after that it all fell apart. Once the internet and television went out there was no new information. We thought about going to Walter Reed and seeing if we could find you but it never happened. Seemed like a pipe dream. Before the internet failed we heard that the hospital was overrun by the dead, and everyone simply assumed you died, too."

Trump scoffed. "As you can see, they were lying, like they always do." He realized the news media was defunct. "I mean, like they always *did*."

"Yes, Sir. I'm at your disposal, Sir, whatever you need, just ask. Now that you're here, we can get back to making America what it once was."

A shadow appeared at the tent entryway and Trump looked past Morrigan to see a large man in camo clothing enter. He was big, over six feet and Trump, who was no slouch in the height department, had a feeling the young man had a good two inches over him.

The new arrival was all muscle, with thick, curly black hair. His skin was tan, but it didn't look like it was from being in the sun. With the curly dark hair and dark skin tone, the man must have had mixed race parents. Trump was fine with that, as long as the man obeyed orders like Morrigan seemed to want to do.

Morrigan nodded as the man spoke, then waved him away. "Thanks, Thames, you can go." The large man retreated back out of the tent.

"Something up?" Trump asked.

Morrigan appeared to be thinking, and was staring down at the floor. He looked up and at Trump after the question sank in. "Huh? Oh, no Sir, I was just getting a report from Corporal Thames. I had a team scavenging for food and weapons; they found a new settlement of people, I guess. Our search party talked to them. They were nice and friendly. They're about thirty miles from here. On the outskirts of Baltimore. Maybe we could trade with them. That is, if we had something to trade. So far, I only have enough for my men, and I'm not gonna trade any of our weapons, that's for damn sure. There's about fifty of us here, Mr. President. Women, too, but to me, they're all my men."

"What are you going to do then? Just make nice with those people and hope for the best?"

Morrigan shrugged. "I guess. What else can I do?"

Trump pointed to the sidearm Morrigan wore on his right hip. "Do you have more of those?"

Morrigan, glancing down and seeing the gun as if for the first time, nodded. "Of course, Sir. We were stockpiling weapons long before the dead started running around. We thought it would be for a Civil war, but…" He shrugged. "So, yes, Sir, we have plenty of weapons to defend ourselves with."

Trump nodded; he'd already known the answer to his question, and he usually did before asking. It was a way to gain control of a conversation. He remembered the firepower Morrigan's people had used on the dead to save his ass. "Then why don't you use those guns and take what you want?"

"Sir?"

Trump began to become frustrated, but he wasn't in control here, not yet, so he calmed himself, knowing to get his way he needed to become Morrigan's friend, and not just his superior.

"Captain, do you know how I became President of the United States?"

Morrigan looked as if he was going to reply but Trump was already talking again. The question had been rhetorical, he hadn't expected an answer.

"I became President by taking what I wanted. That was true then and from what I've seen so far of the state of the country, and heard from you, it's even truer now."

"Sir, are you suggesting…?"

"Fuck yes I'm suggesting it," he snapped, hopefully using the full power and respect of being the President of the United States. "You go in there, guns blazing, and take whatever the hell you want and you kill anyone who gets in your way. That's how you get power son, real power. You take what you need and fuck anyone else."

Trump felt a wave of exhaustion sweep over him and he knew he needed to lie down again. He slid back down onto the bed; recumbent, he let out a loud sigh of relief. "Look, son, I'm tired, really tired. I need to rest now. We can talk more later, and I'll explain it all to you in more depth. You'll see. It'll be beautiful, amazing. When I tell you it'll blow your mind."

Morrigan stepped over to the bed and gazed down at Trump, who looked back up at the captain, seeing nothing but worship in the man's eyes. Trump was pleased. He knew he could use that worship to his advantage, as he'd done with others for years.

"But before you leave, I need you to get a few things for me."

"Anything, Mr. President. Whatever you need."

"Come closer."

Morrigan closed the two foot gap until his knees brushed the side of the twin bed, the frame and mattress scavenged from a nearby home, as were the others within the tent.

Trump told him to lean in closer, as he didn't want to talk any louder than necessary, the fatigue slowly claiming him.

Morrigan placed his ear only inches from Trump's mouth, and as he nodded a few times in understanding, Trump informed the captain what he required.

***

When Donald J. Trump awoke from what was basically normal rest, he felt refreshed. The IV had been removed from his arm and it was still daylight when he peered out of the tent opening. It was around seventy-five degrees out, which was very comfortable. The exact time was unknown and he didn't think it was relevant anyway. Nurse Tammy was nowhere to be seen, but he had a feeling her, or someone like her, was within earshot.

On a small table beside the bed was a bowl of stew and a glass of water. The moment he saw it his stomach rumbled. He spared no time in consuming it. He ate quickly, not remembering the last time he was so hungry. The stew tasted like the best meal he ever had. Better than any cheeseburger or chicken nuggets or taco he had the pleasure to devour during his life. When the stew was gone, he even licked the bowl clean, and though still hungry, it took the edge off his hunger. He downed the water in three gulps, the liquid tasting like the finest wine.

With his immediate need for food satiated, his eyes darted across the tent to see the items he'd requested waiting for him.

There was a battered wardrobe rack scavenged from a clothing store a few feet across from him. From a cursory inspection, it looked as if Captain Morrigan had found everything that was requested.

Tentatively, Trump sat up, and when he didn't feel faint, he slid off the bed, careful not to collapse as soon as he was upright. But he felt fine. Strong.

He even felt the urge to urinate, which was a sensation that he hadn't felt after waking in the hospital. He quickly used the bedpan. Only a slight trickle came out but he figured that was to be expected.

He crossed the tent and sat down in the chair Morrigan had used previously, then began to remove the pajamas he was wearing. He began to put on what Morrigan had fetched for him.

First were the black socks, wool, by the thickness, which was fine. He hadn't specified the material he'd wanted.

Next were pants. Dark blue, with a tight crease down the front. A leather belt to hold them up. Black shoes, polished to a mirror finish were the next things to get on. The fit was comfortable, and he wondered if his shoe size had been checked while he slept.

The white, button down shirt was donned next, followed by a red tie, which he made sure to make a little shorter than it should be. The shirt was a little tight, but not too much. When he slid into the dark blue business jacket to complete the suit, the tightness wasn't visible. And the jacket fit pretty well, if not as perfect as the ones he had custom fit at the White House.

There was a flag pin on the lapel, a note attached as well. He pulled it off and read it.

Mr. President,
I believe I've found everything you asked for, including two more items you didn't, but I think you'll want. The flag pin is from my personal collection, and the last item was found in a costume shop in downtown Bethesda.
When you're dressed, please exit the tent. I have one last surprise for you.
Your loyal servant,
Capt. T. Morrigan

It was obvious what the remaining item was, as it was the only thing remaining on the wardrobe rack. It was in a white plastic bag, hanging from a hook, but the moment he removed it from the bag, a wide smile came to his lips.

There was a small mirror hanging from a tent pole in the center of the tent, and he used it so he could see how to affix the item to him, then he turned, squared his shoulders, and walked out of the tent.

He was blinded for a few seconds upon exiting the tent, but after blinking a few times, his vision cleared.

Two men, guards by the looks of them, stood on either side of the tent. Both guards were armed with assault rifles and had sidearms and knives strapped to their bodies.

One man turned, saluted and said, "Mr. President, Captain Morrigan instructed us to escort you to the far side of the camp."

The other guard was talking into a two-way radio, Trump overhearing words like, "He's awake, Captain," and "We're bringing him to you now."

"Oh, okay, then, let's go," Trump said, feeling out of his element but acting as if he was in complete control, a bluff he'd used far too many times in his political career. Most of the time he had no idea what the hell he was doing, which was the way he'd gone through life, if he was ever honest with himself. He'd always lived for the moment, dealing with each issue as an increment in time. When all options failed in that segment of time, he would simply move on to the next segment, and see how he could get what he needed. His entire life was living in the moment, and damn the consequences of future or past mistakes.

The two guards escorted Trump through the camp, which he saw was as basic as a camp could be. Cooking stoves were scattered around between the tents, and port-o-potties were off to the side. Over the tent roofs, Trump saw burned-out homes. It appeared the camp was placed inside a park of some kind, which was then within a gated community. Behind some of the houses, he could see the eight foot, iron spiked fence going to each point of the compass

Weaving through the tents, eventually he was led to another tent, where the guards gestured him inside.

"Please go straight through to the other side, Sir," one guard said. He was a young man in his twenties with more craters on his face than the moon, and more acne than any man should have to suffer through. Trump wondered if the apocalypse had affected the man's access to acne cream. Not that he cared one bit either way. The issues other people dealt with daily were irrelevant to him. Only Trump mattered to Trump.

Hesitantly for a moment, Trump did as requested. He entered the gloom-filled tent, which was empty, devoid of anything but the grass it had been set up on, and crossed the ground inside until he was at the far side of the tent. A wooden step two feet wide protruded into the tent at the exit, and another after that. Whatever he was about to go out into, it appeared he was climbing upwards.

Squaring his shoulders, and not knowing what awaited him, he stepped out of the tent and back into the daylight, taking the steps cautiously for fear of tripping.

There were only four steps, luckily, for as he ascended he was already feeling winded. The second he was outside, voices were raised, and he found himself on a very small stage, no more than eight feet across and six feet in width. At the back of the stage, the remnants of wood and tools could be seen, the stage hastily erected for him, he assumed, as even sawdust could be seen blowing across the stage due to the light breeze.

Captain Morrigan stood at the far end of the short stage, a bullhorn in his hand. He quickly moved closer to the president and stood by his side. Trump gazed out over the heads of the Lost Sons of Freedom, who were all gathered before the stage as if Trump was doing one of his rallies.

Trump, no stranger to showmanship, knew immediately what was occurring and he smiled widely.

Morrigan took a step forward to the side so he was now facing Trump, though he turned his head slightly so the bullhorn was in the direction of the crowd.

"Men and women of the Lost Sons of Freedom, I'm proud to give you Number 45, the one and only true President of the United States. With him leading us, we can once more Make America Great Again!"

The crowd went wild, cheering, hooting and clapping. A few shot their guns in the air. Trump could see all the weapons, the camp heavily armed. That must have explained why, along with the fencing around the gated community, they weren't concerned with making noise and attracting any zombies to the area. Anything that showed up at their front gate could be easily mowed down and destroyed.

"Trump! Trump! Trump!" the crowd chanted over and over.

Trump stood tall at the center of the stage, his face impassive. He looked as if it was nothing new to have him adored, but deep inside he was filled with exuberance.

The breeze continued to blow, and Trump liked the way it fluttered the blonde wig on his head, a perfect copy of his once trademark locks. Captain Morrigan had done well in finding it. The uniform Trump always wore when he played President was complete due to the wig. With it on his bald head, he looked exactly as he had before suffering a heart attack.

As he gazed out over the camp of his new, screaming, chanting and adoring subjects, he mumbled under his breath, "I'm back."

Chapter 10

Two days later, Donald J. Trump was feeling completely like his old self. After having eaten many meals of solid food, he had his strength back, too.

On his face, was a nice shade of pumpkin orange, thanks to makeup he'd asked for. He thought he looked wonderful, and everyone agreed. No one had the courage to tell him that he really looked like a giant Cheeto.

He was sitting in his command tent, which were also his living quarters.

After his welcome rally, he'd quickly taken control and instructed Captain Morrigan what he would need. There was no doubt Trump was now the man in charge.

The rally from two days previous had gone as well as Trump could have hoped. He'd given a speech, one full of lies, but then his fans had never cared too much for the truth. The truth was depressing, but his lies told of a world waiting for them to conquer, where the walking dead was a mere impediment to rebuilding America.

By the time he was finished, they'd been cheering and applauding so hard the undead would have heard them in Washington, which was only a mere seven miles away.

Trump had asked Morrigan about that, curious how D.C. had fared after the fall of civilization.

"Washington is a plague town, Sir," Morrigan explained. "Zombies are everywhere, corpses littering the streets as well. It's filled with disease and is a cesspool too dangerous to enter."

"So what else is new?" Trump said with a sneer. "Sounds like the Washington I already knew. And there's no longer a danger to the China Virus? It's gone for good?"

"No, Sir. Once the dead started running around and attacking and killing, it decreased the population on the planet in less than a week. With no way it could spread person to person, plus no air travel or any other travel really. It only took a few weeks for it to be eliminated completely."

"See?" he said proudly, feeling vindicated. "Didn't I say it would disappear? That one day it would just be gone, like magic." He left out the part about all it taking was a Holocaust and only about one percent of the population not dying in said apocalypse. Just a few minor details not worth bringing up, really.

The camp was setup in a large park, set within an area of Maryland called Locust Hill Estates. Mostly luxury homes, before the dead began to walk the homes went for a million dollars or more. But sometime recently, a major conflagration had broken out, and soon, every house in the complex had caught fire as well. Only foundations remained now, the burnt husks of the houses surrounding the camp on all sides. Some still had their roofs, however, with only their skeletal frames remaining. But the eight foot tall wrought iron fence that ringed the community still remained, along with the guard house and the two rolling gates at the north and south ends. Guards had been positioned there, along with heavy weapons, and other men patrolled the perimeter daily. Given the state of the country it wasn't a bad set up.

It was midday. Trump was studying a map of Baltimore, Morrigan hovering over him.

"Show me where these people are located," he instructed Morrigan.

Captain Morrigan leaned over and studied the map for a moment, then, with a Sharpie, he circled an area just outside of Baltimore. "They're here, Sir."

Trump nodded, barely looking or caring. He was just going through the motions like he always did.

"You need to send a messenger to them. I want you to have him explain that I'm in charge again and that I expect them to accept me as the rightful President of America. And in doing so, they need to pay taxes in the form of food and whatever else you, my dear Captain, might need or want. Explain that to Make America Great Again—I love saying that—we need supplies. As citizens of the United States, they need to contribute. We'll need more recruits, too. We need to continue to build our army so we can destroy the zombies and bring Law and Order back to this great nation."

"But what if they refuse?"

Trump shrugged. "You said they didn't look like they have much in the way of guns, am I right?"

"Yes, Sir. From what we saw they did have guns but nothing like we have."

"Good, then you tell them they have two choices." He leaned forward and steepled his fingers, elbows on the table. "Submit or be killed. If they ignore me we'll wipe out every single one of them, and use them as an example to any other groups we find, so they know we mean business."

Morrigan hesitated, unsure of what to say. He respected the President immensely, but what he was suggesting, it didn't fit into the captain's world view.

Trump shifted in his chair and looked up at Morrigan, seeing the indecisiveness swirling within the man. "Captain, when I was in office, I didn't get as much done as I wanted. Do you know why that was?"

"No, Sir."

"It was because the goddamn Democrats stopped me at every turn. We say the United States is a democracy but you know what it really is?"

Morrigan shook his head, enraptured by Trump's lecture.

"The United States is a place where the weak get to control the strong. Every time I tried to stop illegal immigration, who was it who stopped me?"

"The Democrats and the Liberals."

"Yes. And when I tried to get rid of all those fucking DACA kids, what happened?"

"The same, Sir," Morrigan said, slowly warming to the ideas Trump was feeding him.

"Yes. And what happened every time I tried to pass laws stopping gays and the rest of their foul ilk?"

Morrigan's eyes were brighter now. He was getting into the mood. "The fucking Democrats, Sir. It's always them. The bunch of no-good Democrats!"

"That's right! And if those people over there don't want to fall in line and help us rebuild this country, that must mean only one thing. And that is?"

"That they're Democrats, Sir. Filthy, no-good Democrats!"

"That's right. There's no more Senate now, no more Congress. There's no one to stop us from doing what's right. What God wants us to do!"

Morrigan was fully onboard and he nodded his head emphatically. "Yes, Sir, I understand now. I'll send someone immediately. We should have an answer back in a few hours or less." He began turning to leave the tent and carry out his orders.

"Good, good," Trump said, smiling widely, as if Morrigan was his best friend. "Now that I'm back, the free ride is over." He paused before adding, "Oh, and one more thing, Captain."

Morrigan stopped at the tent opening, glancing back at Trump. "Yes, Mr. President. Whatever you need."

Trump nodded. "Now that I'm fully recovered, I got an itch I need to scratch, if you know what I mean."

"Sir?" Morrigan asked, not understanding, but as Trump stared at him, revelation slowly came to him. "Oh, yes, I understand. I'll have it taken care of immediately."

"Good, please do. And make sure the age is within my preference."

Morrigan saluted and exited the tent, Trump leaning back in his chair as he gazed down at the map of Maryland.

It had never been a state he'd never really given much thought to, but now, it would be the first one on his renewed grab for power. One state at a time, he thought. And with no one to stop him, oh what fun it was going to be.

They used to make cracks about him wanting to be an autocrat, well, they didn't know the half of it. And now, it was all within his grasp.

Fifteen minutes after Morrigan departed the tent, another figure entered.

Wearing camo like Morrigan, the moment Trump looked up he could tell that the new arrival wasn't the captain.

Even the drab camo shirt and pants did little to hide the shapely figure within.

At around thirty years old, with long dark hair and a full chest, the woman who entered would have looked good in an empty potato sack.

"Mr. President. I was told you had an itch you needed scratched." She smiled seductively.

He stood up and walked over to the king-sized bed that he now called his own. Sitting down, he stared at the beautiful woman before him. "I do. Can you help me with that?"

"Yes, Sir, I think I can help you with that and a whole lot more." With a sexy swing of her hips she went to the tent opening and stuck her head out, talking to the guard stationed there, telling him not to disturb the President until Trump said it was okay. Trump always had a man watching him, much like the Secret Service had once done. She then closed the flaps and walked over to him, while simultaneously pulling off her shirt to expose her bra and the perfect globes with in it.

"My name's…" she began, but Trump raised his hand to stop her from talking, then gestured for her to come to him.

"I don't care." Trump laughed and began to undo his tie and unbutton his shirt as she got down on her knees before him, another supplicant kneeling at the altar of Trump. "I'm going to enjoy this."

Chapter 11

Under a heavy ceiling of storm clouds, thick black smoke merged with the dark clouds to become one, constantly swirling overhead.

There was a slight breeze coming off the ocean, which was less than a mile away. But the scent of salt was lost in the aroma of burning gasoline and charred human meat.

Donald J. Trump, the rightful leader of the United States by his opinion, stood on a hill just outside of Baltimore. He wore a long black overcoat, the tails swaying in the wind. Underneath the coat, was a white shirt, sans tie, and blue pants. A pair of loafers were on his feet. He knew he would be walking today, and he hated walking.

Holding a pair of binoculars to his eyes, he watched the closing battle where there had once been an enclave of surviving humans. Though the defenders had tried their best, the fight was over before it even started.

Two weeks earlier, after sending a messenger with Trump's ultimatum, the man had returned with a reply half a day later. It hadn't been what Trump had expected. Instead of welcoming him back as their President, the enclave had told the messenger to 'fuck off,' in those exact words, and had refused to comply with any demands asked of them.

Angry and offended that the enclave would be so insulting, Trump had ordered Captain Morrigan to begin planning for an attack. First spies had been sent to study the enemy and to get intelligence on what sort of true defenses the enclave had. Then, once all the intelligence had been gathered, the attack had begun, with thirty of Morrigan's people sneaking up to the perimeter of the enclave the night before and secreting themselves in strategic hidey holes, the rest attacking the main gate and another group at the rear.

When the attack had been sprung in the early hours of the morning, just as the sun was cresting in the east, the enclave never knew what hit them until it was too late.

Having to deal with two groups of attacking foes, when the hidden men and women had popped out of their holes after receiving a planned signal, and flanking the enclave's defenders, the fight had been over almost immediately.

Trump had to give credit to Morrigan for his planning skills. Though the man was in reality only playing army, as he was just a leader of a homegrown militia, he was in fact a competent tactician.

The last few gunshots could be heard, as the remains of the resistance within the enclave were dealt with.

Trump wasn't alone on the hill. Beside him, was his personal bodyguard, the brick wall of a man, former Corporal and now Major Thames, who'd received a battlefield promotion from Trump weeks earlier. Morrigan was somewhere down below, leading the attack on the enclave, or the routing of it. On Thames' shoulder hung an AR15, and a .45 was strapped on his hip. He had more than enough firepower on him to protect the President. He and Thames had talked weeks ago about what the man would be responsible for. Thames was fully under the President's control, and worshiped Trump like an acolyte to a cult leader. He would do whatever Trump wanted, and that included killing someone if told to. So far, Trump hadn't acted on this, but he was looking forward to the first time he did. For now, simply knowing he had that kind of power was invigorating.

Thames' two-way radio crackled and the man put it to his ear. After listening for a moment, he turned to Trump. "Sir, the captain says the fight's over. If you'd like to come down and inspect the scene, it's safe."

"Ask him if he's sure? And I mean, really sure," Trump said. Though he acted tough, in truth he was a coward. There was no way he would ever go into that enclave if there was even the remotest possibility of danger.

Thames did as instructed, and after receiving a response, added, "The captain said the enemy has been pacified. It's safe, Sir. He says he guarantees it with his life."

Trump scowled and pursed his lips. "He better, because if he's wrong, he just might have to."

"Yes, Sir."

"Let's go then."

The walk was only a few minutes, and Trump reveled in the fact that he wasn't even winded when he reached the main gate of the enclave. His thinner body, now more lean after his coma, meant he was physically able to be more active. It was nice not to become winded when he rose from bed in the middle of the night to use the bathroom, or after banging one of the whores he would have sent to his tent late at night. Of course, the women were just members of the Last Sons of Freedom, not true prostitutes. But to Trump, all women were whores, especially the ones willing to fuck him.

The enclave had taken a fleet of RVs and school buses, wrapping them around their living area. Then they'd packed the opening beneath the vehicles with whatever could be found. It wasn't a perfect wall but it worked well to keep the dead out.

As Trump reached the gate, he saw many other corpses scattered around, signs of the zombies that had been attracted to the fighting. But his men had more than enough firepower to stop any that arrived.

As Trump studied all the prone corpses, he began to get an idea. If the dead could be used as a weapon, it would be much easier to pacify unruly settlements. It was only the hint of an idea, a kernel at the back of his mind. He made a note to discuss it more with Morrigan once they returned to their camp.

Trump was able to see inside the enclave at the burning homes and other structures of unknown use. A church was located within the protective perimeter. It was now a roaring inferno, its steeple alight, resembling a giant candle burning against the lightening sky.

Trump smiled upon seeing the devastation, enjoying it immensely. These people had refused to join him or pay tribute. So they had to die as an example to anyone else who defied him. He was especially enjoying the fall of civilization today. He was now the ruler he always wanted to be. A dictator that proclaimed something was law and it was; no discussions, no one to ask to put it to a vote.

"Is it safe to go inside?" Trump asked Thames, despite already being informed it was so. "I want to have a better look around."

Thames held his AR15 in his hands. "My job is to guard you with my life, Mr. President. That's what I'll do."

Trump only nodded. "I want to talk to Captain Morrigan." He began walking through the missing gate, which had been blown off its hinges and lay off to the side of the opening. Wood splinters were everywhere, the remnants of the stockade fence gate. It had been built to keep the dead out, not determined human beings.

A few of Trump's militia joined up with Thames, wanting to keep the president safe. One was a bearded man in his forties, the other, in his thirties with blonde hair and stubble to match, a large and colorful tattoo of a snake on his neck. Both men had blackout paint slanted across their faces.

"It looks like we win," Trump said proudly, seeing nothing but corpses scattered everywhere he looked.

"Hell yes, we did. We kicked their asses, President Trump."

Trump looked over to see it was the blonde man who had said this. The name on his camo shirt was Hodgkins. He made a note of this. The man was gung-ho, and Trump had learned a long time ago that men like him could be useful. If he promoted him to a higher rank later, the others in the camp would become more motivated as well, in the hopes they might be next.

"Mr. President!" a voice called from the left.

Trump turned to see one of Morrigan's men stepping around a half-fallen brick wall, dragging a grimy and scared little boy of around seven, with a dirty stuffed rabbit still clutched in his hands. The pitiful waif's left arm was bleeding from a deep cut, droplets of blood splattering onto the ground. Tears left runnels down the boy's dust-covered face. He wore a teddy bear shirt and pajama pants.

"I found this brat hiding over there," the man said, dragging the child behind him. He carried an Uzi with folding stock extended, the butt on his hip, the barrel aimed at the sky.

Trump looked at the rugrat, his face devoid of emotion. "Good for you, soldier. But what were your orders about anyone found alive inside these walls?"

The soldier paused for a moment before saying, "We were told to kill anyone we found. Scorched earth, no survivors."

"Right, so you already know what you need to do." Trump glared at the soldier, the hair on his blonde wig blowing gently in the light breeze. His own hair was growing in slowly but was nothing more than peach fuzz. But in time, he would be able to toss out the wig for his own hair, of course, he might have to use a come over, as his hair had never been completely natural. Not for years, anyway.

The soldier went pale under his Pittsburgh Pirates baseball cap, as he came to the realization of what Trump wanted him to do. "But, Sir, you don't mean you want me to..." He gazed down at the crying child, who held his hand as if it was a lifeline. He swallowed the lump in his throat. "You can't mean it. Please..."

"So you're refusing to obey a direct order from your President," Trump said flatly. He glanced at Thames, who saw the look and began to move slowly away from Trump, but closer to the soldier and his small charge.

"No, of course not, Sir," the soldier said, stammering. "It's just..."

His reply was cut off when a shadow loomed over him from behind and Thames reached out and grabbed the man, pulling him against his chest. A thick forearm encircled the soldier's neck, while a meaty hand clutched the chin.

With one massive twist, Thames snapped the soldier's neck, the man squeezing the trigger of his Uzi, the bullets shooting high in the sky. When the giant let go, the man dropped to the ground like his bones had been substituted with pudding. The body slumped in the dirt, immobile, the man's eyes still open but seeing nothing.

The child, who only a moment ago had been holding the soldier's hand, stared with enormous blue eyes in absolute terror, before he took off running, his small bare feet slapping the ground.

Trump gestured to Hodgkin's. "Deal with that."

Hodgkins did as instructed without hesitation. He leveled the M16A he'd been holding with the muzzle pointed down and raised it to waist level, then triggered a short burst.

The bullets stitched the child's back; the small boy spun in a circle three times, arms out flung, the stuffed rabbit spinning away, before the body slumped to the ground. His teddy bear PJs were immediately soaked in blood, as was the ground around the tiny corpse.

"Good job, Hodgkins," Trump said. "Or maybe I should say, Lt. Hodgkins."

"I'm only a private, Mr. President, Sir," Hodgkins said.

Trump stared at the man as if he was an idiot, but then decided to overlook Hodgkins' contradiction. "Not anymore you're not. As of right now, you're a Lieutenant. And you're part of my personal bodyguard detail along with Major Thames here. You report directly to me, no one else." He spit onto the ground after tasting dust. "Do you understand?"

"Uh, yes, Sir, I get it. Thank you."

"Good, now make sure that small creature doesn't get back up again. Gotta shoot the head, right?"

Hodgkins nodded, and jogged over to the still body of the child and pumped one more round into the small skull. The bullet did much more damage being the head wasn't as large as an adult's. Lost youth sprayed into the air, the bits of skull fragments and brains falling in a V pattern where Hodgkins was standing.

Trump didn't even pay attention, uninterested in the tiny tot's murder. He gazed wistfully at the men surrounding him. More than a dozen had appeared now that the battle was over. Many had blood spatter covering their camo clothing. A few had seen the murder of the boy but their faces showed no hint of disgust, which Trump was watching for. "Let everyone understand this. I respect strength and men who appreciate the chain of command without question. Only by these values do we show that we deserve to survive and lead others. If we're not strong, then we're no better than the weak-minded pieces of shit we've exterminated here this day. These people didn't want to support the growing call to rebuild America, they wanted to be left alone, while we do the work. But they had no problem basking in the success once we finish and this country is restored to what it once was. They were losers, and there's no place for losers in our rebuilding of the country."

"Hell yes," a soldier said from the back of the crowd.

"Fucking pussies, all of 'em," offered another man.

"Kill 'em all!" another shouted.

Trump gazed out at his men and a few women with satisfaction, and at the destruction of the surrounding enclave. Fire belched from the church, tongues of flame licking skyward out of the shattered stained glass windows. The tall spire collapsed after one of its structural supports finally burned through. In a tower of sparks it fell into itself.

It had been a good day. Trump believed he'd accomplished something here that he never could have done as President before the world had collapsed. He was the ultimate authority with his militia, and soon others would join, whether they wanted to or not. Such was necessary to rebuild America. Sacrifices would have to be made. Of course, none by him.

Captain Morrigan appeared from behind a low structure and walked over to join the president. He saluted crisply

Trump did the same, only not as tight, his hand more like a wilted piece of lettuce. "We've done a good thing here, Captain, one history will remember as being the day America started its climb back to greatness. Wait till you see it when it's finished. It'll be beautiful, amazing to behold."

"Yes, Mr. President."

"Has everything been done as we agreed?"

"Yes, Mr. President, Sir. No survivors remain, scorched earth." The church roared with flames as a counterpoint. A nearby building had begun to burn as well; some embers from the church had reached it. Soon, the defying enclave would be nothing but ash.

Trump planned to use the destroyed town as an example to others who thought to resist him.

Though how that would happen without social media or television media, was unknown. Actually, he hadn't thought that far ahead.

He gazed out over the abandoned buildings of the now empty enclave, smoke from the fires hovering low to the ground, obscuring some buildings from view.

He was confidant that the lesson given today, though hard taught, would ensure that other settlements fell in line.

His great plan had begun.

In glorious fashion.

Morrigan was turned away from the president and talking to a few of his men, along with Thames, who were filling the captain in on what had happened to the unruly soldier who had disobeyed orders.

Trump patted Morrigan on the shoulder as the captain spun back around to face Trump, who cast a brief glance down at the soldier Thames had killed by snapping the man's neck. "Did you really have to kill Dewey, Sir? He was a good guy. I'd known him for years. I mean…" He trailed off, not having words to understand why one of his own men had been killed in such a way.

"Sorry about that, Captain, the responsibilities of a leader. Sometimes tough things need to be done." He glared at Morrigan, his lips tightening into a line as he glanced at Thames as well. The large man shifted slightly so he was standing closer to Morrigan.

The captain seemed to be thinking as he looked at the body of his friend, eyes closed, as if the man was sleeping, despite the dark bruises of a snapped neck.

Morrigan was silently wrestling with his own morals; conflicting with his devotion to Trump and his personal code on which he lived by. Every man had one, some stricter than others, but each day a man, or woman, had to look at themselves in the mirror and accept their choices. Either good or bad.

Thames had slid a little closer to Morrigan, who didn't seem to notice the ominous figure behind him. Thames glanced at Trump, waiting for a nod, which was all the large Black man needed to fulfill the order.

The next few seconds could go either way, and Trump stared at Morrigan, looking for a sign of dissension.

But it never came.

Finally, Morrigan's shoulders seemed to sag slightly, as if in defeat, or acceptance. "I understand, Sir. It had to be done. But I'll miss him."

"And that's okay." Trump patted Morrigan's arm, as if to console the man, despite him being the reason the soldier was dead. He did a similar gesture often to people to acquire their friendship. It was a small thing, but people didn't realize it meant nothing to him. It was just a way to control people. Others felt a kinship with Trump by such a gentle act, but to Trump it was all just part of the show. "Why don't we leave this place? I think we've done all we can here." With a nod to Thames, the looming Black man moved away from Morrigan.

Morrigan nodded and turned to a few of his underlings. "Have everyone make a pass through this place and take anything worth saving, then it's time to move out."

On the ground, Dewey's eyes snapped open, the mouth opening and closing. Gurgling sounds from a shattered voice box meant the normal sounds a zombie would make were now garbled. Trump pointed at the dead creature with a casual wave of his hand, getting Morrigan's attention, who acknowledged the president.

"Deal with that, Captain."

Now Morrigan had to put a bullet in his murdered friend's head, adding insult to injury already given. Trump enjoyed kicking a man when he was already down, even if it was someone who was supposed to be an ally.

With Thames and Hodgkins flanking him, Trump was already walking out of the enclave and back to his waiting command vehicle, a simple Ford pickup truck—nothing as grandiose as a Hummer or a limousine—to return to their campsite.

When the single gunshot sounded, he was barely paying attention.

Chapter 12

Another week passed uneventfully, Trump enjoying the safety of the camp. At night he would keep warm with a willing female body, and in the day he conspired with Morrigan on growing his influence across the state and then beyond.

"We need to get a better home base, this camp is too small once we start bringing in new recruits," Trump explained to a rapt Captain Morrigan. "We need someplace defensible, someplace like a fortress, but close to Washington."

Morrigan pointed to the map spread out on the desk. "Well, Sir, there might be two places that are worth considering. They were found when I sent out scouting parties when I was trying to figure out where to go that was safe back when it all started. I considered them as good candidates, but in the end decided to set up here in the Estates." He pointed with a finger at the map. "Over here, about three miles from Washington is a shopping mall." His finger slid across the map to another spot a few miles away from the mall. "And this is the factory district. Lots of giant buildings we could use here, a lot of them empty and abandoned. We could simply take this camp and transfer it to one of the factories, and then have the added protection of the cement walls of the building."

Trump considered the options, his mind quickly going to the shopping mall. Lots of luxuries there, he figured. He liked the good life and toughing it out in his tent was barely a tolerable option. He had to use a chemical toilet for Christ's sake!

"I like the shopping mall. Let's go there."

Morrigan hesitated, not saying a word.

Trump could tell something was amidst. "What's the problem?"

"Well, Mr. President, the mall is full of zombies. You know, like a shitload of them. It would take a lot of ammunition to kill them all and it would be a risk to my men."

"*Your* men?" Trump asked.

"I mean, your men, of course, Sir. Sorry."

"Yes, all right then." Trump looked sideways at Morrigan for another few seconds, the man studying the map. Trump searched but saw no sign of deceit in his visage. Satisfied, Trump returned his attention to the map.

Morrigan might become a problem in the future, Trump thought, thinking back to when Thames had killed Dewey.

Every now and then the captain seemed to forget who was in charge around here. Trump made a mental note to watch the captain more closely. But for the time, he was still useful, and Morrigan's lapse in judgment could be overlooked.

"Captain, you say the mall is full of zombies, right?"

"Yes, Sir. When the scouting party checked it out they couldn't go inside, there were so many bodies at the door, pressed up to the glass. They went to more than one entrance, too, and on all sides they found it was full."

"Yes, about that. I was thinking about how we could use those creatures to help us if a settlement refuses to obey me. Somehow you need to remove them from the mall and get them into some kind of containment, like trucks or something. I don't know exactly. I'll leave the complexities of the operation to you."

"Sir?"

"I only have an idea about how to use them you see. It's a beautiful plan, tremendous in its simplicity, but how to fully go about it exactly I'll leave to you when the time comes. You're the tactician, after all."

"Whatever you need, Mr. President, I'll do it."

"I know you, will, Captain, and I appreciate it." Trump looked at Morrigan and gave the man a wide smile. "I know you're loyal to me." But he thought, *And if you ever act like that isn't the case, I'll make sure you're removed from your command with extreme prejudice.*

"I'll get to work on a plan to capture the zombies at once."

"Good, now leave me alone." Morrigan turned to leave and Trump added, "Tell Thames to come in, I need him."

"Yes, Sir," Morrigan said and left. There were low voices heard from the tent opening, and a moment later, Thames entered the tent. He'd been standing guard at the opening, which both he and Hodgkins did on a rotating basis, even when Trump was asleep. They were Trump's personal bodyguards after all.

"You need me, Sir?" Thames asked.

"Yes, I'm getting that itch again, can you see that someone comes over to scratch it for me?"

"Right away, Sir," Thames said, and exited the tent. Trump heard the man talking on his two-way, ordering up a nice piece of ass for him to play with.

One thing that had been a welcome change since the apocalypse was that he was able to get laid a hell of a lot more, and not have to worry about tabloid nonsense causing problems.

There were plenty of women in the camp that worshiped him—just like the men did—and they were happy to lay with him whenever he wanted. Just another perk at being in charge, he thought with a grin.

Anxious to have a little fun, he went to his makeshift bathroom—a few tarps hung in the corner to hide the toilet from view—and took a small bottle that contained little blue pills off a shelf. It wasn't that he needed to use the enhancements, but he liked the way it helped him perform. And the ladies thought he was a stallion who never grew tired.

Whistling to himself, he prepared for his upcoming guest.

One week later, to the day, Trump stood in the rear bed of a GMC pickup truck, a pair of field glasses in his hands pressed to his eyes. On the ground, leaning against the truck and both smoking cigarettes, Thames and Hodgkins waited for orders. At the moment, there was nothing to do but wait, as the president gazed across the parking lot to the Maryland shopping mall. Trump was parked as far away from the mall as he could possibly be, where the pavement ended and a row of privacy trees prevented him from going back any more.

There was a lot of activity around the mall, all of it focused on the north entrance, which was where the doors were wide open to allow the zombies to exit, the soldiers hooting and calling to get the dead's attention.

An elaborate maze had been built out of scrap wood scavenged from the area. Everything from old wooden pallets to front doors of empty homes was being used to build the maze. It resembled a cattle maze, a way to herd the zombies from one spot to another, and remain in control.

There was a bank of glass doors at the north entrance to the mall. At the farthest left and right doors the wall of the corral, about six feet high, began. It started as wide as the full set of doors and then slowly shrunk down, so that it resembled a rodeo cage, where the bulls or horses would wait until it was time to go out into the yard, or the thin walkway cattle would be forced to move down after being offloaded from a truck and into the slaughterhouse. If the cows ever thought they were going somewhere good, they were in for one hell of a surprise.

With this setup, the zombies, though exiting the mall enmass, were soon forced to walk single file through the three foot wide maze.

The winding maze allowed a lot of zombies to filter out at once, and Morrigan and his men were able to keep control, if just barely. There were many times where a weak spot in the maze began to break and fall outward, and only the quick thinking of the men pushed it back into place, where others would re-secure the wood with nails or screws.

At the end of the maze, which extended more than half out into the parking lot from the mall proper, was a gate built to slide up and down like a guillotine.

Box trucks taken from rental companies, as well as a couple of bread trucks, and one UPS truck, waited for their turn to back up to the sliding gate, where the zombies were loaded until no more could fit.

So far, three box trucks had been filled without incident, and the next one, the bread truck, was backing up to the gate. It was easy to see it was a bread truck; there was a giant loaf of bread painted on the side with a smiling, cartoonish face at the end of the loaf. From where Trump stood, he could faintly hear the backup beeping sound the vehicle made as it moved in reverse, even over all the noise his men were making.

Something kicked an empty soda can, the can bouncing across the parking lot. Trump turned to see two zombies stumbling out of the trees lining the lot on all sides. After weeks of seeing the undead, Trump was accustomed to them, and now he barely acknowledged the two shambling forms.

"Someone take care of those?" he mumbled while looking through the field glasses again. His wig hair blew gently in the wind.

Both soldiers had been ready, having already seen the two approaching creatures. Hodgkins slapped Thames' on the shoulder, signifying the two zombies were his to kill, then pushed off from the GMC's front fender and took a few steps closer to them. He leveled his M16A at waist height and sent a tri-burst at each figure.

The bodies took the bullets in the chest, the rounds blowing out their backs to little effect. Large holes were blown out of their torsos and abdomens, and slick, gleaming organs slid out to splatter onto the pavement. Glistening in the sun, the viscera resembled giant reddish-black slugs. One zombie's intestines popped out, to splash onto the ground before its stumbling feet. One foot caught the intestine and it began walking and forcing more sausage-like links out of its body. Its foot miraculously kept landing on the hanging rope, to force out more entrails with each step. The zombie didn't seem to mind it was unraveling with each step it took, however, and kept moving forward.

"Shoot 'em in the head, man. The fucking head," Thames said from behind him.

Hodgkins snapped his head around and glared at Thames. "Don't you think I know that?"

"Then do it, bro. You're makin' us look bad in front of the Man."

Frowning, Hodgkins adjusted his aim and sent another tri-burst at the undead pair, this time focusing on their heads.

Both skulls erupted in a spray of blood, brains and bone fragments, the trio of gore pattering across the asphalt like rain. Both bodies dropped to the ground, their neck stumps spouting dark ichor, the heads vaporized by the onslaught of bullets.

Trump didn't see the zombies go down, his attention focused on the box trucks near the mall. The bread truck was filled and it rolled off, the UPS truck pulling up next. This went on for over an hour and a half, each vehicle filling with zombies, to then leave and allow another one to replace it. Only one box truck wasn't needed, all the zombies swarming out of the mall finally exhausted.

"That's the last of 'em," Morrigan's voice crackled amidst static on Thames' radio. "Tell the president he can come over if he wants to."

Thames glanced up at Trump, who was already climbing out of the rear bed of the GMC. He hopped to the ground with far more agility than he would have six months ago. With less body fat, he felt ten years younger and was able to move much smoother than he used to.

Thames, seeing Trump had heard the radio, was already moving around to the driver's door, while Hodgkins jumped into the rear bed.

Trump slid into the passenger seat, and as soon as he slammed his door closed, Thames started the engine and drove over to the mall.

Trump felt in his coat pocket for the .45 he now carried. In a world filled with walking corpses, a gun wasn't something you went without. It was a much-needed tool, no different than a cell phone before the world collapsed. He always made sure the weapon was with him, for to forget it could mean his death. And he'd come too far in a short time to let something as annoying as death get in his way.

The GMC rolled up to the north entrance, where a section of the maze was being removed so Morrigan and his people could enter the mall.

Trump climbed out of the pickup and walked over to Morrigan. "What's going on? Are they all gone?"

"Yes, Sir," Morrigan said. "The trucks are being moved to a safe location, close, but not too close to our camp."

"Good. What about in there? Is it safe to go in?" Trump gestured to the mall's interior.

"I sent a small team in already, Sir. Just waiting to hear back from them."

"That's good. Very good." Trump smiled. So far everything was going how he hoped it would.

Morrigan's two-way radio crackled and he answered it. "Go ahead, Rogers, What's it look like in there?"

"Not good, Captain," the voice on the radio replied.

"What do you mean? Explain yourself."

"I think it would be better if you just came inside, Captain. But watch yourself. A few dead fucks are inside some of the stores and they're coming out. Not too many though."

"Is that all?"

"No, not exactly. Like I said, you need to come in and see for yourself. There's really no way to give a full description of what it's like in here. The smell alone is something you need to experience firsthand."

Trump, listening, glared at Morrigan angrily. "What the hell does he mean by that?"

"I don't know, Mr. President, but whatever it is, I'm sure we can fix it. Nothing a good cleaning won't cure," Morrigan said, hoping to placate the president.

Trump looked like he was going to yell at Morrigan, but at the last instant before it was going to happen, Trump held back, using something he rarely used, namely self-control. So without saying anything, he began walking to the mall entrance, weaving around the wooden opening and through the glass doors. Behind him, Thames, Hodgkins, Morrigan, and five others the captain directed to follow, all entered the shopping mall, and what they believed would be their new home base.

Chapter 13

It took less than a minute for Trump and the others to realize the one-story shopping mall was going to be hopeless as a new base of operations.

It was for multiple reasons, but each reason alone was more than enough not to stay.

The odor was the first thing.

Like a dead cat baking in the hot sun all day, the smell was almost too much to take. Two of the soldiers behind Trump began to vomit, their previous meals splashing across the floor. Not that it mattered, the aroma of their puke was nothing compared to the miasma of decay filling the mall.

The place was a charnel house on steroids. Everywhere the eye landed, the surface was covered in blood and viscera; horizontal or vertical.

Organs hung on park benches and plastic trees, blood splatter so profuse it was as if someone had carted in a giant balloon fifty feet in diameter and popped it in the center of the mall. Corpses were scattered down the large walkway that divided right and left sides of the building, their abdomens having exploded from internal gases, spraying their insides across anything within range. The stores stood silent, some with their gates up and others still locked, only a few being the latter.

Offal and urine covered every surface as well, and mixed in with the blood, it was like the most massive Jackson Pollack painting ever attempted.

It was hard to talk, as breathing through the nose was all but impossible. Flies and maggots were everywhere, and dozens of rats hopped and pounced from body to body, searching for special morsels. One rat popped up amongst a pile of bodies, a juicy eye hanging from its mouth. Thin ocular nerves hung from the eye, swaying back and forth like the tendrils of a jellyfish.

Seeing the intruding humans, it turned and bounded away, to be lost in one of the many stores lining the walkway.

"Filthy things," Trump said under his breath.

A zombie stumbled out of a GAP store, a name tag still on its shirt. The name wasn't readable; it was covered in blood. The creature's face was half-eaten, bone glistening past the gristle that was its cheeks.

Thames was the first to react. He casually leveled his rifle and shot the zombie in the head, dropping it immediately with half its face missing.

A few more zombies appeared, and they too were dispatched quickly.

"This is hopeless! Hopeless!" Trump screamed. His face might have been turning red with anger but no one could tell with his orange makeup on.

"We can clean it up, Sir," Morrigan said, understanding instantly why Trump was upset. "A little soap and water and this place will be as good as new."

"No, it won't. This place is disgusting. Look..." He pointed at a circle of prone bodies off to the left. They had begun to dissolve into a putrid puddle, the mishmash of liquids seeping under a large rectangular planter set in the middle of the wide corridor. "That gunk is *under* that thing. Under it! The only way to get rid of the smell of death there is to remove it, and the whole damn place is like that." He gestured off to the right, where the entire wall was covered with gore. "All that has to be cleaned up." He pointed into a CVS, where the shelves were covered with viscera. "None of that is useful, it's all contaminated!" His hand shifted to the store beside it, a Pretzel store. It was covered in intestines, or what looked like intestines. "I'm not getting a pretzel from there, are you?"

"Ah, no, I guess not," Morrigan said.

Trump looked at a trio of men walking towards him, the soldiers having come from deeper in the mall. "You three, does the whole place look like it does down here?"

"Worse," one man said, a redhead with two days of stubble. "I mean, Mr. President, Sir," he corrected.

"Exactly." Trump turned to Morrigan. "Forget it, I'm leaving, and so are you and my men. But before you vacate this shithole, have them go through the place and take anything that's not covered in shit. Your idea was a stupid one, Captain. I should never have listened to you." He began walking out of the mall, but stopped and turned to glare at Morrigan. He pointed at the man. "Sad, Captain, so sad." He called out to his bodyguards, "Thames, Hodgkins, get the truck, we're going back to camp."

Morrigan watched the president leave, and when Trump was out of the mall, he let out a silent sigh of relief. Trump was a demanding son-of-a-bitch, and though he worshipped him and was pleased to be part of his initiative to rebuild America, it was pretty tenuous sometimes. The man was prone to mood swings, for one. One moment he would be in a good mood, contemplating the future, and the next he would be raving about some past offense by one of the Democrats or someone from the news media. The Fake news media, as Trump called it.

Morrigan walked over to the open glass doors and peered out, watching Trump climb into the GMC, while Hodgkins hopped into the rear bed; Thames was driving. Trump took off his wig, and rubbed his newly-grown gray stubble with his hand. Yes, it was gray, the blonde hair he showed the world was nothing but a façade, just another part of the costume he wore when before the world. Soon, however, he wouldn't need the wig anymore.

Morrigan thought back to when he'd found Trump cowering on the roof of the black SUV, naked and terrified, grateful for being rescued, looking as pitiful as a human being could ever be. It was a far cry from the man he now served.

Turning, he faced the men standing nearby, waiting for orders. A few seemed to be looking at him differently, as if the respect he once commanded had waned slightly.

Trump insulting him in front of the men hadn't been good for Morrigan's image, and he felt a twinge of annoyance at Trump for doing such a thing. It was disrespectful; something a bully did to make himself look bigger than he was.

That dressing down was the beginning of growing a tiny seed of dissent deep in his heart that he was slowly tending. He didn't even know he was doing so. The seed had been planted when he found out Trump had ordered Dewey, a good friend, murdered for no reason that was justified in Morrigan's eyes.

That same seed had just received water for the first time, thanks to Trump dressing him down before soldiers Morrigan still felt were his men to command, not Trump's. But there was no seedling sprouting yet, only a bare patch of dirt.

"One of you go and get the couple of empty trucks left and back them up to the doors, the rest of you, well, you heard the president. Strip this place of anything useful. It's a bust, we won't be staying."

No one said anything in reply. Some simply nodded, others just turned and moved off to get to work in search of salvageable items.

Morrigan waited in the center of the wide hallway, his rifle casually slung over his left shoulder. As he watched the open doors, he heard sporadic gunfire from within the mall. His men had already come across more zombies. Maybe the president was right, maybe the shopping mall was too far gone to be saved.

It wasn't like he would ever know; his orders had been given. With extreme prejudice.

With nothing else to do, he pulled a marijuana cigarette out of a pocket and lit it.

Maybe if he was a little high, he wouldn't feel so slighted by the president, the way he'd been rebuked before his men. Maybe then, it would all roll off his shoulders.

Chapter 14

Donald J. Trump opened his eyes.

This time was much more pleasurable than a month before.

Glancing over his shoulder, he saw the opposite side of the bed was empty. It should be. When he finished the previous night, he told the woman to leave. He didn't need to waste time talking to her, as there was nothing he wanted to say to her, nor listen to anything she might want to say. She had one use and only one use, and when his lust was fulfilled, he discarded her, much like all the others he'd slept with since coming to the camp.

The sun was already up as he sat up in bed. A shadow came through the tent opening, and Trump recognized the silhouette of Thames immediately.

Thames was completely loyal to Trump, so much so that he knew he could order the large soldier to kill Morrigan, and it would happen without hesitation. To most men, that sense of insane loyalty shown him would seem strange, almost impossible, but not to Trump. He'd managed to get people to support him his entire life, and once he became president, that power over others increased tenfold.

Morrigan was pulling away from Trump; he'd seen it a few times in the past weeks. One day soon, there might be a time when Trump's hold over the captain had waned enough that the man could become a threat. At that time, the misguided captain would have to be removed from his position, with extreme prejudice. But not today.

Today, Morrigan was still under his power and obeyed Trump unquestioningly.

Voices came from the tent opening, low and unable to decipher, but it didn't matter; a second later Captain Morrigan stepped into the tent. His rifle was slung over his shoulder, but Trump still slid a hand under his pillow, touching the .45 pistol hidden there.

The world was different now. He'd come to accept it wholeheartedly and in fact, relished it. It was a world without laws, with the exception of the ones he proclaimed as true.

The new world was one Trump was thriving in. He was now the autocrat he always wanted to be. No one other than himself could make a decision. No one could tell him 'no.'

It had been a week since the shopping mall mission and he was anxious to do something. He'd considered doing a rally for the troops, but so far had delayed it.

If Morrigan was coming into his tent this early, or early to Trump, as unknown to him it was ten in the morning, maybe it was a sign there was something relevant happening. Something he could become involved in to occupy his time.

"Mr. President, our radio operator picked up a transmission from a settlement about fifteen miles from here, on the west side of Washington, D.C." Morrigan stopped before Trump's bed, standing tall. He didn't salute however. Trump ignored it.

"And?" Trump sat up, wincing from a pain in his back. He wasn't getting any younger, that was for sure.

"We don't know too much more than that. The transmission was from their home base to someone on a salvaging party, from what the radioman told me. But he was able to triangulate their location."

"If they were so close, how come you never found them before this?" Trump asked, annoyed.

Morrigan shrugged. "I don't send my people that way. There's nothing worth it there, and the only practical way would be to drive through the city of Washington. It would take three times as long to go around the city." He shrugged. "Wasn't worth the risk."

"I see, but it sounds like it's worth the risk now, if we can get them to give in to my demands and supply us with goods."

"Yes, I suppose. What do you want to do? I say we should ignore them. They're too difficult to get to and maintain control of. Even if we manage to get them to support us but then they reverse their allegiance, I'll need to deploy a large group of my people there, and with them alone without reinforcements, it could get bad. It could get real bad, real fast..." He let his words trail off.

Trump stood up, grabbed his gray bathrobe and donned it. "I don't care. Reach out to them, but don't tell them too much about us. Tell them we want to meet them. In fact, tell them I'm going to go personally to explain what will happen next. But don't tell them more than that. Let's wait until we're eye to eye to explain everything."

"That could be dangerous. Is that wise?"

Trump turned and glared at Morrigan. "I say it is. But I'm not going alone, and by that I mean just myself and bodyguards. I want us to load up and go in force. I want them to see an army outside their doors. Call it my way of getting an upper hand on them. I assume once they know it's me, they'll be relieved to see me and want to join us immediately, but if for some odd reason they don't..." He paused and added, "Well, once they see our firepower and numbers, I figure they'll fall in line easily. I want a lot of men there, a lot."

"But what if they resist like that other place did?"

Trump flashed a wide smile, one filled with malevolence, rather than mirth. His teeth were chillingly white against his orange-covered face. "Then we'll wipe them out, sift through the ashes, and take whatever's left."

* * *

The next morning, with only the faintest of light touching the east, ten vehicles rolled out of the camp.

With Thames driving, Trump was in the first vehicle, a brand new Ford truck taken from a nearby showroom. On the cab's roof was a 40mm mounted turret gun. Hodgkins rode in back, holding onto the heavy-duty gun as he stood and watched the road ahead. Lying in the bed beside Hodgkins was a set of golf clubs. Trump had asked for them earlier and they had been provided. Trump hadn't asked where they came from, he didn't care. He was planning to take up golfing again. He missed it since waking from his coma, and wanted to get back into the game. Having the clubs with him meant he could play at any opportunity given. Perhaps, when this envoy mission was completed, he could see about playing a few holes on the way back to camp.

The pickup he was riding in had been so new that the odometer only had twenty miles on it when he'd gotten into the cab, and those miles had come from being driven around the showroom and parking lot for potential customers, along with mechanics who had needed to service the vehicle. It had been found with a service tag on it as well. It had been sold to someone, and four days after the dead began to walk, was supposed to have been the scheduled pickup time of the vehicle. But the customer had probably been a little busy by then to swing by the dealership, and the showroom had closed anyway, given the unimaginable emergency. Trump believed some of the twenty miles put on the truck was from being driven from the dealership to the camp, too.

Sitting in silence, Trump felt slightly uncomfortable. Something had been gnawing at him and he didn't know what it was. The feeling had begun after speaking to Captain Morrigan the previous day. It was something about the conversation that bothered

Trump, but he just couldn't put his finger on it. But after the captain left the tent, it just felt like the usual supplication Trump received from the man had been missing. But it wasn't a tangible thing he could point at and say, "There, that's it, right there."

So he decided to let it go. For the time being anyway. But he might choose to revisit the subject later, if he remembered.

To distract him from his previous thought, Trump ran other scenarios in his head of future power grabs, while the landscape rolled by outside his window. Zombies were seen wandering, either close to the convoy or far off the road, half hidden in the tall grass. He was anxious with what he hoped was to come. He wasn't just going to do a meet and greet, oh no. He felt he had enough firepower to demand capitulation right there and then. No negotiations, no discussions. Submit or die horribly. Morrigan had no idea of course, not that it would have mattered.

It would be a smooth transition if the settlement simply accepted him as their rightful president and obeyed, but deep down, he hoped they refused. He loved dominating people in business, and this new role he was playing was simply him taking it to the next and perhaps ultimate level. The fact that he cared little for other people's pain and suffering allowed him to fulfill that role easily.

One example, if one needed to be submitted, was that when already over a hundred thousand people had died of Covid-19, the only things Trump was concerned with were tweeting about the upcoming election and how it would be rigged, thus cementing his mail-in voter scheme and getting him a second term in office.

When Trump could have used the Defense Production Act to comply companies to make N95 masks, those masks would have saved thousands upon thousands of lives. For both medical workers and private citizens. Where an N95 mask filtered out 95% of all airborne substances, including coronavirus, instead, Trump ignored it completely and America citizens had to settle for wearing bed sheets made into masks on their faces. If one more example was needed, after taking office in 2016, Trump never bothered making sure the mask stockpiles on the Federal level had been shored up, and three and a half years later, when accused of screwing up, when masks were in shortage throughout the country, along with other forms of PPE (Personal Protected Equipment), such as gowns and gloves, and even a simple swab to test for the virus, he blamed former President Obama, saying the cupboards were bare when Trump took office.

If you move into an apartment and the cupboards are bare, you don't wait three and half years to go grocery shopping, unless you want to starve to death. And even if you do, you can't then blame the former occupant for not leaving you any food, and then attack them for not doing so as well.

Since waking from his coma, Trump had found he liked the violence of the new world. But there was a reason why he could never show or feel empathy, it was because of his father, and the way Trump was raised by the man. Perhaps not a perfect ideology in the normal world, now, with the new rules and norms in place, it was as if his father had been raising him to survive in this exact world. Sure, the normal one had been ruthless, business being a dog eat dog world on a daily basis, but now, where all he had to do was point at someone and either Thames or Hodgkins would kill them without hesitation, if that was his desire, for a despot like Trump, it was like he had died in that hospital and gone to his own personal Heaven.

Behind Trump's Ford truck, coming from one of the vehicles following his, the staccato burst of an Mk19 or M2 .50 caliber—Trump didn't know military weapons, so had no idea what was what—filled the crisp air of morning.

Morrigan liked to let his men use the walking dead for practice targets, to make sure they were honing their marksmanship.

Over Trump's shoulder, if he'd bothered to look, zombies were popping like balloons after being struck by the high caliber rounds. Each time a powerful bullet hit a body, the force of the impact caused the torso to all but disintegrate, spraying bits and pieces of human body parts in all directions. A pinkish, reddish, blackish mist always hung in the air after each zombie shot.

He had to admit, though Morrigan and his men and a few women were basically *playing* army, the captain ran a tight ship. Trump wondered why Morrigan hadn't enlisted in the real military, but then the thought was lost, as he really didn't care about anyone but himself and the fleeting curiosity was already gone, even faster than it had percolated.

Trump took off his MAGA, bright red baseball cap and rubbed his scalp. His hair was slowly coming in, though it was as gray as a battleship. The more his hair grew, the more the wig became unbearable to wear. It was hot and uncomfortable. So today he'd decided to wear the cap, which was also a trademark of his. He had learned early in his career it was all about brand name recognition.

It had been less than an hour since they'd left camp and Trump was already getting antsy. "How long till we get there?" he asked Thames, sounding more like an impatient child than the President of the United States.

Thames checked his watch, then the miles on the truck. "About another forty minutes, Sir. We're taking the long way around to avoid going through Washington, so it's gonna take a little longer than if we went straight through." He glanced at Trump. "You gonna kick all their asses, Mr. President?"

Trump shrugged. "Perhaps, if they're too stupid to know what's good for them."

"They'll listen to you, Sir. You know what's best for them."

"I know that, Thames. The trouble is making others who don't understand my greatness see reason, too. But it'll work out. It'll be amazing, you'll see."

The rest of the ride was in silence, which was unusual for Trump. Whenever he had a captive audience he loved to talk, but Thames was different. There was no reason to keep talking to strengthen Thames' loyalty. The man had been a die-hard supporter of Trump from before the president had been found on that SUV, naked and vulnerable. Thames hadn't only drunk the Kool-Aid, the man had mixed it for the others in the camp. And Hodgkins was almost fully indoctrinated in the ways of Trump as well.

The only thing Trump was unsure of was if his two personal bodyguards would lay down their lives for him if necessary. Yes, they said they would, but talk was cheap, and Lord knew Trump knew how cheap talking could be. He made a career out of it after all. Hell, it had netted him the presidency.

Almost an hour later, the Ford pickup finally slowed to a stop and Trump looked out the front windshield, pulled from his thoughts. He'd completely tuned out the outside world while he was contemplating his future goals. He'd been fully absorbed with coming up with more machinations to solidify his power.

Morrigan's vehicle pulled up beside Trump's and the man climbed out of the cab of a similar looking vehicle, only a different color. The camp had raided a Ford dealership, so their convoy looked like a Ford truck commercial.

They were on a rise on the highway, Washington, D.C. at their backs, and as Trump gazed around the area, he saw nothing that looked like any kind of settlement.

Morrigan was talking to the people in another vehicle with four men inside; Trump briefly recalled noticing that the vehicle had already been waiting for the convoy as it had rolled up. It had been a scouting party Morrigan had sent out a few hours before Trump's procession had departed camp. The four men had reconnoitered the settlement and surrounding area, and were now reporting to Morrigan.

When finished, Morrigan left the men and went to Trump's passenger door and opened it, gesturing for the president to exit the vehicle. "This way. I want to show you the settlement."

"Are we going to walk there? You know I don't like to walk."

"No, of course not. It's not far." Morrigan handed Trump a pair of field glasses. "Use these, so I can show you the outlying wall of the place."

"Ah, of course, I knew that." Trump got out, wincing slightly as he did so. He may have dropped some weight but he was still in his mid-seventies. One other thing he benefited from since the world collapsed was that he didn't eat fast food any more, as there were no longer the restaurant chains in existence. He was eating, if you could believe it, (make gagging noise here), vegetables.

And on a daily basis!

But his private cook did wonders with the produce and there had been a few times Trump had been able to stomach it. But still, if given the chance, he would wipe out an entire village for a cheeseburger and fries

Morrigan, Trump and the president's two bodyguards walked a little ways off the road, through a line of trees and then stopped. They were overlooking a low valley, more of a dip in the land. There was a small river at the bottom of the rise Trump was on, and across the river, were the signs of human activity. A few zombies could be seen wandering on this side of the river, but the moving water prevented them from threatening the settlement. In fact, Trump watched as a zombie stumbled into the water, thinking it could walk across easily. No sooner did its foot slide into the river, than it was knocked off its feet from the current to splash in the water. It was quickly taken downstream, sinking from sight before it was out of view.

The settlement had made their home in a wide open plain, perhaps once farmland. This was due to the large ranch house set in the center of the twenty acre mostly square plot of land. Like the spokes of a wheel, other structures spiraled outwards from the ranch house, all one story, quickly fabricated square cubicles, no more than seven or eight feet tall and ten to twenty feet wide. A few tents were also scattered about, but it seemed that each day, the tents were being replaced with the wooden and metal structures, which were made out of whatever the settlement could salvage from the surrounding area.

The first squat building had clean lines, as if a lumber yard had been raided for supplies, but as the spiral extended outward, the cubicles took on a more Mad Max type look, due to the piecemeal way they'd been built. Trump looked outward from the spiral to see a windmill, the blades slowly turning in the gentle breeze. Smoke columns were sporadic around the settlement, showing where cooking fires were in use.

Near the back end a few large eighteen wheeler semis were parked, the containers being used for living or some other similar reasons. The sound of multiple, heavy duty generators carried to the hill Trump stood on as well.

The river was a natural barrier to protect them from the walking dead, and the other three sides were also protected by makeshift walls of cars and other four wheel transports. A forklift running on propane was even now, as Trump watched, shoring up a piece of a wall on the north side. Piling mostly-flattened vehicles three high, it made a decent barrier for the settlement. A school bus, with metal plates welded to its center between the front and rear tires, was the main gate. It would roll forward and backwards when someone needed to enter or leave the place, which happened even as Trump surveyed the settlement.

All in all, it was a pretty stereotypical apocalyptic settlement someone would find in a world where the dead walked. Predictable and convenient, if not unimpressive.

"I was planning on setting a mortar team on this ridge, Mr. President," Morrigan explained. "If there's any resistance I can rain hell down on that place in a few seconds of notice."

"Uh-huh, that's good," Trump said, barely listening, his eyes locked onto the settlement.

Morrigan continued, "My scouting party didn't notice any heavy gun emplacements, but they did see a few people that looked like sentries with guns; small caliber mostly. By the way they were standing watch, my men said they were probably just on the lookout for zombies, not an attacking force."

"Uh-huh, good, Captain, that's excellent."

Morrigan frowned, but then forced himself to stop and only set his lips in a firm grimace. He didn't know why he was disappointed that the president wasn't interested. He was never interested in the logistics of any military-type action Morrigan had worked on, even though Trump always had to interject himself into the equation. He always criticized Morrigan's plans, though Trump never had an answer to the issues he wasn't pleased with. But that was just how the president was, and the captain had come to expect such behavior, but now found himself not accepting it the way he used to.

That seed of dissention inside him, after being planted and watered, had just been given its first sprinkling of fertilizer to help it grow. Morrigan was starting to pull away from Trump, though he would be hard-pressed to admit it. Others had done this over time, mostly the men and women Trump had taken on to join his administration at the beginning of his term, but as time passed, those people had come to see that Trump wasn't who he pretended to be, and in fact was not someone to be looked up to or admired at all. And so those people had left the administration, and every single one had had to suffer through Trump's rants of how stupid and terrible they were. The irony of it all was that Trump liked to brag that he only hired the best people to be on his team, and therefore it was his judgment that would allow them to join him. So if these people, once they left the administration, were so terrible and incompetent, what does that say about the person who hired them?

But Morrigan still wanted to believe, desperately in fact, that only Trump could save America, and make it great, like it once was.

As a white man, Morrigan had become sick and tired of all the black and brown people trying to take what was rightfully his. He longed for the day when the white man was at the top of the food chain again, and to be white meant you had a golden ticket in life.

But not anymore. That is, before the dead had began to walk. Then, it was all about the blacks and browns and any other damn color under the rainbow, plus the gays, bisexuals and the ones who were born one gender but said they were the other—he didn't know the politically correct name as he'd never looked into it enough to be truly informed. He'd gotten his news from far right channels, and only those.

It seemed like nowadays the white man was always the guilty party, like Morrigan had to suffer for what had come before him. He harkened for the days of old, where whites were respected and had money and power.

Not like the world was now, or right before the dead began to walk. Morrigan, aside from playing army, had worked in a car wash. Not an educated man, as he never went to college and barely managed to graduate from high school and from the Midwest, he blamed everyone else for his lot in life. When he couldn't get a better job, it was the Blacks' fault. When he couldn't afford a house, it was the Brown people's fault.

When he couldn't afford a car because he smoked and drank his salary away each week, it was some other nationalities' fault say, oh, why not the Muslims?

It didn't matter to Morrigan, it was all interchangeable. It was always someone else's fault though, never his. So when the Lost Sons of Freedom had come along, he'd joined immediately, finding like-minded, disenfranchised men and women who thought just like him.

And when Trump had become the 45th President, spouting his rhetoric of taking America back to the old days, and doping immigration bans and blocking some countries, mostly Muslim outright from being allowed to enter the U.S., and to build a wall across the Mexican border to keep all the goddamn illegal out, well, he was completely on board.

When Trump said, "Make America Great Again," he meant 'great for the whites,' to go back to how it was before all this equality bullshit and affirmative action had taken over the country.

And now, here was Donald J. Trump, standing beside Morrigan, an ex-carwash jockey, the right-hand man for the one person who could save America from itself. Morrigan was still far from walking away from Trump, and if the urge arose, he would shove it down deep inside him, where it couldn't get out. He not only wanted to support Trump, he *needed* to support Trump.

Still, that seed was there, and it wasn't going away anytime soon.

There was a battle raging within Thomas Morrigan, between good and evil, only the man didn't fully know it yet.

"We're all set to go to their gate and talk to them whenever you're ready, Mr. President. Sir," he said.

Trump lowered the binoculars and handed them back to Morrigan. He flashed the captain a wide smile, one that always enamored whoever was the recipient of it, Morrigan included. "Let's go down there and say hello."

Chapter 15

"Hello, inside the town!" Trump called from beside the pickup truck with a bullhorn. He was standing, the passenger door between him and the town for protection. Thames and Hodgkins had demanded it, so Trump was at least able to duck down behind a small amount of cover if things went sideways.

Trump hadn't liked being told what to do but had relented, knowing the men were looking out for his safety. And Trump didn't want to risk getting shot if he didn't have to. But after seeing the settlement through the binoculars, he was pretty confident he wasn't in any real danger. With everything he'd observed himself, and also what Morrigan had told him after being briefed from his scouts, was that the settlement was non-hostile to strangers.

Still, Trump was glad he had on a bullet proof vest under the black leather jacket he was wearing. He also wore a white button-down shirt and blue slacks, with casual loafers on his feet. The day had turned into a comfortable one, a gentle wind blowing in from the west, but with his red MAGA ball cap on, there was nothing on his head to flutter in the wind. He missed that sensation.

When Trump had called out, he was already aware that his people were being watched from inside the vehicle-wall. Tops of heads could be seen moving about, as the men and women at the metal and fiberglass vehicle-wall stayed low and out of sight.

Along with Trump's pickup, there were two other vehicles behind him, both with heavy weapons bolted to the roofs of their cabs. A .40mm mounted turret gun and an M2 .50 caliber machine gun. Both were manned, the soldiers ready to rock and roll at a moment's notice. Captain Morrigan had positioned himself so that he was standing a few feet behind Trump, watching the president's back.

The other seven vehicles were parked a ways back, just out of sight of the settlement. Morrigan had told Trump it wasn't a good idea to spook the town, though Trump had wanted to go in with all the pickups and their weapons exposed, hoping to scare the town into submission. Morrigan had managed to talk Trump out of it, knowing how the man was. When you thought you were a hammer, everything else appeared to be a nail. In the end, Morrigan had tricked Trump into thinking it had been the president's own idea to leave a few vehicles out of sight.

"What do you want?" a voice called from inside the wall.

"To talk, for now."

"About what?" the voice asked again.

"Well, your surrender to me for one thing." Trump stood tall and despite his guards' wishes, stepped out so he was in full view. With his red MAGA cap on and his orange, makeup-painted face, there was no question who he was. If anyone had ever watched the news or read a newspaper or gone online, Trump's face was well known. Too much, in fact. Like the ultimate bombardment of neural ads, before the dead walked, it seemed Trump was in every facet of every American's life, and many other countries as well. He was always saying something outlandish, or offending someone. Whether he was insulting the Gold Star parents of a fallen veteran, calling John McCain a loser for being a POW, saying that "Losers get caught," when referring to McCain's prisoner status in the war, or calling Covid-19 the Kung-flu, it never ended.

Every day, since before he was elected the 45th President of the United states, Donald J. Trump had managed to insinuate himself into every facet of most people's lives. Whether they wanted him to or not.

So when Trump stepped out from behind the passenger door, there was an audible gasp from behind the wall, one so loud it carried back to Trump.

He grinned widely, enjoying the attention. He fed off it; it was almost as if to live, he needed the adulation of others, and food was only an annoyance he needed to deal with to maintain his body. But his real nutrients to survive was the love of others, strangers most of all.

At the wall, multiple voices began talking at once, a quick staccato coming so fast it was almost hard to understand it all.

"Holy shit, it's Trump."

"Bullshit, you're lying."

"No, he's right fucking there!"

"It can't be."

"Well, it is, look for yourself!"

At the wall, a man rose up from the crouched position he'd been in, exposing himself from the shoulders up, the shock of Trump being at the gate distracting him from safety "Fuck me it is him." He stared at Trump, his eyes wide in amazement. But the look of surprise quickly turned to one of anger and hate.

He flipped off Trump with both middle fingers. "You suck, Trump! I thought you were dead! What the hell are you doing here, what the hell do you want?"

"To surrender to me, for starters." Trump ignored the man's taunts, at least for now.

"What? Dude, I know you've always been unhinged, but that's the last thing we'd ever do. In fact, most of us are Democrats in here and the few Republicans we have are moderates. No one in here liked you, I mean likes you. You're the worst President we ever had, you lying son-of-a-bitch."

"My friend, you have me all wrong. I'm here to help you."

"What?"

Trump put on his best reality show face. "I'm still the President of this country, and it's my job to fix this country from the terrible state it's in. I'll bring it back to power. It'll be beautiful, trust me. All you have to do is agree to me being your rightful ruler, which I really already am."

"Are you fucking serious? There is no more government. Washington is nothing but zombies now."

Trump sneered. "Sounds like it's the same to me." He turned to some of the soldiers. "Am I right, guys?"

Laughter broke out amongst the men, Thames and Hodgkins snickering as well. The Trump show was in full swing this day.

"Make jokes all you want, Trump, but no one here accepts you as the ruler of anything. So why don't you just fuck off and leave us alone. We've got work to do, something you know nothing about." He paused and then added. "No one voted for you in here. You've heard the saying, 'Not my President?' Well, yeah, that's how we all feel."

"Then you're all losers," Trump snarled, his temper completely exploding. "Okay, that's it! I'm through trying to be nice. Open that gate and let me inside and submit to me now or so help me, I'll burn your whole damn village to the ground and kill everyone in there." He grinned malevolently. "And if you're still alive after I destroy it all, I'll make sure you suffer in a special way for the disrespect you've shown me here today."

"Fuck you. Go ahead and try! A few machine guns bolted to a couple of pickup trucks don't scare us!" He looked at his fellow guards. "Am I right, guys?"

Voices sounded, everyone agreeing with the dissenter. Trump was so angry he thought he was going to burst. Acting impulsively, he took his .45 pistol out of his jacket and began shooting at the big mouth guard. He didn't hit anything, and everyone at the wall ducked down, but it made Trump feel better. Unfortunately, as he wasn't thinking straight, he didn't realize what his shooting would set in motion. Both Thames and Hodgkins, seeing their Commander in Chief begin shooting, also did the same, and once that started, so did the other men standing near Trump.

Bullets pockmarked the wall, doing no damage but making the guards keep their heads low. An air raid siren erupted within the walls and a hive of activity began as men and women began running to assigned emergency stations.

In a small lull in the shooting, Big Mouth stood up, leveled a Kalashnikov down to the ground, and began firing, using up half of the thirty round clip in a few seconds.

The rounds crawled across the dirt directly in front of Trump, small geysers of soil erupting when each bullet impacted. Trump only stared in utter amazement that the guard had the audacity to shoot at him. But then he was being tackled and forced to the ground behind the pickup as the passenger side window shattered, spraying bits of safety glass everywhere.

Trump's mouth was opening and closing like a fish as he struggled to make sense of what was happening. "I don't understand this. Don't they know who I am?"

"I think that's the problem," Morrigan said, partly lying on top of Trump. "If they're Democrats in there, they hate you. They'll never surrender to you."

Morrigan slid off Trump so he wasn't lying fully on him, then pulled the president closer to the rear bumper, wanting to keep him safe.

Meanwhile, all of Morrigan's men were returning fire with renewed earnest, keeping the guards' heads down but not doing much else. The large caliber guns mounted to the pickups began chattering, filling the air with a wall of sound that caused the ears to ring and everyone to immediately get a headache.

Larger and deeper bullet holes stitched across the crushed cars making up the wall of the settlement, hundreds of pockmarks appearing as if by magic. Some rounds went straight through the cars, exploding out the far side; if anyone within the settlement was hit, it was unknown.

The sentries were firing more, however, and it was evident there were sniper holes in the wall for them to use. The windshield on Trump's pickup grew multiple holes as bullets went right through it and into the leather seats. Then it shattered as more impacts weakened it enough that it collapsed in on itself.

Trump rolled onto his side, his face covered in dirt, the light brown dust mixing with his makeup; with his sweating it made a thick paste on his face.

"Don't just sit there staring at me, you fucking idiot!" Trump yelled at Morrigan. "Do something! Stop them from shooting at us!"

Morrigan paused for another heartbeat, then nodded. Taking his two-way radio from where it was attached to his belt, he said into it, "Mortar team, light 'em up, over."

"Understood, over," came back.

Thirty seconds after Morrigan gave the order, nothing happened, but then there was a whistling sound coming from somewhere overhead, and a moment later, the windmill inside the settlement erupted in flames and wooden splinters flew across the surrounding area. Then another mortar round landed just behind the vehicle wall, its explosion sending up a spout of dirt and gravel that peppered the sentries lining the wall.

The other pickup trucks rolled up to join the three already parked before the gate, the men debarking and running for cover, wherever they could find it. One man got down out of a blue pickup carrying a LAW anti-tank rocket tube. He was a short man with red hair and freckles, a ginger by the pale complexion of his skin. With an evil grin on his lips, he aimed the LAW at the bus that was the gate, and fired.

A white back-blast smoke trail appeared behind the rocket as it shot out of the tube. The man discarded the empty launch tube and ducked for cover just as the rocket struck the school bus dead center.

There was a blinding flash of light, despite it being daylight, and every one of Morrigan's people had to cover their eyes or risk impaired vision. But no sooner did the initial explosion begin to fade than the gas tank caught and sent the entire bus jumping off the ground a good two feet. It landed heavily, bouncing on its tires, askew of the gate, orange and red flames filling it from steering wheel to rear exit door. The tires began to pop from the heat as dark black smoke roiled into the air, the wind catching it and wafting it sideways across the wall. Coughing and hacking from the fumes of burning tires and gasoline, the sentries were as impaired as if tear gas had been used. Plumes of smoke, taken by the wind, blew across the wall, impairing the guards even more.

Another mortar landed within the settlement, blowing up a shack and vaporizing anything that was inside it.

People were running every which way within the walls of the settlement, not knowing where to go. Not that anyone could blame them. Where do you run when the danger is falling randomly from the sky? It was about as easy as dodging raindrops. Outside the walls, zombies began appearing through the trees. Attracted to all the noise, they were drawn to the settlement like ants to a picnic.

The first time anyone among Morrigan's people knew there was any danger from behind them, was when one of the soldiers, a small man with a balding pate and an arm tattoo of a scorpion, shrilled in agony when a zombie came upon him from behind and sank its teeth into his arm. Rearing back, the zombie took a large piece of the man's camo arm sleeve along with a decent chunk of flesh. The irony was that the part of the tattoo that was the stinger on the scorpion was what was removed along with the chunk of meat.

The man could only stare in horror as blood shot out of the large wound in his arm, crimson spurting with each beat of his heart. Panicking, he took off running, completely forgetting any form of discipline. He didn't get far for his cowardice, however. He barely made it thirty feet before two more zombies came out of hiding and tackled him. A flurry of arms and legs, all jumbled into one, rolled around on the ground, shrieking coming from somewhere in the middle. Then the screaming stopped abruptly, but not the feeding.

Trump had his head buried in the dirt, his arms over his head, as the world around him exploded with fire and fury. "Are we winning?" He yelled to no one in particular. "Did we get them all yet?"

Morrigan looked up from where he'd taken cover beside Trump, seeing the burning wreckage that was the school bus gate. There was a wide opening now in the settlement's defenses, and he knew now was the time to finish the fight. "Mortar team, hold fire. I repeat, hold your fire! We're going into the town now. I don't want you killing your own people, over."

"Affirmative, holding fire, over," came back on the radio. "How's it look?"

"It looks good, great job, guys, you fucked 'em up real good, over."

Despite the machine guns still chattering, with the loss of the mortar fire, it seemed almost quiet. There were no more sentries returning fire along the wall, and Morrigan felt confident enough to stand up.

Upon doing so, he raised his hand above his head and then pointed at the opening in the gate. "Okay, let's get in there, men!" He pointed to one of the trucks. "Use your car to make that opening wider, we're all right behind you!"

A man saluted quickly, the salute as sloppy as a person playing Army could make it. Most of the men on the captain's team just went through the motions, and were far from ever being Marine or Army material, even as grunts.

But being part of the Lost Sons of Freedom gave them something that had been missing in their lives before the world went South. Now they had a belonging, and a feeling there was a purpose in their lives. The Lost Sons were no different than any other group out there in the world, whether it was a church or a biker gang. All most people wanted was to feel they belonged to something, that there were other, like-minded people around them, willing to show support when needed.

That was the main reason the Lost Sons had such a large membership, even if some of the people, like Morrigan, may have had other reasons for joining. Besides, it wasn't like the Lost Sons was the first group of mostly angry white men and some women had founded, and at least his people didn't run around in bed sheets and wear pointy hoods. Hell, they even had Thames as a member, their proof they weren't completely racists, even if Thames was only half black on his father's side.

The pickup truck surged forward, crashing into the burning school bus, pushing it a foot more to the side. Backing up, the driver rammed the rear bumper again, this time shoving it a few more feet. Then he didn't back up, but floored the gas pedal. Smoke billowed from the rear of the pickup, the tires spinning, but the school bus was pushed another meter. With more than enough room now, the pickup shot through the opening, the other pickups following close behind, the men whooping and cheering over their victory.

Trump stood up, seeing Morrigan in the upright position also. He felt foolish lying on the ground, now that the danger had passed. He would never admit to anyone how truly scared he felt only moments ago.

"Jesus, Mr. President, that sure went sideways fast," Morrigan said as he watched the opening, seeing the last pickup disappear into the gate opening. Meanwhile, Thames and Hodgkins shot at any zombies surrounding them, their weapons more than sufficient to stop the sporadic amount that were appearing.

As for the two zombies still feeding on the small balding man, they were left alone to feed. Until they became an actual danger, neither man was going to waste ammunition on them. The balding soldier was no more than a pile of dark red carrion, his ribcage torn open, cracked like a dozen wishbones, the zombies scooping out handfuls of entrails and glistening organs. Their slurping and chewing was loud enough to carry back to the four men, only Trump making a face in disgust. Morrigan, Thames and Hodgkins had been dealing with the walking dead longer than Trump and had become more desensitized to the undead's animalistic urges.

Wanting to feel at least a little safer, Trump climbed back into the pickup truck, ignoring the safety glass crunching under his ass. At least the door was still intact, if not the window.

Morrigan began walking towards the gate, his M16 in his hands.

"Wait, where are you going? Don't leave me here!"

Morrigan turned and looked at Trump, seeing the man in a new light yet again. Covered in mud, his face looking more like a clown, his voice taking on an almost whiny tone, a small part of Morrigan wondered what the hell he saw in this fool of a man. But it was only a flicker, like a pilot light trying to relight, but then going out. As soon as it flickered there, it was gone.

That seed had just received a little more nourishment deep with Morrigan.

Morrigan gestured to Thames and Hodgkins. "They'll keep you safe. I need to go in and coordinate the assault. Once it's safe, I'll call on the radio so you can come in and inspect the…the whatever's left, I guess."

He didn't wait for a reply, but turned and jogged to the gate. At the frame of the gate, he paused, swung his head around slowly, and when it looked clear, he slipped into the town and was gone from sight. Two of the pickups were parked thirty feet ahead and he wanted to join those teams and see what was happening.

Trump watched the man go, seething inside, but not so much for the way Morrigan had responded to him, but for the awareness of being so vulnerable.

Each time Thames or Hodgkins shot a zombie, Trump flinched, and it angered him to do so. He glanced at the .45 still in his hand and touched the grip of the .45 as if he was caressing it. At least he was armed, something he always did now.

Crossing his arms over his chest like a petulant child, Trump sat in the pickup and waited to be told he could enter.

Chapter 16

"Tell President Trump he can come inside, the town is secure, over." Captain Morrigan's voice came out of the two-way radio lying on the dashboard of the pickup truck, amidst all the safety glass.

"It's about damn time," Trump said and gestured for Thames, who was sitting behind the steering wheel, to get moving. Hodgkins was standing outside the truck, and as it began to roll, he simply walked alongside.

Another dozen zombies had been put down since Morrigan had gone inside the makeshift town, but after that, the area had been devoid of further living dead.

"Where did Morrigan get all the weapons in use today?" Trump asked, the thought just coming to his head.

Thames just shrugged. "We hit a National Guard facility that had been overrun by those dead fucks, Sir. We cleaned it out and once we got inside, it was fucking payday. There was a shitload of stuff. We raided the place and took off."

"Why didn't you just stay there and make it your home base?" Trump asked, mildly interested. "Seems better than where you are now, I mean, where we are now at the camp."

Thames shrugged again. "Well, Mr. President, the place was mostly destroyed, a lot of fire damage, and almost all the perimeter fences were down. It had been a helluva battle before the guardsmen lost. It looked like most of the dead fucks had wandered off after that, which was why we were able to get in there without too much of an issue. The captain decided it wasn't worth tryin' to rebuild, plus it would make us an easy target for others that showed up. Luckily, we were the first ones to find it, I guess."

Trump only nodded, satisfied with the answer.

Thames maneuvered the Ford through the gate opening and slowed to a stop a few feet inside. The school bus still burned, snapping and popping a constant background noise. There was a Lost Sons sentry standing at the gate, on orders from Morrigan to keep watch for danger, either living or dead.

Bodies were everywhere, each one with at least one new hole in their heads. Morrigan knew what he was doing. Anyone killed by gunfire in the battle needed to be shot in the head or else eventually a zombie would be created.

Off to the side near the wall, one corpse hadn't been gotten to in time, as the soldiers made their way through the bodies. Like in an old black and white voodoo movie, one of the corpses with large holes in its chest and torso, slowly sat up, hands reaching outwards. But that's as far as the newly awakened zombie got, before a soldier walked up to it, aimed his pistol at its forehead, and blew half its brains out the back of its skull. The body slumped back to the ground, killed for the second time that day.

Trump climbed out of the truck, safety glass cubes sliding out under his ass as he did so. It tinkled to the ground and glistened in the morning sun. He wiped his ass of anything that was still stuck there, then realized he was covered in dust from head to toe. His black leather jacket was all but obscured in brown. He began patting his arms and legs, and seeing what Trump was doing, Hodgkins joined him and tried to help. But the man didn't know his own strength and he was slapping Trump much harder than necessary. Though dust clouds puffed up with each blow, the president had to endure the pummeling. At least until he shoved a hand in Hodgkins face and yelled, "Enough, goddammit, I'm not a fucking drum set!"

"Sorry, Sir, I was just tryin' to help," Hodgkins looked down at the ground, a scorned puppy look on his face.

Someone snickered, and mumbled, "Moron." It was barely noticeable, but Trump's hearing had always been excellent, and he caught the word as the wind blew his way, against the speaker. He looked up to realize off to the left, out of sight when he'd first driven inside the settlement, were about twenty-five men and women lined up.

He didn't recognize any of them, and from their clothing, he assumed they were what was left of the haphazard town. Captain Morrigan was standing off to the side, along with ten of his men. Trump made the assumption that the people were prisoners. More men of the Lost Sons also stood behind the prisoners, all with weapons leveled at the twenty-five people.

Standing tall, Trump walked over to the prisoners, Morrigan joining him as he approached. Hodgkins and Thames were two feet behind Trump, following him like the loyal hounds they were. Morrigan tried not to think that Thames used to be his loyal man, that is, before Trump appeared.

"Mr. President, these are the survivors we managed to round up. There really wasn't much resistance. Evidently, only the guards on the wall had firearms, the rest didn't have much in the way of guns. Once we were inside the walls, it wasn't hard to round them all up."

"Did any fight back?" Trump asked.

Morrigan wiped his mouth with the back of his hand, as the man gathered his thoughts. "A few did, but they were easily dispatched."

"You mean killed, don't you?"

"Yeah, I mean, yes. We killed them. We had no choice. They attacked us."

One of the prisoners standing near Trump and Morrigan, who had heard every word of the conversation, spit at the ground, loudly. "Animals. Thought you were bad when you were president, now look at you. Raiding and killing like a tin pot despot. I guess you found your true calling, Trump."

The president walked over to the man, his two loyal hounds close behind him. If the man tried anything, he'd be dead before he could touch Trump.

"I know that voice. You're the guy who said those things about me and shot at me."

"Yeah, that was me." The man stood taller, or at least squared his shoulders and raised his chin proudly. "If I'm gonna die, I'll die like a man, Trump. I'll admit it. My only regret is that I missed. I wanted to put a bullet right through that fat pumpkin face of yours, you giant Oompa-Loompa."

A few of the other prisoners laughed at that, despite the taut situation.

"Shut the fuck up, all of you. Don't laugh at me." Trump raised his index finger and pointed accusingly at the others, roving from person to person. "Next one who laughs I swear to God I'll have their tongue cut out right here in front of everyone."

The man laughed defiantly, despite the warning. "God? *God?* Oh, please, you got a lot of nerve even uttering His name. You're about as Godless as they come. How you managed to fool all the evangelicals is a mystery no one will ever discover." He looked around at the Lost Sons of Freedom. "But I see your cult is growing once more. You got all these idiots to follow you, now." He looked at Morrigan. "You have no idea what a fraud this man is, do you. You just drink the Kool-aid with a smile every time he pours you a cup and do his dirty work. I bet he never gets his hands dirty and why should he? He always has gullible fools willing to do it for him. He might be a moron, but what does that make you?"

Trump lashed out with his right hand, backhanding the man across the face. "Don't call me a moron. I went to an Ivy League school. I'm as smart as they come!"

Spitting blood, the man raised himself up after reeling backwards from the blow. "Sure you are, Trump, you're as smart as they come. You're a real stable genius." He wiped his mouth clean of blood. "You might want to fix your makeup, sweetie, you're orange base coat is running."

A few more people managed a few titters, but most of the prisoners could see what was happening wasn't going to go well and remained silent.

The vein in Trump's forehead was bulging, his anger so powerful he could barely contain it. He remembered the .45 in his pocket and reached for it, but stopped suddenly after withdrawing it. He saw the look in the man's eyes. He wanted Trump to kill him, that was the reason for one insult after another.

"No, I have a better idea with what to do with you," Trump said and put the gun back into his pocket. "I have an idea that even you will think is 'smart.' " The anger washed away from Trump's face, leaving only a calmness that made the man swallow a lump in his throat.

Something had just changed in the power struggle between the two men, but the man couldn't put his finger on it. Trump's demeanor had shifted from angry to something far more devious.

Trump raised his voice so the other prisoners could hear him. "I take it you all feel the same as this man? If you don't, now's the time to say something."

No one spoke, all eyes glaring at Trump, both the men and the women.

The man Trump had been sparring with grinned. "I told you, Trump, we're all proud Democrats here. We'll die before we'd ever follow you and your gang of assholes and wanna be Republicans."

Trump grinned slightly. "We'll see about that." He turned to face Morrigan. "Captain, I need you to do a few things for me. I want to make an example of this guy. And when we're done, I'll ask the rest of them one more time if they're all against me."

"Whatever you need, just tell me and I'll make it happen," Morrigan said.

Trump smiled even wider, his white teeth almost flashing in the sun against his orange and dirt-encrusted face. "I know you will."

Chapter 17

It took an hour to prepare everything, the prisoners, under armed guard, having no choice but to stand and watch.

It didn't take long for everyone to figure out what Trump had in mind for their hapless colleague with the big mouth.

Every now and then a gunshot would sound from the front gate opening, where a few of Morrigan's men stood guard, taking down any zombies that appeared.

Trump sat in a folding chair taken from a shack and watched silently, while sipping from some ice tea taken from the same place as the chair. The beverage was warm, but manageable. He called over to Hodgkins, who was standing a few feet away. "Go to our pickup and grab me my nine iron from the back, would you?"

"Yes, Sir," Hodgkins said and jogged off. Thames stood at Trump's right shoulder, his massive height partially blocking out the sun and keeping Trump a little in the shade. It was slightly warm out and Trump was getting warm, too, but he kept his black leather jacket on. He thought it made him look cool, and he wasn't about to lose any edge he might have over the prisoners. His head was hot under his MAGA ball cap as well, but he would never consider taking it off and exposing his short hair, and he hated to admit, thinning hair, for others to view.

"What you wanted done is all set, Mr. President," Morrigan said. He was following the orders of his president but his heart wasn't in it. Morrigan had never been a brutal man, and even after the dead began to walk he hadn't changed much. He'd only killed when being threatened, and hadn't sought murder for its own sake.

But since Trump had become the Lost Sons' defacto leader, he'd found himself doing things that went against his moral code. Still, his duty was to follow, and Trump to lead, or at least, that's what he kept on trying to believe. It was why he'd attended countless rallies for Trump. But seeing what was about to occur, something inside him caused him to speak up.

"Mr. President, I have to tell you, I think this is wrong," Morrigan said. "What you're doing to that man is inhumane, and I respectfully request you reconsider."

Trump turned slightly in his chair to stare at Morrigan. "Go on."

"Well, it's just, we don't need to do this. I'm sure the prisoners will see reason if we simply talk to them. This is barbaric, and I might have done some bad shit since the dead began to walk around, but I never did anything this bad. It's wrong, just plain wrong."

"Duly noted, Captain, but I'm in charge and I say nothing changes."

"But," Morrigan began.

Trump raised his hand, stopping him from continuing. "But nothing. I said it's going to happen." He leaned forward slightly in his chair. "If you want to understand real power, my friend, then you need to wield fear. Fear is real power." He leaned back and sipped his tea. "Do you understand me? You are loyal, right?" He lowered the glass from his lips. "Because if you're not, we need to have a serious discussion about your future with me."

Morrigan read the warning clearly and wasn't about to push it any more than he had. He sighed heavily and his shoulders sank. "No, Sir, there's no need. I'm loyal."

"Good, then we don't have anything else to discuss."

Hodgkins returned with the nine iron and Trump took it. Standing, he tossed the glass of tea away from him, not caring where it landed. The crystal glass shattered upon impact when it hit the hard ground. He hoped the simple disregard of something such as a glass of ice tea might hold more meaning to the prisoners. A similar thread would be when one neighbor kept his land immaculate and the house beside him didn't, but let the grass grow wild and the trash pile up. To the first neighbor, doing such a thing seemed beyond the normal way to live, it seemed against his code of normalcy.

Unfortunately, no one was looking at Trump, for there was something much more interesting in the wide open area just beyond the gate opening.

The man with the big mouth was recumbent in the dirt, each of his limbs having a heavy chain wrapped around them. The chains were set up so that the man was spread-eagled, and if the eye was to follow the chains, each one was attached to the rear bumper of an idling Ford truck.

The vehicles were facing to all four points of the compass, a limb coinciding with each pickup.

Big Mouth was about to be drawn and quartered.

Trump strolled over to the prone man, swinging the golf club as he walked. Upon reaching him, Trump gazed down at the hapless man and placed the club on his chest.

"What's your name, asshole," Trump demanded.

"Fuck you."

"If you say so. So, Fuck You. What I'm doing here is a little experiment." He made sure to raise his voice so the rest of the prisoners could hear. "See, I've been told when someone dies, as long as their brain's intact, they come back from the dead. Now, I haven't actually seen that happen and I gotta admit, I'm curious."

Big Mouth said nothing, but his lower lip began to tremble as the reality of his predicament truly set in. He was about to be torn apart by the limbs, left to bleed out in the dirt, baking under the hot sun, and there was nothing he could do about it.

"What? Nothing witty to say to me now?" Trump asked with a sly smile. He was gloating and he loved every moment of it. When someone fucked with Trump, he always made sure to fuck the other guy twice as hard in return.

Big Mouth summoned up as much courage as he could manage and yelled out so that his fellow townspeople could hear him. "Don't do what this asshole says! He's nothing but a make believe dictator. Even if the 2020 election had happened, he wouldn't have won! Biden was gonna kick his ass! Not because he was a better candidate, but because everyone's had enough of Trump. All of you, keep fighting, don't stop for anything! Don't let the fuckin' Republicans win, they'll destroy what's left of this country!"

Trump laughed. "Nice speech, I hope you enjoyed giving it, because it's the last thing you'll ever say." He raised the golf club in the air, the signal having already been worked out with Morrigan to pass on to the pickups' drivers. "I'm going to enjoy this immensely."

Trump leaned forward slightly, club still raised, and said in a soft voice so only Big Mouth could hear, "And I would have won the election and gotten a second term. By a lot. It would have been a landslide. A tremendous victory. It would have been probably by eighty million votes or more. But I was cheated by the fucking dead walking and spoiling all my plans." He grinned. "But at least I can take out some of my frustration on you." He stood up and took a few steps back, not wanting to get sprayed by arterial blood.

"Fuck you!" Big Mouth yelled.

"You first," Trump said and then casually lowered the golf club.

Each of the pickup drivers were all watching Trump diligently, knowing that if they screwed up, there would be hell to pay.

So when the golf club was lowered, they were ready.

Simultaneously, each pickup's transmission was slammed into 'Drive' and each driver floored the gas pedal.

There was no slack in the chains attached to Big Mouth, so things went very bad, very fast. There was the slightest bit of tension on each of the chains, so it took only seconds before human limbs of bone and flesh were tested against metal and steel.

The human side lost terribly.

The first limb to come off was the left arm. Evidently, the driver had been just a little faster on the uptake when given the signal to go. Big Mouth shrieked in absolute agony as his arm was torn from its socket, arterial blood flying outwards to splash the nearby prisoners. Trump actually began to laugh at the gory sight. Finally, all his inhibitions on how he wanted to rule were gone. He could do anything he wanted, do anything to anyone he desired. He had enough sycophants following him that all he had to do was wish it and it would come true. Though not the ruler of the entire country, at least in his small fiefdom around Washington, D.C., he was the master of everything. It was a thrill he'd seldom felt in his life, even when he had been sworn in as the 45th President of the United States of America.

The pickup with the first severed arm continued driving for another twenty feet, the arm bouncing end over end at the tip of the chain. A plume of dust covered the area from the spinning tires of the four pickups.

The second limb to go was the right leg. Like a turkey leg being pulled free from a cooked bird, the limb peeled off the pelvic bone, the man's pants ripping as well. The tearing sound from both the material of his pants and that of his flesh were terrifyingly similar.

More high-pitched screaming filled the day as the second limb was yanked off.

Trump realized, under the shrieking and screaming, there was an underlying sound, one that was the actual noise of tearing, like wet paper, as each limb came clean off in succession, along with the ripping of clothing. When the third limb was pulled free of the body it belonged to—the left leg—he knew to listen for it and was able to pinpoint the exact moment that the limb was severed; there was a ripping sound followed by a meaty *thwack*.

The fourth and last limb remaining to come off was the right arm, which didn't actually come off, despite Trump's hope that it would. With the other three limbs gone, there was no tension to allow it to be yanked off as well, so instead, Big Mouth started to be dragged behind the pickup truck, the torso bouncing and rolling around to be covered in dust.

The driver, seeing this happening in his rearview mirror, slammed on the brakes and stopped fast. He'd only traveled twenty-five feet before seeing this and he put the truck into 'park' and let the engine idle, waiting for whatever would come next. The one limbed body being pulled behind the truck rolled a few times and came to a stop in the dirt.

Trump walked over to the whimpering shell of a man. Though each limb spurted arterial blood with each beat of his heart, somehow he was still alive. But he wasn't thinking clearly. Lost in a void of utter agony, his eyes were rolled up into his head and his mouth hung slack, a mewling sound coming from his throat.

"Drag him back to the others so they can see him better," Trump ordered anyone within hearing. Thames and another man were the ones who did the deed. Unhooking the remaining arm from the chain, they then used the same arm to drag the legless torso back to the other prisoners. Thames did it alone, as with his size and the limbless man weighing barely a hundred pounds now, due to missing body parts, it was a simple task for him to do so.

Thames let the body slump to the ground a few feet from the prisoners. Many were uttering curses and whispering angrily. Morrigan, seeing this happening, cocked his rifle in full view of the prisoners; the motion a warning.

"What now?" Morrigan asked Trump quietly, so no one else could hear. He tried not to look at the mewling creature on the ground. It was too stomach churning. Blood was barely seeping out of the three open wounds, most of the blood from the body having already pumped out, and Big Mouth was only a few heartbeats from death. Already, his complexion was taking on the color of a piece of parchment.

"Now we wait for what comes next," Trump said confidently.

"You bastard, you can't do this to us! We have rights!" an old man screamed from the middle of the prisoners. "You'll burn in hell for this!"

Trump looked up, spotting the man immediately. Short brown hair and wearing nothing but a T-shirt and jeans, his feet devoid of footwear. He must have been asleep when the shooting started. He appeared to be in his sixties or around there.

Trump glanced over at Hodgkins, who was already returning the president's gaze. "Kill him," Trump said flatly.

"Sir!" Hodgkins said, and in one smooth motion, pulled his sidearm from his hip, leveled the weapon at the man and fired. The old man's mouth was still open, more protests about to spill out, when the bullet entered into the opening. The bullet clipped a few teeth as it entered the rear of the mouth, then was deflected upwards into the skull. The top of his head blew off, a round piece of skull almost lifting upwards to pop back down, as if the old man was a cartoon character with a hat that had blown off his head after eating something too spicy to handle. Bone and blood sprayed the closest prisoners, and more than one yelled in terror. Only the threat of gun muzzles leveled at them kept them from doing something they would most definitely regret.

"Anyone else have anything to tell me?" Trump asked as he watched the crowd. No one spoke, and most lowered their eyes to the ground, averting their gaze, not wanting to make eye contact with the president. Others cowered in fear, and a few were sobbing. "That's what I thought." He looked down at the pitiful excuse for what had been a human being. Big Mouth wasn't moving anymore, nor making sounds. Trump placed the golf club on the man's chest and shoved slightly, shifting the body a little, as if he was poking it.

Trump shifted the club so that the tip was near the corpse's face, then slowly, he began taking practice swings, but would stop just shy of the man's head.

He glanced at the prisoners. "Don't judge me, folks, I'm a little rusty. But I'm getting back into it, I promise."

No one said anything, knowing better. Trump was talking for an audience of one at the moment, something he often did, even when he was standing in front of thousands of people.

Trump did this for another two minutes, and then, on an upswing, Big Mouth's eyes, which were closed, snapped open and his mouth cracked apart until it looked as if the dead man would dislocate his jaw. Trump smiled, not feeling threatened in the slightest. Trying to roll onto its side, the zombie reached for Trump with its only hand; a futile attempt barely worth acknowledging.

Which was Trump's plan all along. After all, it wasn't as if he would truly put himself in danger on purpose. Oh no. Trump knew once the man had his arms and legs torn off, he would be as helpless as a baby.

But the facade of danger was still there, which was all Trump needed.

"Oh, look who's awake. But not for long." Trump raised the golf club over the head of the snarling zombie and brought it down as forcefully as he could manage. The top connected with the zombie's nose, shattering it and sending blood flying off in tiny droplets that splashed onto the ground. Raising the club again, Trump wiggled his ass as if to get into a better position, and this time lowered the club like it was an axe and he was an out of shape lumberjack. The club imploded the undead man's right eye, popping it like an egg and cracking the socket. Viscous fluid squirted out from around the nine iron, to then sloppily roll down the creature's cheek. But the animated corpse was still very much animated.

Trump frowned, especially when he saw the faces of the prisoners. Of course they were terrified of him, but there was something else mixing in with their visages; a lack of respect.

The dead man was snarling and growling, ignoring the wounds to his head. Big Mouth felt no pain and so was unfazed by the abuse he'd just suffered.

Trump was growing annoyed. Even in death, Big Mouth was defying him. He needed to finish this now or the entire show he'd put on to break the prisoners' spirits would be worthless. Bringing back the golf club as far over his shoulder as he could, as if the zombie's head was a giant golf ball, he swung for all he was worth. The club connected with the left temple of the zombie, cracking it and sinking a few inches into the brain. A wet squelching sound carried into the air and the body went still.

Trump withdrew the club from the corpse's head, a slug like slime coating it, as well as a few gobbets of brain matter. He gestured to Hodgkins who ran up to him. "Clean this up," he ordered and tossed the club to his bodyguard.

Hodgkins said nothing, though he made a disgusted looking face, but it was gone as fast as it appeared. He knew better than to show distaste for a request by Trump. He walked off to deal with the task.

Squaring his shoulders, Trump walked back to the prisoners and stood before them. "That was fun, people. I enjoyed that. And I tell you what. I'll do it again and again until I get what I want."

"So what do you want?" a brave soul at the front of the pack asked, then added. "Mr. President."

He liked that, it was subtle but it was a sign of respect. "What do I want?" Trump fixed his leather jacket, as the zipper was off kilter. "Why, I want your loyalty. I need recruits. Now, none of this had to go down like this. This was all bad, very, very bad. That man there?" He gestured to Big Mouth. "He's pathetic, a loser." He looked at the others, making eye contact with each one. That is, the ones who would meet his gaze. "Are you people losers, too?" He waved to them. "You have my permission to talk amongst yourselves for a few minutes, to make up your mind. But be warned, I expect complete loyalty. If you can't give it, then too bad for you."

"What if we don't want to join you?" the same brave soul asked. His question was asked with respect, no malice in the tone.

Trump shrugged his shoulders and pursed his lips. He nodded his head to the corpse on the ground, the gesture obvious. "You'll end up like this poor bastard if you don't join me." He locked gazes with Morrigan, who sauntered over to see what Trump needed. "How did this place fare from the fight, Captain?"

"It's mostly intact, Sir," Morrigan explained. "The windmill is trashed and a few shacks were destroyed, but the rest is fine. There's even a vegetable garden at the rear of the settlement."

"That's excellent, excellent. I propose we move our camp here, then. Once we get the gate repaired, it's safe as a bug in a rug." As if to emphasize his point on security, a shot rang out from outside the walls, another zombie being put down.

Morrigan seemed to consider Trump's suggestion.

"Trouble, Captain? I want to move here and that's final. You don't have a problem with this, do you?"

"No, Mr. President, of course not. I was just thinking of the logistics of having to move our camp all the way here, that's all."

"Well, that's your problem. As for me, I'm tired. I want to lie down. I'm going to go find someplace to take a nap. If anything comes up, deal with it, but leave me alone."

"But what about the prisoners?"

Trump waved an errant hand over his left shoulder as he joined Thames and Hodgkins, who handed Trump his golf club back, now cleaned and shining in the sun. "I told them their options. If they don't want to join me, kill them all and be done with it." He sighed. "I'm bored."

It took only a few minutes for Thames to find a suitable two-room shack for Trump to relax in, and quickly search it for anyone hiding within. It was empty. It was a Spartan home, with only the bare necessities to live on.

Trump didn't understand it at all. There was so much to scavenge from the surrounding area, why not take some for yourself? He stretched out on a clean-looking bed, with fresh smelling sheets in a second room barely big enough to hold the bed.

He closed his eyes and was already drifting off when he heard a lone gunshot. This one was closer, within the walls, and not a sentry shooting zombies. He cracked open one eye, cocking an ear to see if any more shots were forthcoming, but after a full minute passed and none did, he smiled slightly and closed his eyes again. Evidently, there had been another holdout with the prisoners, and

Morrigan had had to make another example. But once that prisoner was dealt with, the others must have quickly redefined their motivations in life and had sworn allegiance to him.

Of course, they wouldn't be trusted right out of the gate, but would be watched closely, always a Lost Sons of Freedom member paired up with one of the prisoners. But in time, they should be absorbed into the camp and any past grievances would be forgotten. At least that's what Trump assumed, and if that wasn't so, there was no one who could talk him out of it, even if he let them try.

He was snoring in minutes, his conscience clean. As long as it was something furthering his personal agenda, that he was doing something to better his life and only his life, it was all good with him. The carnage he'd perpetrated meant nothing to him. He wouldn't even give the day's occurrences another thought. It was done, and like always, he was the winner.

And winning was all that mattered.

Chapter 18

The bright-white golf ball soared across the fairway, slicing through the air before coming down on the green with a few bounces. It began to roll across the roughshod, un-manicured green of present day and amazingly, was heading directly for the flagstick on the seventh hole.

If there had been a crowd, a gasp would have been elicited as the tiny ball made its way unerringly. But just before it would have hit the flagstick, a tattered, desiccated foot stepped directly in the path of the ball, knocking it askew to miss the hole entirely.

Donald J. Trump, wearing a red windbreaker, black khakis, and his trademark MAGA hat, didn't move after teeing off as he watched the ball bounce off the zombie foot. He was like a statue, staring in awe at the bad luck he'd just received. It would have been a hole in one, for Christ's sake, if not for that piece of dead shit walking around ruining his shot.

He spun around and glared at Captain Morrigan, who also held a club, as he'd been forced to play with Trump this morning. He hadn't wanted to but then, it wasn't like he could tell the president no.

The two men stood looking at one another. Behind them, set higher on a hill, were the remains of the clubhouse. It had burned to the ground weeks ago, only a few pieces of rebar and stone jutting out of the wreckage. The odor of burned building was long gone.

Trump had been a little bothered upon seeing the building destroyed. He'd come here, to Sterling, Virginia, many times during his presidency. Too many times according to the Fake news media.

They would constantly complain how people were dying from Covid-19, and he was playing golf.

So people were dying. What did they want him to do about it? He was the president, not a scientist, though he liked to think he played one on TV when he did his press conferences. Forget an apple a day. A cup of bleach is even better to keep the doctor away. Or better yet, stick a flashlight up your ass to kill Covid instantly.

Other than the clubhouse being destroyed, the Trump National Golf Club was in decent shape. The grounds were overgrown of course, to the point playing a round of golf was ridiculous, but Trump didn't care. He'd told Morrigan to have a few of his men trim a little, taking down the high grass in strategic places, such as where he would tee off on each hole, and around the flagstick at the end.

Of course, there had been dozens of zombies wandering the grounds when Trump had arrived that morning, but he didn't care. So Morrigan had no choice but to have his people risk being hurt to destroy the creatures. All so that Trump could play a round of golf and pretend the world was fine.

But indulging Trump wasn't over yet. Once he began playing, the rule to kill a zombie was not to use guns. Blades only. He said he didn't want to be distracted by gunfire when he was teeing off or putting. Morrigan thought it was ridiculous, especially when he had to play with Trump and realized the man was terrible at the game.

And worst of all, Trump cheated constantly. For no reason, too, for though Trump might be bad at the game, Morrigan was even worse.

Playing golf with Trump had eroded Morrigan's loyalty just a little bit more, another piece of the rock chiseled away. It had been a slow thing, taking weeks, if not months, but when Morrigan looked back when he had first found Trump, trapped naked on that SUV, he should have realized something.

The man wasn't a winner, like he so often touted, he was a loser, a large one actually, but one who always had an edge to cover up his losses.

The seed that was planted inside Morrigan had just sprouted into a full-fledged seedling, and was now beginning to grow.

"Have someone deal with *that*," Trump pointed with his nine iron at the zombie that had blocked his shot. It was the same club he'd used to bash in the head of the troublesome man previously. "And I'm taking that as a hole in one. Best damn shot I ever made and there's no one around to see it."

"Ah, okay I guess," Morrigan said flatly.

"You know, my friend, if the club house was still intact, I might have considered setting up shop here."

"Really?" Morrigan was surprised at that. The grounds were so wide open with almost no fences. There was no way to secure the perimeter without manning it with more than a dozen or more men, and even then there would be holes an enemy could sneak through. They had been set up in the new settlement for over a week as of today, the move taking days. The former prisoners had already been absorbed into the camp, and for the most part had accepted their fate. In many ways, to them, it didn't really matter who was in charge. They quickly found out that their lives didn't change too much from before Trump had arrived. They still got up each morning, worked the day, and went to sleep each night. They didn't have dealings with Trump or any of the higher-ups either, so mostly their lives went back to normal, that is, the life they had before Trump had forced himself onto them.

A wild chicken came into view down below in the tall grass. Trump's eyes went to it like a heat seeking missile. "Look, over there."

Morrigan spun around, dropping his club and reaching for his sidearm, expecting danger, but relaxed when he saw it was only a chicken.

"Have someone grab that and cook it up for me for lunch. Fried chicken will be fantastic. You know, I've been craving fried chicken for a while now."

Morrigan gestured to a soldier, one of three standing off to the side of where Trump was teeing off. Thames and Hodgkins were the other two men.

The man had been carrying Morrigan's golf clubs, which had been salvaged from a Sporting Goods store, and was playing caddy. When the world collapsed and the dead walked, golfing wasn't high on many people's lists—unless you're Donald J. Trump—so it hadn't been hard to find a set on store shelves for Morrigan to use.

Thames was Trump's caddy, and Hodgkins was just along for the ride. Morrigan didn't even give Thames or Hodgkins orders any longer. The two men were completely under Trump's spell and followed him without question. There had been a few times when this had caused Morrigan concern, but whatever the issue was it had usually resolved itself. Besides, the settlement was large and Trump mostly kept to himself, leaving Morrigan the duties of running the settlement, so most days, the different factions didn't even see each other.

Morrigan gave his caddy orders, but having been within hearing of Trump and Morrigan, the man already knew what was needed and ran off down the slight incline to chase the chicken. There was a lot of squawking as man and fowl ran around the course.

The chicken darted into the treeline bordering the fairway and the man dashed after it. For a few moments there was no sound, but then a scream split the morning and the man appeared, running back out onto the fairway, holding his arm, which was bleeding profusely, and yelling for help.

At first, no one understood what was happening. The wound seemed much too large for it to have been from the chicken, perhaps pecking the man when it had been caught. But then a zombie stepped out of the trees, bright red blood covering its mouth and chin.

The man was still screaming as he ran back to where Morrigan was standing, along with Trump and his bodyguards.

Trump pursed his lips, annoyed. He waved the club he was holding at Thames and Hodgkins to get their attention. "One of you shoot that man and shut him the fuck up. He's been bit so he's already dead, am I right? Besides, he's a loser for getting bit in the first place and I can't stomach losers."

Both Thames and Hodgkins nodded and began moving across the grass to where the yelling man was running right towards them, thinking they were going to help him, not execute him.

Morrigan, seeing one of his men about to be killed in cold blood, couldn't just stand there and watch. The caddy was under his protection, and he'd be damned if he would let Trump have the man murdered in cold blood, despite the current situation. "Thames, Hodgkins, halt, goddamn it!"

Both men did as ordered, the tone of Morrigan's voice enough to make them pause, at least for the moment.

Morrigan began walking towards them, as the screaming man tripped and fell about twenty feet from the two bodyguards. Another soldier, seeing the zombie, shot the creature in the head, forgetting the rule of no firearms on the golf course. Blood and brain matter splattered across the tall grass and the zombie toppled to the ground. The soldier who killed it grabbed its feet and dragged it off the course, which is what the men had been doing all day each time they killed one.

Trump, seeing his direct order being disobeyed, walked down the fairway and joined Morrigan, who had stopped halfway to Thames and Hodgkins. Trump closed the gap and positioned himself in front of Morrigan, thus blocking the captain from moving.

"Just what the hell do you think you're doing?" Trump demanded, enraged. "I gave those two an order."

"I don't care. I'm stopping them from killing that man."

"But why?"

"Because it's wrong, that's why. That man is one of us and we don't kill each other."

"He's been bit. He's gonna die!"

"Maybe, but if he is, it won't happen today and he deserves the right to at least say goodbye to anyone he cares about."

"That's bullshit. He's contaminated, he's already dead."

"I don't care. No more killing." Morrigan got right in Trump's face, who realized whatever control he had over Morrigan was gone. The defiance was written all over the man's face. Morrigan was through listening to the president, the facade Trump portrayed to the world had been pulled away and Morrigan saw him as he truly was, a sham—which made the man a liability in Trump's eyes.

That seedling inside Morrigan had finally blossomed into a beautiful flower and it was standing strong.

Not wanting to go head to head with Morrigan, and feeling a little intimidated, though he'd never admit it to anyone, Trump stepped backwards and nodded. "Fine, Captain, have it your way."

"Good, and once we get back to town, things are gonna change there, too," Morrigan said, his newfound power emboldening him. "It's time I took back my role as leader, like it was before I saved you from those zombies." He locked eyes with Trump. "You owe me, you know. If it wasn't for me, you'd be long dead by now."

"I understand completely," Trump said, sounding cowed. "We'll do it the way you want."

Morrigan grinned and walked past Trump, going to the fallen man, who was surrounded by three other men who'd gone to his aide. Only Thames and Hodgkins were looking at Trump and Morrigan, the rest occupied with the fallen man, trying to bandage his wound.

As Morrigan turned his back on him, Trump saw the perfect opportunity to ensure he didn't lose power, or lose face with Thames and Hodgkins, who'd witnessed the disrespect Morrigan had shown him. As Morrigan passed him, his back to Trump, the president pulled out the .45 he always carried on his person, and in a smooth motion, flicked off the safety, placed it an inch behind Morrigan's head, and squeezed the trigger, shooting the man in the back of the head.

The bullet penetrated the skull but ricocheted away almost immediately, punching another hole in the side of the skull, but not making the shot a killing one. Morrigan fell forward and went to his knees, a hand going to his head, as if that would help with the pain he suddenly felt. Morrigan touched his head and then moved his hand before his eyes, seeing the blood on his fingers and palm. It took a few extra seconds for him to try and understand what had just happened, but slowly, he figured out what had just occurred. He'd been shot from behind.

His hand went down to the sidearm on his hip, but as he was disoriented from the shot to his head, his motor functions were off and he slapped the gun but couldn't get his grip around the weapon.

Both Thames and Hodgkins stared, not understanding what had occurred. It was Trump who snapped them out of their shock.

"Don't just stand there looking like a couple of idiots! Kill him, you morons! Finish what I started!"

It was the test of loyalty Trump had been wondering about. Would the two men follow his orders without question, and kill their former leader, or would they balk and become difficult.

Both men stood and stared at Morrigan, who was still struggling with his sidearm. He couldn't seem to figure out how to remove it from its holster. Blood spurted from his head as well, soaking into his shirt.

It was Hodgkins who broke the spell, and Trump wasn't surprised by that in the least. After all, it was Hodgkins who had killed the child found in the rubble of the village without remorse when Trump had told him to.

Hodgkins leveled his rifle and fired two times, hitting Morrigan in the back, saying, "Sorry, Captain, but he's the fucking President of the United States."

Morrigan opened his mouth in response but nothing came out but blood, which coated his lips and dripped down his chin to splatter the grass beneath him. He slumped to the ground, dead. Thames walked over to tower over Morrigan and shot the dead captain in the head, this time making sure the bullet destroyed the brain, and the man would not come back from the grave. In doing so, he cemented his loyalty to Trump.

The president smiled. He had a small amount of blowback on his orange-colored face, small spots of red, like freckles, covering his cheeks and forehead. He gestured to the men down at the bottom of the hill; they'd witnessed the murder of Morrigan firsthand.

"No witnesses, men, we need to keep it all clean," Trump explained calmly.

"Sir," Hodgkins said, and Thames only nodded. Both men spun around on their heels and aimed their weapons at the crouched men surrounding the wounded man, and together, began firing into the quartette of bodies.

Not expecting an attack from their fellow soldiers, and not getting what was going on with their captain being shot, the three crouched men never so much as got their weapons out. Bodies were riddled with bullets, the men falling away from the prone soldier and exposing him to gunfire, too, which so far he remained untouched.

Getting to his hands and knees, the wounded man had forgotten his bleeding arm and began trying to crawl away, but Hodgkins jogged down the hill after him. Upon reaching the retreating man, Hodgkins kicked him in the side, flipping him over onto his back. The man raised both hands in front of him, as if that could ward off more bullets, and he pleaded for Hodgkins not to kill him, begged for his life as tears rolled down his face.

Hodgkins, ever the cold-blooded killer, ignored the pleas for mercy and shot the man twice in the chest and then once in the face to ensure he wasn't going to rise again.

Turning, he walked back up the hill and joined Trump and Thames.

"Well done, son, well done. For this, you both deserve a reward. How do you both feel about being Captains?"

"That would be awesome, thank you, Sir," Hodgkins said with a wide grin.

"Yeah, thanks, Mr. President," Thames echoed.

"Good men, very good men. I knew I could count on you." He gestured to all the bodies now littering the golf course. "I have an idea. Why don't you grab a few dead zombies that have been taken off the fairway and toss them near the bodies of our departed fellow friends? Anyone asks, we say they got attacked by zombies and the foul things got the better of them. Poor Captain Morrigan fought bravely but in the end was overwhelmed."

"That's an excellent idea, Mr. President," Hodgkins said, already understanding that Trump needed constant praise. And if the newly-commissioned Captain wanted to stay on his good side, Hodgkins needed to always be patting him on the back.

"I know it is. That's why I came up with it." He tapped his forehead. "Nobody is as smart as me, nobody. Okay, you two, off you go. Hurry, before more of our people show up and we have to kill them, too. That would be bad."

His two loyal bodyguards ran off down the hill, darting into the trees and coming out with the corpses of fallen zombies. They quickly began staging what would resemble a kill zone, at least if no one looked too closely.

Meanwhile, Trump decided to make his hole in one a mulligan. He turned, walked a bit, stepped over the corpse of Morrigan as if it was nothing more than a fallen log, and went back to the area to tee off yet again. Maybe this time, without a damn zombie on the green, he could sink the shot yet again. And why not? He'd done it before and he was sure he could do it again.

After all, he was Donald J. Trump.

He could do anything he set his mind to.

Chapter 19

It was three weeks to the day, after Trump had killed Morrigan and ensured his control over the Lost Sons of Freedom, when he was informed about another settlement on the Maryland/Washington line.

In those three weeks Trump's army had found four other settlements. Three had been absorbed into his army, and one had defied him, and so had been destroyed. If someone was to visit the settlement today, all they would find is ashes and charred human skeletons.

It was coming on noon, the day cool but comfortable. A stage had been built in the courtyard before the gate, the same spot where Trump had drawn and quartered a man weeks ago, to then cave in his head with a golf club after the man had died and returned as one of the living dead.

Trump was about to give one of his trademark rallies. It was his way of keeping the people riled up, making them believe it was them against everyone else, and only Trump could lead them to a better world.

Checking the Rolex on his wrist, Trump walked out of the large shack that he called home. But it was a shack in name only. Built strong, it was made of wood, the walls within covered with plasterboard, the floor poured concrete and then carpeting. No expense had been spared to make his three-room home something that befitted someone of his stature. And by no expense, he meant labor, for if it could be scavenged, it was free. His toilet might have been a chemical toilet still, but it was a top of the line one, as good as anything he'd used that operated with running water

As he stepped outside, the music at the rally was already playing, the generator powering the speakers and audio system running smoothly. Off to the west, solar panels were being installed on dozens of roofs, and a small solar farm of panels was being set up outside the perimeter walls, after a technician had been absorbed into the camp from the last town they'd come upon. Soon, electricity would be plentiful and they wouldn't be beholden to generators and finding fuel to run them.

Thames and Hodgkins were waiting for him in the street, and they took up escort behind Trump. It was a short walk to the stage and his adoring fans.

Before he reached the stage, Trump had to round a corner, and once he did this, the sound of the crowd came to him in force. Chanting and calling out, everyone was singing to the music, and when he finally arrived and stepped onto the stage, the army of Trump went wild.

Hodgkins and Thames stood on the stage as well, directly behind the president. While, on the ground, surrounding the stage, more than two dozen trusted men with an assortment of rifles, watched the crowd. There were four elevated platforms as well, where Trump's men watched for signs of an unruly agitator. It had happened a week ago, when Trump had been giving a speech.

One of the prisoners from a settlement two weeks ago had bided his time, playing along with joining Trump's team, only to wait for a chance to strike. Luckily, the attack had gone terribly wrong. The man had acquired a pistol, but before he could get off a shot, one of the snipers in the elevated posts had seen him and shot the man dead in the chest. It had put a hell of a damper on the speech, but Trump, ever the performer, had charged onward, making a few jokes about the dead man and then finishing his speech—to the adulation of the crowd.

While he was finishing the speech, one of the men on the ground had gone to the dead man and rammed a steel blade into the ear, thus ensuring the corpse wasn't going to rise as a zombie.

Trump gave a speech about how they needed to keep expanding their power with recruitments and more tribute. He decreed that any of the towns they dominated would soon be upping the amount of tribute. After all, it wasn't as if they could refuse, for defiance was death!

They also needed to be on guard for those goddamn Democrats. Before the dead rose they had tried to stop Trump's rise to power, but they were mostly gone now, and he was the last one standing. With him as their leader, they would rule the entire country. They would Make America Great Again, once and for all, and this time he really meant it.

The crowd had cheered and applauded and it couldn't have gone better.

Trump exited the stage to Hail to the Chief playing him off. Yes, it was supposed to be played when he entered, not exited but Trump liked the song and who was going to argue with him?

As he walked back to his home, he was smiling from ear to ear. His hair had mostly grown back and he didn't wear his MAGA hat unless he chose to.

He was the undeniable king of his domain, no, a God! Nothing could stop him now. He thought about Captain Morrigan for the briefest of moments, thinking what a fool the man had been. But the man was gone, probably still rotting on the golf course where the body had been left.

His lunch was waiting for him when he arrived back home, his private chef having prepared it to Trump's exact specifications. A hamburger and French fries were on the table, the meat for the burger taken from a freshly slaughtered cow a day previous, the potatoes for the fry's part of tribute from one of the settlements.

He wasted no time in sitting down and digging in. As he closed his eyes and savored the burger on a homemade bun, he could almost think he was back in the White House, having a late night snack at eleven p.m., after binge watching Fox News for the past three hours.

As he finished lunch a messenger arrived; he asked to speak to Trump. Thames checked with the president first, wanting to know if he would talk to the messenger.

"Send him in. Maybe he's got news of something interesting. I've been getting bored around here."

The man entered. He was a short fellow with short, reddish brown hair and freckles. His cheeks were wind burned. He wore a plaid shirt and jeans, and had just ridden in on a dirt bike, which the camp had many and used for exploring. The bikes were easy to maintain and used little gas.

The man looked excited about something. "Mr. President, I found another town, Sir. It's a big one, too."

Trump perked up at this. Lately, his expansion of power was the only thing keeping him going. The only true rush he felt was when another settlement was taken into his army, absorbed like an amoeba to an outside cell. He gathered he'd already either combined or destroyed any other settlement within a thirty mile area surrounding Washington, D.C., but evidently he was incorrect.

The messenger looked exhausted and thirsty, but Trump didn't even so much as offer the man a glass of water. As stated many times, Trump didn't have much empathy for anyone but himself, and could care less how the man was feeling, or his needs.

"No shit? Where is it? Why haven't we found it before this?" Trump demanded.

"It's on the north side of Washington in Maryland, on the Maryland side of the Potomac, Sir. They've taken a decent section of Kempton and walled it off. They've used the dead in Washington as a barrier, making a giant horde that someone would have to go through to reach them. Every bridge is blocked by zombies. I was able to get through them only because I had to make a detour and then, I only made it because I was on my bike. I found them completely by accident."

Trump stood up from his chair, hamburger bun crumbs falling off his shirt. "So they're using Washington as cover. Clever. That's why we never found them before this, despite how close they are. Morrigan told me Washington was nothing but death and I never thought to disagree. They're using the dead as cover for their little town."

"Yes, that's what I thought when I found them. The guards on sentry duty took me in at first. They were shocked I'd found them. I thought they weren't going to let me go at first, especially when I told them about you and how you're rebuilding America." He swallowed the knot in his throat. "It looked like they would kill me then."

"Yes, I would have," Trump said under his breath.

"I don't understand, Mr. President."

"Nothing, go on."

"Oh, okay, well, I was brought to a small building they used as a council chamber. There were a bunch of people, all sitting around this big table. They argued a lot but also discussed stuff normally. They asked me who I was and I told them everything. They seemed to each have a vote in what happens in the town and the majority vote was what would happen. It seems they run things like a democracy."

Trump blinked a few times at the man, not saying anything. "You told them everything? Right there, when you were inside their walls with no way of escaping, and told them they were to submit to becoming part of our community or risk us attacking them and taking what we want?"

"Yeah, exactly. That's what I was told to do if I found any survivors living somewhere."

"You're not too bright, are you, fella," Trump said and touched his hand to his forehead, while closing his eyes in annoyance.

The messenger looked at Trump and cocked his head to the side, like a dog would. He didn't fully understand.

"They let you go so they could follow you back here, you idiot!" Trump screamed and then grabbed the man by his shirt. Trump was a good foot taller than the man and though not muscular, the extra height was still imposing to the younger, smaller man. "They let you go so they could trail you back here."

"But….but how do you know that?"

"Because that's what I would do, damn it." Trump walked away to the far side of the room, his eyes creased as he concentrated on scenarios.

"There's more, Sir, and I think you'll want to hear it."

Trump spun around to face the messenger and his lips were pressed close together. He had just about enough of the moron standing before him, but he managed to say, "Go ahead, speak."

"Well, I got a good look at everything; like I was told to do if I found anybody. I figured they let me go because they're not afraid of what I told them. I mean, they didn't even take my gun when I was with them, though there were armed guards standing next to me. They were really friendly, actually. Too friendly, if you ask me."

"What do you mean?"

The man began to explain everything he'd witnessed, from the stockade and concrete brick fences twenty-five feet tall, to the elevated sniper's nests on all four points of the town, each one manned with an M60 machine gun with 7.62mm ammunition.

"They have their act together, Mr. President, and are well organized. Much better than the other places that've been found and taken over in the past few weeks. In size, I'd say they're as big as we are, in numbers and in weapons, or at least from what I saw. It wasn't like they were trying to hide any of it, and I think they were kind of proud to show it all off."

"Sounds like they're a bunch of Democrats, the way they acted," Trump reasoned. "They believe everyone's got good intentions and we all want to work together and all that other happy horseshit. Bunch of fucking socialists, if you ask me." He began pontificating, more for himself than the messenger. "I ask you, why would I want to work and amass wealth just to give it to others who aren't as smart as I am and can't do the same thing? I made my money fair and square, or that is, I managed to get others to give it to me, and then the Democrats come along and want to tax the shit out of me and give it to poor people. Like a fucking reward. I earned it, its mine. And it's not like all these Democrats, worth millions themselves, ever said, 'I'm giving all my wealth to the poor and I'm only keeping enough to live on and have a small home somewhere. The rest goes to everyone else.' Fuck no. They make their money and keep it, and all the while they're giving speeches about how the rest of us that are wealthy need to give our cash away."

"Its funny you say that, Sir," the messenger said. "From what I heard at the council meeting, it's mostly Democrats that are running the place."

"Ha! See, I knew it. Bunch of goddamn pussies, the lot of them. We'd all be better off without them. They're all weak cowards that need someone like me to make them stronger. That's how they were in the Senate and Congress as well. All they did was bitch and complain, but never did anything but talk."

"I got the idea that some of them were Republicans, too, that is, I was told by their leader when they talked to me, but even those were all open-minded people who were happy to be a part of the group."

Trump grunted. "They sound like they are nothing but a bunch of RHINOs along for the ride."

"I don't understand."

Trump glared at the man, exasperated. "It means that their 'Republican in name only.' They're not true Republicans!" He pointed at the door. "That's enough, get out of here, we're done here."

The man didn't argue, but spun on his heels and exited the house.

"Thames, get in here!" Trump yelled.

A moment later, Thames entered the house. "You needed me, Sir?"

"Yes. It looks like we might have company. Double the guards on the walls and send out a few scouts to watch the area around us."

"Trouble?"

Trump looked at his second-in-command, the promotion happening after Morrigan had been killed. Thames was the new Morrigan except his loyalty hadn't faltered as of yet. "Might be." He quickly explained all he'd learned from the messenger, about how the man might have been trailed back to their base camp, and followed it up with, "Those trucks we filled with the dead from that shopping mall, have a crew check them out and make sure all the trucks are in running condition."

Thames right eyebrow rose up in a query.

"I've been saving them for a rainy day, and from what that little shit told me, it's about to fucking pour out."

"We gonna pay this new place a visit, Sir?" Thames asked.

"Eventually, but for now, I think we need to get more info on what we're up against. They're a match for us in both firepower and manpower. We need to play this right."

There was a knock at the door and Thames went to it. Opening it, he began talking to someone.

Trump waited, annoyed that he was waiting at all.

After a full minute, Thames pulled his head back and called to Trump. "It's the messenger again, Sir, he says he forgot to tell you something, thought it might be important."

With a heavy sigh, Trump waved the man in. "Fine, let him in, but it better be fast. I've run out of patience for that idiot."

Thames stuck his head out the door again, said a few things, probably telling the messenger to be quick and that Trump wasn't in the mood any longer, and stepped aside to allow the man access.

The messenger scooted inside and quickly walked back over to Trump, who was standing in a posture that showed impatience to anyone astute enough to realize it. "Sorry, Mr. President, I forgot to tell you something. I think it's important. At least, it seemed that way to me when I was talking to…"

"Just tell me, for Christ's sake!" Trump snapped.

The man stopped talking when he was cut off. He gathered his thoughts to be as succinct as possible. He was bright enough to sense he was pushing his luck with Trump. He closed his eyes for a heartbeat, calming his thoughts and then said, "It's about the leader of the town, though they have a council there is kind of one person who seems to be more in charge or at least the one who presides over the meetings. When I told the council and her about you, she laughed. There was a lot of talk after that, but finally she got everyone to stop talking and she then called me over to speak to me."

"And?" Trump coaxed. "So help me, get to the point or I will tell Thames to shoot you in the fucking head right here and now!"

"Yes, Sir," the man said, visibly nervous but snapping back to focusing on what he had to say. "The leader of the council, she told me that she knows you personally."

"Oh really? Who is she?"

"She said her name was Nancy Pelosi, and that she was the Former Speaker of the House before the world went to shit."

Chapter 20

Around two weeks, give or take a day, from the day the messenger reported to Trump about the new enclave, Trump was still waiting for an attack from Pelosi's people. If the messenger had been followed, there was no sign of either scouts or a messenger from Pelosi's side. Trump found he had even more disdain for Pelosi if this was true. If she simply let Trump's messenger go and hadn't tried to trail him, the decision was even more foolhardy than he could have imagined.

Trump hadn't been idle in those two weeks and now, was on his way to pay that nasty woman a visit.

"I'm going to enjoy this," Trump said with a grin as he sat in a bright red pickup truck, Thames driving, Hodgkins in the rear bed, his knees pressed to the back window as he held onto the .40mm turret gun mounted to the cab.

There was a feeling of déjà vu, Trump thought, as the pickup, along with every able man and woman that could fight, rode in vehicles behind him. But there was one difference. When last he rode in a pickup truck like this, he'd gone to talk to the settlement. Though giving an ultimatum, at least the people inside the place had been offered the option of submission. Not this time, however. This time he was going to war. He knew Speaker Nancy Pelosi would never submit to his rule, nor secretly, did Trump want her to. So there would be only one option. Scorched earth.

"The box trucks with the dead in them, are they in position yet?" Trump asked Thames, who picked up the two-way radio on the dashboard and spoke into it. A reply came back quickly, Thames nodding as he listened, the speaker to his ear. Satisfied, he tossed the radio back onto the dashboard, careful not to knock off the bobblehead stuck in the center.

"All set, Sir, when the signal is given, they're ready to go."

Trump nodded. "Good, and the hats, did they manage to do what I wanted? It matters to me, Thames, I need Pelosi to see that when it all goes down."

Thames nodded. "Yes, Sir, say said they got the hats on as ordered. They lost two men doing it."

"Excellent about the hats, not so much for the two losers stupid enough to get killed. This will be big, Thames, my boy, very big. I always think big, do I not?"

"You sure do. I'm proud to serve under you, Sir."

Trump smiled, his teeth bright against his orange makeup. "As well you should, Captain, as well you should." He leaned back and tried to get more comfortable. Not wanting to deal with the living dead in Washington, they were taking the long way around, having to go far out of their way and then circle back until they reached Kempton Bridge located on the north branch of the Potomac. But the end result would be they would make it to their destination safely.

"What about the forward attack party, are they there yet?"

Thames did a repeat with the two-way radio, and reported, "All went as planned. They're in position now and ready to go at your signal."

"Good. This will be a tremendous victory for us. They'll never see it coming." He was wearing the black leather jacket again, his .45 in his right pocket. Between his knees, handle up, was his nine iron. He liked the way he looked with it, and if all went well, by the end of the day, it would be covered in blood once more. Nancy Pelosi's blood, to be more accurate.

He had named the club Lucy, but as of yet had not said it out loud. It wasn't that he would be ashamed if others thought it was silly, for Trump was a man who never felt shame. It was a feeling he simply never used.

Trump fixed his MAGA hat more firmly on his head, glancing at Thames to see the man also wearing one. His entire army all wore the red ball caps. They were found in a strip mall, the entire small store dedicated to Trump paraphernalia. Trump had taken a small bobblehead from all that had been taken for himself, and stuck it to the dashboard before leaving this morning. He thought it was amusing to see his head bouncing around on the dashboard.

The toy's face was bright orange and to most people would have looked silly, but to Trump, the bobblehead looked fantastic, a miniature him he could admire.

After making their way around Washington D.C. to avoid the masses of living dead in the city, the convoy went north, making their way down winding roads, most lined with homes. Many of the houses looked in perfect condition, while others were nothing but scorched wrecks with only the foundations remaining. Many had corpses lying supine on the overgrown lawns, the soft parts, such as eyes and tongues long gone thanks to the animal life predominate in the area.

In a once quaint neighborhood, the convoy rolled up on a spot where a giant car crash had occurred, later, when emergency services had arrived, they had been attacked and killed along with any survivors. The remnants, now months later, was a massive amount of vehicles blocking the road.

But normal rules of vehicle law didn't apply anymore, so it wasn't hard to drive over the sidewalk and onto the grass of the city park adjacent to the crash. One at a time, the convoy rolled over the tall grass, more than once the pickups bouncing as something hidden beneath the grass was run over. No one wanted to consider what they were driving over, and it wasn't mentioned again.

Zombies were seen wandering around, of course, and Trump had orders not to molest the creatures unless someone was personally in danger of an attack. But that didn't mean more than one of the pickups didn't swerve in the road to take out a wandering corpse.

Thames wasn't above having a little fun and Trump allowed it.

While driving down the center line of a two lane highway, a female zombie had stumbled out from the shoulder and onto the road. Thames, with an evil grin on his lips, had steered the front bumper of the pickup directly at the zombie. When impacting it, the head had snapped clean off, while the torso and legs had gone underneath the vehicle. There was a vibration as the body thumped the undercarriage, and then the pickup had processed the body and spit it out the back end. The following pickup, too close to swerve, had no choice but to run over the headless corpse as well, the same process transpiring.

The third vehicle along with the fourth did the same, and by the time the fifth truck had ridden over the corpse, it was nothing but a flattened mass of red paste with a few splintered bones jutting out of the zombie pâté.

"Excellent," Trump grinned. "I hope to do the same to Nancy when we get there."

Thames glanced at Trump. The road was clear for the moment, no cars or zombies on it. "You don't like her, Sir?"

"No, not at all. I dislike her immensely. That's why we're not negotiating with her and her people. Waste of time, it'll go nowhere. She'll never submit to me. She's a terrible woman, Thames, so argumentative. Nasty, nasty personality. I tried working with her and the other Democrats but it was too hard. She's a piece of work." Trump pursed his lips in thought. "Not even good for a mercy fuck. Hell, she's eighty for Christ's sake. I like 'em much younger, much." He looked up at the roof of the cab, as if he was gazing higher to the sky and beyond. "I miss my daughter."

"Which one, Sir?"

"Ivanka of course, why, is there another?"

"Tiffany."

"Oh, yeah, right. I forgot about her. She doesn't matter. It's Ivanka I like. You know, if she wasn't my daughter, I would have loved to…"

"Yes, Mr. President, I heard the story, we don't have to get into it." Thames made a face. Even he had limits and banging his own daughter was one of them.

"Huh? Oh sure, sorry. I was just reminiscing. I had a lot of fun in the White House, you know. Good times. I was the best thing to ever happen to this country. Before me, it was a joke, but then…"

"But then the coronavirus came and the dead rose, Sir."

Trump's braggadocio faded. "Yeah, there was that."

"Can I ask you a question, Sir?" Thames said.

"Sure, shoot."

"It's about the coronavirus. I lost both my parents from it, Sir, within days of each other. Neither of them wore a mask. They listened to what you said, that we were okay. That we were, how did you say it? 'Rounding the corner.' So they went out one night with friends, to a karaoke bar, none of them did anything to protect themselves from the virus, the simple things anyone can do to be safer. They both got it—the virus. That was one of the only times they went out and didn't wear a mask. A lot of places made them if they wanted to go inside, like a supermarket. So I gotta ask you, President Trump, Sir. Knowing what you know now, would you have done anything different? You know, like telling people masks were good and you not having like a thousand rallies without following CDC rules while running for re-election?"

"I would have won, too, Thames. It would have been a landslide. Old Sleepy Joe would have been such a loser. Not me, though, I would have been the winner. I'm always a winner."

Thames never got an answer to his questions, for before he could prompt Trump, the two-way radio squawked and Thames answered it. After tossing it back on the dashboard he said, "We're five minutes out from the bridge, Sir. Then we're almost there."

Trump laughed out loud. "Then it's go time! Time to teach those fucking Democrats a lesson they'll never forget!"

Thames glanced at Trump for a second. He'd really wanted answers to his questions, but as he looked at the president, who had completely ignored his queries, Thames realized at that exact moment, he probably never would.

Chapter 21

"Park that truck there, over there, you idiot, otherwise they can't get through!" Trump yelled to a driver. He was standing on the roof of one of the pickup trucks, far away from the action, safe from any danger. But that didn't stop him from directing the operation going on before him, at the end of the Kempton Bridge. He used his nine iron as a pointer, waving it around like he was leading an orchestra.

Thames was standing on the ground below Trump. "Did you know, Sir, that Fairfax Stone is located just down there?" He pointed to the north of the river. "It's at the tip of Maryland's southwestern corner and is believed to be the origin of the Potomac."

Trump looked down at his new captain, a look of annoyance on his orange-covered face. "And I give a shit about that, why?"

Thames looked downtrodden. "No reason, Sir, just a little trivia I picked up somewhere."

"Focus, Thames, focus!" Trump snapped.

"Yes, Sir. Sorry, Sir."

The bridge was a two lane structure, more like a highway than a bridge. It reminded him of the causeways that connected parts of Florida.

The bridge was occupied by more than two hundred zombies, possibly more. It wasn't like he was bothering to count.

The zombies were a credible deterrent to stop anyone from crossing the bridge, that is, if said people didn't have the resources that Trump did.

With all the vehicles and armaments Trump's people had, it wasn't difficult to deal with the zombies, and do it in a way that didn't waste ammunition.

That was due to a fortunate occurrence that had happened to the bridge in the recent past. About ten car lengths onto the bridge, a wide hole the size of a standard vehicle was in the guardrail. At the same time around when the dead began to walk, a car or small truck had lost control and broken through the guardrail, to plummet into the Potomac River below.

Trump had seen the hole and quickly figured out how to solve the hundreds of zombies that were marching towards them as they sat parked on the highway.

Moving the pickup trucks so that they made a wall, he had the vehicles near the hole curve inward so that the zombies had no choice but to walk in that direction. The entire bridge had been blocked by the pickup trucks, only the hole remaining. Of course, the dead didn't step through the hole willingly, that would have been too easy, but rather they tried to get at the soldiers standing behind the pickup trucks. But as the horde began pressing at the trucks, the vehicles shaking and rocking from the press of bodies, eventually, that pressure began forcing some of the bodies to the side, directly to the hole.

It wasn't long before the first zombie, though not choosing to do so, was forced off the bridge to tumble down to the river, where it hit the water like the surface was made of cement. The body quickly sank into the murky river to be washed downstream.

That zombie wasn't the last, the plan working perfectly. As the initial zombie struck the water, a second one was already tumbling out into thin air, followed by a third and fourth. It took a little while, but within half an hour, more than fifty percent of the zombies were off the bridge and in the river.

A few soldiers climbed out onto the guardrail, getting close, but not too close, to the hole in the bridge. They catcalled and whistled to draw the zombies closer. With no reasoning skills whatsoever, the zombies did exactly that, and soon, more were falling to the water, after being grabbed by their loose clothing by the soldiers bold enough to risk it. Another two dozen were disposed of that way, until there were less than fifty zombies remaining on the bridge.

Trump nodded, pleased with how it had all worked out. "Okay, that's more than enough gone. Gunners, take out the rest so we can get this show back on the road."

Ten men with M16s, Uzis and Kalashnikovs, jumped up onto the rear beds of the pickups blocking the bridge, and began shooting with unparalleled joy. There was something about killing zombies that most of the men loved to do. Perhaps it was because though the walking dead still looked human, despite the undead being as far from a living being as a thing could be. But many of the men had a bloodlust within them, and shooting down zombies for target practice was one way to feed that lust for violence and bloodshed.

The zombies, helpless as the day they were animated, absorbed bullet after bullet, unable to defend themselves. Torsos were shattered, blown apart to spray viscera in all directions. It took only seconds for the pavement of the bridge to be covered in a soupy black and brown gore that had been the zombies' insides.

Bodies danced a jig as round after round impacted them, some spinning around from the shots, to then receive a final tap to the head. Some looked like dancing marionettes, the bullets striking them causing the bodies to pirouette before falling down.

It was a massacre, there was no question of that, and after a full two minutes of firing, every zombie was down and either completely dead or flopping around with missing limbs or severed spines.

"Good enough," Trump said to Thames.

All the smoke from the weapons had blown away as fast as it appeared, thanks to the brisk wind crossing the bridge. The wind also helped to dispel the odor of the dead bodies, too, and kept any flies from bothering them, which was a welcome break.

"Tell everyone it's time to leave," Trump jumped down into the rear bed and crossed the space until he was standing by his own pickup. Hodgkins appeared as if from nowhere, never too far from the president. He took his responsibilities to protect Trump seriously.

Thames gave orders quickly, yelling at the men to get them moving. The pickups were loaded with manpower and one at a time the vehicles backed out of the wall they'd made and began driving down the bridge.

Squelching, crunching sounds filled the area around the bridge as truck tires crunched over the collapsed bodies. Heads were pulped beneath wide tire treads, chests caved in to splatter up into the undercarriages. When the last pickup had passed through the sludge that had been the remains of the animated corpses, the first crow had already appeared.

In no time, more than two dozen crows were feasting on the road kill; one with a juicy eye that had escaped being popped, another with a still flopping tongue, another with a piece of rotting cheek.

There would be quite a feast today on the Kempton Bridge, and every creature that took part in it had Donald J. Trump to thank for the bounty they were receiving.

Chapter 22

The approach to the Democrat compound was nondescript, the street lined with suburban homes. All were derelict and most were missing large portions, the parts salvaged by the compound.

Trump's convoy stopped fifty feet before the main gate to enter the compound, the other pickup trucks pulling in to the side and behind him. Any vehicle with heavy artillery mounted on its cab made sure to park so that it had an unobstructed vantage point. Turret guns, M2 .50 caliber and Mk19 heavy guns all aimed their barrels at the wall

The street ended at a large stone wall twenty feet high, the wall going off into the distance on both sides of the street, through yards and beyond. It was as if a giant line had come down from above, segregating the compound from the outside world. The roofs of homes could be seen over the wall.

On either side of the gate, ground had been cleared and crops were growing. A few corpses lay here and there, ones that had been killed but not removed yet. On the ground before the gate, dozens upon dozens of dark stains dyed the pavement brown, the residue of past kills of zombies that had wandered too close to the compound.

Sentries walked the wall, the gate made out of giant slabs of metal. The hinges were fourteen inches wide and custom made by the looks of it.

Trump had to admit he was surprised with the compound's defenses, which were impressively better than past enclaves his army had come across. Though he'd been briefed about the compound's defenses, to see it in person was far different. Evidently,

Pelosi wasn't as much of a wimp as Trump had first thought, or for once in her life she'd let someone else take the lead, at least as far as the defenses for the compound.

The moment Trump's pickup drove up and stopped, the tower overlooking the main gate was on alert, and the M60 machine gun on the tower platform immediately shifted its muzzle to face the convoy. The sentries became a hub of activity as they ran back and forth along the wall, visible to the men below on the ground only from their chests up.

Within thirty seconds of Trump's people arriving, a siren began to sound within the compound, alerting the residents that they had company.

Trump slid out of the passenger seat and stood up, making sure to fix his bright red tie, which was like a beacon as a target with the white shirt and black leather jacket. When all was in order he reached into the cab and plucked his club from where it was leaning against the seat. He cocked the golf club over a shoulder, the handle in his hand, the silver orb of the club facing the sky.

Without a care in the world, as if he was going for a stroll in a world that didn't exist any longer, he walked about fifteen feet and stopped before the gate, then peered up at the faces gazing down at him. He ignored all the weapons glistening in the sun, all of them aimed at him. One itchy trigger finger would end up having him peppered with bullets, and before the smoke cleared he would be nothing but a bullet-riddled corpse. He had confidence no one would shoot him, already forgetting past adventures when the exact scenario of being shot at was what had happened.

Behind him, men and women exited the pickups to take cover wherever they could. Every truck manned with heavy firepower was standing ready, prepared to shoot at the drop of a pin.

Trump had already prepared a signal, and every single pair of eyes was watching and waiting for it, tense for what might come next, but prepared to fight for their leader. There was a tension filling the area surrounding the gate, palpable to anyone with the intelligence to realize it.

"You were the President of the United States," a guard said from the wall. "You're Donald Trump."

"That's me, and I still am President."

"You're not my president," the guard said. "I sure as hell didn't vote for you. Neither did almost all of us in here. And the ones that did wish they could take it back."

Trump wasn't about to go down this road with someone he wouldn't bother to piss on if the man was lying in the street and on fire. "Where's Nancy Pelosi. I want to speak to her."

"I'm over here, Donald," an amplified woman's voice said.

Trump swiveled his head to the left, to the gun tower. Sure enough, Speaker of the House Nancy Pelosi was standing beside the M60, a bullhorn in her hand, pressed to her mouth.

"Nancy, it is you," Trump called, his deep voice carrying easily without enhancement. "Before we start, I've got to ask. What the hell are you doing here in Maryland? After all, you're a representative of California. Shouldn't you be there?"

"Not that it's any of your business, Donald, but I'll tell you. If for anything, it's to get you out of here sooner. I was in Washington with the rest of Congress on Capital Hill when the dead overwhelmed the city. Before any of us realized, it was too late to get out. All the airlines were shut down and there was no way out of the city."

"If that was true, how did you get here?"

"Luck, just dumb luck. Myself and some other members of Congress were able to get out on foot, if you can believe it. We made our way here. Most of them died along the way, it was tough going. But eventually we managed to meet up with some like-minded people. Talented people who knew how to build, and create; not like you, Donald, who only knows how to destroy and divide. Over a few weeks time we managed to get organized and rebuild what you see before you." She stopped and looked at Trump, taking in his outfit as if for the first time. "What is it that you're wearing there? You look ridiculous."

"No, I don't. You're wrong. I look tremendous. You're one to talk about ridiculous. I remember that Kente scarf you wore to pander to the Blacks, you all kneeling for eight minutes of silence. Nice photo-op, by the way, I couldn't have done better myself. Not your best moment."

"Perhaps, but I have to admit I'm impressed you even know the name of the scarf."

Trump shrugged. "I'm not as stupid as you take me for, Nancy."

"Oh, Donald, if only that were true." She gazed out at the army before her gates, and the MAGA hats they were all wearing. "I see you're still converting the masses to your teachings. I don't know what you have in mind here, but I warn you. We have the weapons to defend ourselves." She waved her hand back the way Trump had come. "I thought this might happen when your messenger found us. I hoped when he returned to you, and told you how well equipped we are, that you'd let us be. Leave now and this can all be over without bloodshed." She sighed heavily while shaking her head sadly. "But something tells me you wouldn't see reason; once a fool, always a fool. So we've been preparing in case you did come, Donald. So why don't you tell me what you want, though I have a feeling I already know."

"You got that right. You know what I want."

"I suppose I do. Your messenger explained that as well. I must admit, you're looking well, better than last time I saw you, in fact. But from what I see with you coming here is that you're as crazy as ever."

"That's not true and you know it. In fact, I'm saner than I've ever been. I like this new world, Nancy. Finally, there's no one to tell me what I can and can't do. I'm the law. I will it, it happens."

"That was always you're problem, Donald. You're like a child demanding a cookie before dinner and then pulling a tantrum when you're told no. It's disappointing to see the apocalypse hasn't changed you very much."

He smiled evilly and began pacing back and forth a few feet. "Oh, that's where you're wrong, Nancy. I've changed a hell of a lot since then. But it's sad to see that you haven't. You were a nasty woman before, and you're still one now. You have no choice here. Open the gates and let me in and I promise you no one will be hurt. We can make this a seamless transfer of power. Sure, you have weapons to defend yourself, but I have a hell of a lot more men than you can shoot." He pointed to the open ground where the compound's crops were. "You're food is out here. I can keep you in there until you all begin to starve…and die. Once that starts happening, you'll have a lot more to worry about than empty bellies. But I tell you what. I'm a reasonable man. Always have been."

She scoffed loudly into the bullhorn but he ignored her.

"So here's how it's going to go down. I'll ignore your disrespect today if you come on out right now, get on your knees before me, and admit I'm the man in charge. Do this and I won't kill everyone for making me come all the way here."

"You're all over the place, Donald, just like always. You can't keep an idea in your head for a full minute before you change directions. First you won't kill us, then you will, then you'll spare us. Make up your mind. I wonder how many psychosis you truly have. It's a shame you were never diagnosed. It would be a page long if not more."

He ignored her. "Come out now and submit, or else."

"That will never happen, Donald. I would die first, as would the people within these walls."

"That's sad, Nancy. Very sad. The alternative if you don't is I'll have to kill every single one of you in there. There won't be one lousy Democrat left when my people are finished here."

Her defiance was clear in not responding to him.

"Are you sure?" he asked one last time. He grinned slyly. "If you give in now, despite being difficult, I'll even let you give me a blow job with everyone watching."

She looked horrified, which was exactly what Trump was going for. "You're foul and disgusting, Donald. You know, you made Nixon look like a boy scout compared to you. At least he had the dignity to resign after being impeached! You were a disgrace to the presidency!"

"Perhaps, but I'm still you're president."

"What?"

"You heard me. Technically, I'm still the President of the United States. No election ever happened so it means I'm still in power."

"Even if that's so, it's irrelevant now, just like you, Donald."

"Have it your way, you stupid bitch. Don't say I didn't try."

"What do you mea..." she began, while at the same time, Trump raised the golf club high in the air and snapped it down fast, the silver-egged tip catching the sun and reflecting it brightly.

Multiple things happened simultaneously.

The first one was that four of Trump's men, hidden in the rear of the pickup trucks and covered by tarps, jumped up and threw off the tarps, each one holding an armed portable LAW anti-tank tube. In close to perfect unison, each LAW was fired. With multiple white smoke trails shooting up from the ground, each man had his target already locked in before firing. One rocket struck the main gate, blasting it into metal pieces that were thrown back to pummel anyone standing too close. One either side of the gate, on the walls, men and woman alike were stunned by the blast.

Nancy Pelosi saw none of this. Fortunately for her, the guard manning the M60 was a former Marine, and he spotted the smoke trail coming right for them, and at the absolute last second, shoved her off the platform.

Falling into open air, behind her a massive fireball erupted. The ammunition for the M60 had exploded along with the tower, disintegrating the Marine and everything else on the platform.

Pelosi dropped thirty feet to the ground, and was only saved by landing on a stack of hay that had been placed there after being brought in from outside the walls, the hay destined for the stables at the rear of the compound, where ten horses lived. The farmer's procrastination for days had literally just saved her life. Still, hay wasn't as soft as someone would like when falling from such a high height. She landed hard, knocking the wind out of her, but managed to roll off the pile and to the ground. Standing, she saw her arm was bleeding from shrapnel; all around her was chaos. Explosions were erupting everywhere and fires were flaring up as well. Some residents were already trying to put out the fires, while others were coming to the wall with firearms to defend the compound. Not knowing where to go at the moment, Pelosi stumbled deeper into the compound as she tried to gather her wits about her.

The third and fourth LAW rockets struck the second gun tower near the gate and the last one hit the wall itself, where there was a large congregation of people. The explosions reverberated across the compound and beyond, as fire belched from each impact.

Outside the compound, the instant the LAWs were ignited, every man and woman Trump had with him opened fire at the sentries manning the wall, either with the heavy artillery bolted to the pickups or with rifles and handguns.

Trump, never the brave warrior, had already dashed to the side, running back to his pickup and hiding behind it. Ducking low to the ground, he covered his head with his arms as the world around him exploded. It was so loud! Way louder than he thought it would be. He was petrified, not that he would ever admit it to anyone, and his ego even fought himself on that one.

Gravel chips jumped up from the ground and pelted him as the guards tried to shoot Trump and anyone else they got in their sights. A Molotov ignited from somewhere behind Trump to land on one of the neighboring pickup trucks, the soldier who threw it getting shot just before he could let it fly. The cocktail was a special brew that had dissolved Styrofoam cups in it to make them extra sticky. Many of Trump's people had them to use on the compound.

Screaming sounded as a man in the rear bed of a nearby pickup, who'd been manning an M2 .50 caliber, was engulfed in flames. He fell out of the rear bed and began running into the area between the blasted gate and the pickups. Arms flailing, he stopped shrieking in agony only when someone but a bullet in his torso; as to which side had done it, enemy or friendly fire, was unknown. The body slumped to the ground like a puppet with its strings cut. The odor of burning flesh suffused the area, causing the personnel on both sides of the battle to wince at the smell.

Someone on Trump's side tossed a hand grenade at the gate, the high explosive orb rolling up just inside the opening. Seconds after being tossed, it went off and screams filled the air.

More sentries appeared at the wall, shooting down at Trump's people. In the rear bed of Trump's truck, Hodgkins was firing his .40mm turret gun, peppering the wall with rounds and doing his best to keep the enemies' heads down.

Thames came up and dropped down beside Trump, scaring the shit out of the president.

"It's just me, Sir."

"Is it over yet? Are we winning?" Trump yelled.

"I don't know, Sir, but I just got a report from the other teams. The other towers are down, the LAWS worked perfectly, and at the back wall they broke in and the plan is in motion even now."

Another grenade hit the wall, and went off. Trump ducked lower, as the grenade blew cement chunks out of it and sent stone shrapnel in all directions. Smoke covered the area before the destroyed gate like a low mist, obscuring parts of the wall.

"Good, that's very good," Trump said. "Once they see the surprise I'm giving them, this will all be over and we'll all be the winners."

"Yes, Sir, I sure hope so. In fact I…" Thames stopped talking and Trump didn't understand why. Turning to see what was wrong with the man, his eyes bulged when he saw there was a large hole in the side of Thames' skull. The large man slumped to the ground, dead before Trump's eyes.

"Damn it," Trump said upon seeing his dead guard. He didn't really feel a sense of loss for the man, only sadness at a perfectly good tool now lost. The only person Trump cared about was Trump; everyone else was expendable.

Meanwhile, in the rear of the compound, a six foot wide piece of the wall had been blown out by a specialty team Trump had go in earlier, before his arrival.

The signal for the wall to be blown was when the LAWs took out the gun towers at the rear of the compound along with the rest, and once the hole was there, to begin backing up the box trucks that were filled with zombies taken from the shopping mall so long ago.

All the box trucks were able to park like a fan, their backs facing the wall. As Trump had figured, once the towers were destroyed and the battle at the front of the compound began, no one would be paying attention to the rear. The box trucks had been parked out of sight and then brought in the moment the hole was made.

Razor wire was hastily erected to keep the zombies within the area of the box trucks and the blown hole, and once the rear gates on the vehicles were opened, the men had to quickly retreat to wait for the last one to enter the compound, not wanting to stay in view and distract the zombies.

It was a good thing, too. Trapped within the enclosed box trucks for weeks, the zombies were a special kind of disgusting. Purification had taken hold of every single one, and the skin, now pale and sagging, seemed to slough off the bones like wet sacks of leather.

A giant cloud of flies erupted from each box truck when the door was rolled up or opened sideways, and a two inch carpet of maggots began to spill out as well. Dozens of rats were seen darting amongst the zombies' feet, the rodents able to slither in through any hole in the box trucks they could find to feed on the rotting meat.

One at a time, the zombies stumbled out of the box trucks, falling the three to four foot height to the ground, before picking themselves up and stumbling through the hole in the wall. Many were trapped under the fallen bodies of their brethren, and had to wait until the last zombie had exited the truck, fallen as well, and crawled away before they could rise and follow. More than a dozen got caught on the razor wire and were unable to enter the compound, but the rest did just fine. Attracted by the screams and the reports of the gun battle, they had no problem finding prey upon entering the compound.

One signature Trump idea, and one that had been difficult to enact, was that every zombie to enter the compound had on a red MAGA hat. The hats had been placed there a day ago, when

Trump had been preparing for the battle and had talked with others in his circle of the best way to attack.

The box trucks had been taken out to a field, a small corral built, and each truck had been opened and the zombies taken out. Then, each one had been separated from the pack, the hat stapled to their heads, before then being placed back into the box truck. It had been hard work and more than a few men had been bit and thus had forfeited their lives. Trump could have cared less when it had been reported to him. All he cared about was that his idea had been followed to the letter, which it had.

When the last zombie stumbled into the blasted hole, Trump's attack team followed. Many of the zombies went to the west, the sounds of gunfire and yelling attracting them, so the attack team went east, in the hopes of flanking anyone fighting Trump's team, as well as making sure to cause as much destruction as possible. Some carried Molotov cocktails, made with the same brew as the soldiers out front.

The compound was a roughly square area of streets filled with residential homes, then the wall had been built to make a perimeter to keep the living dead out. While the wall at the main gate was of cinderblocks, other parts were sheet metal, wood from a nearby lumber yard, and even some fallen trees from within the neighborhood, taken from what had once lined the sidewalks. The wall was built to keep out zombies, not a determined army.

The idea of being attacked as if they were a country being invaded had never occurred to the ruling council, or Pelosi. After all, in a world where the living dead would feed on a human being, and there was no discerning what color or party affiliation said human was, the council had assumed any living people would want to band together, not fight amongst themselves. The only enemy was the walking dead, a danger that needed to be fought and could only be overcome, if it was even possible, by all the humans on the planet becoming one force and finally putting away past grudges.

Unfortunately for Pelosi and the council, they hadn't planned on Donald J. Trump, to their detriment.

The battle raged on, both sides equally matched.

At the front of the compound, a pickup truck exploded, the gas tank erupting, only thirty feet from Trump. The blast was so hot he felt it on the back of his neck, the leather jacket he wore being excellent protection. More than half of his convoy was in flames, the men using the vehicles as cover dead or dying. Cries for help filled the air as a few men and women who acted as medics tried to help the wounded. Trump peeked up from his cover, behind the rear bumper, to watch a medic dashing from one truck to another. The woman barely made it ten feet before she was gunned down by multiple rounds. She toppled over and hit the ground hard, her body bouncing slightly when it landed. She didn't move again.

Trump realized he knew her personally. She had shared his bed many times over the past month. She was one hell of a fuck. He'd miss her. But not for the reasons someone might think. He'd miss her because she gave the best damn blowjob on the planet.

Behind Trump, another fireball that had once been a human being ran through the trucks, arms spastically waving, the face engulfed in fire. Another soldier shot the man, the bullets stitching the poor bastard from crotch to neck. The body did a dance and collapsed onto the ground, the flesh still burning brightly.

"Thames, are we winning yet?" Trump yelled, and as soon as the question left his mouth, he realized Thames couldn't answer him, being dead and all. Trump felt more annoyed than sad for the man's death.

"Hodgkins, are we winning?" Trump yelled.

"How the fuck should I know?" Hodgkins shouted back over the roar of the gunfire. It was hard to hear anyone talking unless their ear was less than an inch from your ear. Hodgkins realized he'd just cursed at the President of the United States and he quickly added, "Sir!"

Figures appeared at the main gate opening, and began to stumble out of the compound and into the convoy, while at the same moment, residents of the compound began running out as well. Some of the sentries along the wall stopped shooting, and appeared to be dealing with some other attacker as they fought along the wall, the activity clear to anyone watching.

Trump peered up from around his pickup's bumper to see what was happening, and he tried to take it all in at once. It was frighteningly apparent what was happening, and his heart dropped into his stomach at the realization his master plan to take the compound may have just taken a turn for the worse.

The first zombie that shuffled out of the compound was wearing a red MAGA hat, followed by at least a hundred more, along with many former residents of the compound that were now the living dead.

Attracted by the gunfire at the main gate, the zombies that had been unleashed into the compound had made their way through it like a pack of locusts, killing and eating anyone they came across. Those not fully devoured but dead, soon rose to join the undead horde, repeating the process.

At the same moment, from behind the convoy, as if Trump's people were being flanked themselves, more zombies flooded the road once traveled by Trump's convoy, the dead swarming his soldiers. Attracted to all the explosions and gunfire, any zombies in the surrounding area were drawn to the compound like moths to a flame.

Caught between two undead hordes, Trump realized he needed to reevaluate his options and fast. "Uh oh, I think I made a boo-boo," he said under his breath.

Chapter 23

Going back in time just a little bit, at the exact moment the first LAW rocket was used on the tower platform that sent Nancy Pelosi tumbling to the ground for her life, the sound of the explosion didn't just remain in the vicinity of the compound.

How could it? It was scientifically impossible.

The explosion report rippled outward from the compound for more than a quarter mile, catching the attention of every zombie in the area. Rotting heads perked up at the sound, but it was so quick that they didn't know which way to go, but then another tower was destroyed and another, followed by the hole in the back wall of the compound being punched in. And if that wasn't enough of a trail of noise breadcrumbs, gunfire erupted and continued, undulating but never ceasing.

Every zombie left what it was doing, which wasn't much. Zombies had a lot of free time on their hands and none of them had jobs. If they could have voted, they would have voted Democrat, no question.

The most direct path to the compound was the road leading to it, and one at a time they began to fill it, emerging from abandoned homes, from inside sheds or simply wandering around in the nearby forests, which were many in Maryland.

Soon, the undead were more than two hundred strong, all marching forwards together.

One item to note was that if someone were to have taken a good look at the zombie horde, the procession of animated but rotting flesh, they would have seen that the nationalities of the zombies was quite a melting pot.

Blacks, Asians, Whites, Browns, Muslims, Syrian, Italians and Polish, along with a few dozen other ethnic backgrounds, all walked as one party, the sense of unity they had as the walking dead far outweighing any commonalities they once had as living beings.

In death, finally, they were all equal to one another.

One foot in front of the other, many barefoot and only the white of bone slapping the pavement, the horde made its way in the direction of the gunfire, which was to them, a dinner bell.

Upon reaching the convoy, they slowly infiltrated amongst the soldiers, attacking from behind, the chaos of battle a wonderful distraction for their attack.

Because of this, the MAGA zombies had no one to stop them, as they too, filed out of the compound, some stopping to attack the guards on the wall, others continuing to join in on the feeding frenzy happening around the convoy.

If the zombies had been protesters, then this peaceful protest had turned into a violent one, and this time Trump didn't have shadow soldiers with no names or identifying logos on their uniforms, he had no federal officers to swarm down and attack and arrest the zombies. He was completely all alone, and it wasn't a good situation for him to be in.

Off to Trump's right side, a soldier firing an Mk19, was pulled from the rear bed of a pickup truck by four zombies. The man dropped hard onto his back, at first not understanding what was happening, but when he looked upwards at the drooling and desiccated faces hovering over him, he began to scream, forgetting his sidearm and panicking. The zombies reached out and grabbed him from all sides, sharpened fingernails grown longer in death, digging into his camo outfit. Sinking in deep, blood pooled around gray fingers as the man was torn apart. As teeth and fingers worried at the sockets of arms and legs, it was frighteningly scary how fast the zombies managed to dismember the hapless man, each zombie taking a souvenir with them. The man's shrieks of agony finally died when his head was pulled off his shoulders, the skin stretching taut, like an elastic band, until finally snapping. The shrieks grew louder as the voice box and vocal cords were torn, until finally the severed head's wails were silenced. The zombie with the prized head flipped it over so it was like a bucket, and shoved its mottled hand deep into the skull, pulling out a handful of brains and the flapping tongue. Shoving the meaty treasure into its mouth, it shook its head as it chewed, then went in for more. If a zombie had emotion, this one sure looked like it was enjoying itself. A bowl of plenty, this creature would be happy for quite a while.

The soldier's death was nothing compared to some of the others. Though many zombies were gunned down, there were simply too many for the soldiers to fight.

In took less than three minutes for both sides of the battle to stop shooting at one another, the undead horde taking precedence.

On both sides of the aisle, zombies were dismembering and disemboweling their prey. Democrat or Republican, it was all the same to the walking dead. A meal was a meal.

The sound of gunfire had shifted to the wails of dying humans, pleas for help, for mercy, falling on ears that had long become immune to the plights of living beings.

One such entity, though while not undead, sure was immune to the plights of others' suffering, managed to crawl under a pickup truck and hide.

Above him, in the rear of the bed, Trump listened as Hodgkins fought for his life. All around the pickup, shuffling feet were visible, each foot covered in gore and filth.

Trump could only lay there, his breath blowing bits of dust away from his mouth, as he was so close to the ground, as Hodgkins was torn apart overhead. Trump had barely fit under the Ford when he'd crawled beneath it. If he still had his large belly, there would have been no way, and even now he only just fit.

Hodgkins' screams of being devoured continued, the decibel level of shrieking going up in volume. Blood was dripping down both sides of the pickup to splash the ground around Trump. Wet, tearing sounds floated down to him and the president tried not to imagine what was happening to his loyal servant. And worst off all, the major issue was that Trump didn't want it to happen to him next!

A few quick gunshots sounded from above as Hodgkins did his best to survive, but it was hopeless. Finally, after a tense few minutes, Trump heard Hodgkins yell, "I'm sorry I failed you, Mr. President. Long live Donald Trump!" Then there was one last gunshot and the sound overhead of the pistol falling to the metal of the rear bed. Hodgkins, seeing how hopeless his situation was, had eaten a bullet, thus sparing himself the suffering of being devoured by the undead.

Trump lay there, under the truck and a smile came to his lips. He didn't feel loss for Hodgkins, just like there had been no sadness for Thames' passing.

"What a fool," Trump said under his breath. Hodgkins, like so many others, had become a devotee, completely consumed by the cult of Trump. The president never got over how he could get people to do the wildest things, and apparently it included killing themselves and praising his name as they died, as if he was a deity.

That made him think. He'd never really gone as far as to think himself a God, but then again, he'd never tried.

When all this fiasco of a battle was over, he would have to look into that a little more. Maybe it was time to take it to the next level. The Church of Trump. Why keep beating around the bush. Why not just go for it and become the true God he always deserved to become.

But one thing at a time. For now, he needed to live long enough to escape the terrible predicament he now found himself in.

But like the true coward he was, he did what any man with a yellow streak would do. He hid under the truck, not so much as moving a finger in fear of being discovered.

The day passed, with the zombies feeding continuously, but eventually they ran out of prey or had eaten enough to satiate whatever it was that drove them to feed on the living.

Trump lay silent under the pickup truck, immobile as a statue, even when he heard nothing around him. His stomach had begun to growl more than an hour ago and it scared the shit out of him that the noise would attract the dead to his hiding place. He was starving. He hadn't eaten since early morning and he realized the sun was slowly beginning to set in the west.

Even the odor of burning human flesh, feces and other bodily fluids did nothing to halt his craving for food. He'd always had a cast iron stomach anyway, and some charnel house-like aromas were nothing to put off his appetite.

But with no other choice, he lay still and waited.

Another hour passed, and any screams of pain or for help were long over, and as he looked around his pickup, he found there were no feet moving about, shuffling from vehicle to vehicle.

With night falling completely, it was as if a blanket of silence had also been cast.

Trump waited for another ten minutes, just to be safe, and when nothing stirred, he decided it was time to risk coming out of his makeshift bunker. He ignored the blood surrounding the vehicle; for it was in such abundance there would be no way to drag himself out without getting some on him.

First he poked his head out and looked both ways. In the flickering fires still burning, he saw nothing that appeared to be either a zombie or one of his soldiers. Undulating shadows played across surfaces, causing Trump to think he wasn't alone, but as he saw the shadows remained constant, never shifting past their original spot of origin, he grew bolder and crawled out completely.

Standing tall, he attempted to fix his jacket and pants but quickly gave up. He gazed around the convoy for the first time since ducking for cover.

What had been an army of vehicles, with more than a hundred men and women, was now nothing but a heap of burning wreckage and bits and pieces of bodies strewn everywhere. The familiar odor of burning bodies and gasoline filled the air, along with other disagreeable scents, belonging to things Trump preferred not to think about.

He reached into his pocket, finding the comforting grip of the .45 still there. He pulled it from his jacket. Popping the clip as was taught by Morrigan, he checked it to ensure there were bullets there, then popped the clip back into the pistol and put a round in the chamber. He was as prepared as he possibly could be.

Shocked from seeing the carnage, he left his golf club on the ground, forgetting it. Cautiously, he made his way through the vehicles, giving the burning ones a wide berth.

Nothing living was found, and worse, every vehicle was damaged to the point it was inoperable; whether that was tires being blown out or by bullets having peppered the engines, it didn't look like any were in working condition. And Trump knew nothing about fixing cars or any other item in his life with moving parts. How a toilet flushed was beyond him. Not that he wasn't intelligent enough to figure it out. It was just that he'd never had a need to. His entire life, others had done things for him, to the point he was practically a child when it came to taking care of himself.

And while most people would have been ashamed by this, to Trump it was a badge of honor. It had been a point in his entire life where other people waited on him hand and foot. Hell, if he ever had to make a grilled cheese, he would probably end up burning the entire place down.

Hoping perhaps he could find a working vehicle inside the compound, he made his way to the blown open gate and cautiously entered. Looking from side to side, all there was to see were more signs of death. The guards on the walls had been attacked and devoured, the same as his men had.

Numerous corpses wearing red MAGA hats could be seen, the identifying hats spreading out deep into the compound.

"Looks like my plan went a little too well," he said softly. Still, he couldn't help but take pride in the devastation he'd caused.

Movement to the side caught his eye and he turned that way quickly, startled. But it was only one of the surviving horses from the stable. Trump watched silently as the horse approached, admiring its beauty. The majestic animal trotted past him, through the blasted gate, and out into the night and potential freedom. He watched it retreating for a few more seconds, a gentle smile creasing his lips. Unknown to many, Trump loved horses. So many people had demonized him since he'd taken the Office of the Presidency, but in fact, he was just simply a ruthless man, who had decided early in his life, thanks to the mentorship of his father, that to succeed in life, you did whatever it took to win.

There had been many others throughout history who did the same, whether it was leaders of industry or Caesars harking back to the Romans. What others didn't want to admit, was that he was nothing new. There had been countless more before him, and there would be many, many more after he was gone.

A gargling from his right made him jump and swing the .45 around. But before he squeezed the trigger, he stopped, seeing the danger wasn't immediate. There was a zombie, its lower half blown clean off, along with one of its arms. With only one arm and a hand attached to the limb, it tried to drag itself towards Trump, but it was having zero luck.

"Pathetic," Trump said to the creature. "What a loser."

He walked deeper into the compound, seeing more MAGA hat wearing corpses, but these were bodies wearing camo. His own soldiers. So many had been killed. Trump had to nod in respect to the residents of the compound. Apparently, he had underestimated the Democrats living here. They weren't as much of a bunch of pussies as Trump thought. Both sides had fought hard and it ended as a stalemate, with both sides losing everyone and everything.

Well, not everyone.

Trump had survived, and though it was certainly a massive setback, he could rebuild. There were so many others out there that would flock to his way of anger, of hatred, or hating your fellow man because he was different, or came from somewhere other than being born in America. It didn't matter that Trump's own family, including his last wife, were all immigrants. Trump's family had emigrated from Germany, so he was as much a by-product of immigration as any Latin child born here after their parents had emigrated from another country.

Yet Trump had learned early when running for office the first time, there were so many people who were unsatisfied with their lives. Though many were at a status in their lives that was beyond their control, many others simply didn't have the intelligence or the will to overcome and thrive. Those were the perfect targets for Trump's hate speeches. Instead of accepting responsibility for their own actions, and if they wanted to rise out of their hardships, to work harder than others, it was simply easier to blame others for their lot in life.

Those people simply needed something to hate, something to fight against. If only they would spend all that energy bettering themselves instead of attacking others. But Trump gambled those people would prefer to simply blame others and be done with it. Taking the easier route was simpler.

So yes, though he did lose his army this day, foiled by a bunch of Democrats of all things, he would overcome. Unlike the masses that followed him blindly, he always had an escape plan. When one door closed, he was already walking through the next one that he'd skillfully opened.

Just like outside the compound, there was no one left alive within it. Bodies were everywhere, pools of blood already attracting flies.

In the waning fires still burning within the compound, Trump continued walking, for the moment, not knowing what else to do.

Eventually, he made his way to a low incline deep in the center of the compound. Nearby fires gave off more than enough light to see. There was a lone figure standing on the small hill and Trump raised his .45, figuring it was a zombie.

He stopped walking and just stood still, waiting for the figure to come closer. He could shoot it or run, whatever seemed most prudent when the time came.

"I can tell it's you, Donald," a woman's voice said from atop the hill.

Trump recognized the voice immediately. "Nancy, so you survived." Feeling safe now, he walked up the incline, stopping when he was no more than twenty feet from Pelosi.

Standing with her legs slightly apart to prevent her from falling over, Pelosi said nothing when Trump joined her on the hill. Her right hand was slightly behind her back, out of sight, her left hand and arm by her side. In the flickering firelight of the burning compound, her left arm gleamed dully.

Trump gestured with the .45. "Looks like you got bit, Nancy. I guess I win after all. Last one standing and all that. Couldn't have happened to a nicer woman." He was smirking, his orange and dirt-covered face filled with mirth. "I should wait till you turn and then put a bullet in your head."

"Oh, don't get too excited, Donald. I cut myself, that's all. It's not a bite. I'm not going anywhere, so don't get your hopes up." She stood taller, sucking in air and getting ready to pontificate. She was good at giving speeches. Not that she truly believed in them, of course. She was no pious figure, not by a long shot. The Democrats had been pushing equality for what seemed like forever, but in the end, they always made sure their pockets were lined. When Americans needed help after losing their jobs from shutdowns due to Covid, just before the dead began to walk, when the country had needed to prevent the spread of the virus, instead of passing a stimulus bill, Pelosi and her gang had hemmed and hawed but had refused to agree to anything the GOP offered, because in doing so, they would not have received everything they wanted. The main definition of compromise is both sides not getting everything they wanted. Each side gets a little but gives up a little and in the end, it's still better for everyone. Not this time. But those same Democrats who refused to compromise, and not settling for a smaller piece of the pie, what happened to them? Nothing. They had steady paychecks, along with excellent health insurance. And why they talked shit, Americans lost their homes, rental apartments, businesses and health insurance.

You can't be a party that preaches it's for the people then do nothing to help those people when they're in dire need through no fault of their own.

Republicans are not angels, but Democrats sure as hell are not saints either. It seems the representatives people voted for to look out for their best interests, have forgotten that's why they were put there in the first place. And as for the Americans who voted said representatives into office? Well, they're too busy trying to survive for another day to pay attention to how much they're all getting screwed.

When you're falling from an airplane, a thousand feet aboveground without a parachute, you don't worry about whether you paid the electric bill that month. At the moment, you have bigger problems to deal with, namely hitting the ground and exploding like a bag of minestrone soup.

Republicans or Democrats. If there's one thing to point out is that both sides kind of suck, but it's all there is, so all people can do is make sure there's accountability on both sides' actions.

"You haven't won here, Donald, you know that, right?" Pelosi stated as she took a few steps closer to him, halving the distance between them. "All your people are dead. You have no more army. All you did here was manage to get more people killed—on both sides. All this was for nothing; your constant striving for power, the way you callously flaunt other people's lives." She glared at him. "You know, we lost almost a million American citizens to Covid-19 by the time the dead took over. At last count, before the dead started running around like a bad horror movie, nine hundred and ninety-eight thousand had died on your watch as President! Do you understand the true meaning of that? All the pain and suffering people had to deal with daily, and all of it on your watch!"

Trump raised his left hand and opened and closed his fingers, gesturing that she was yakking away. He began to laugh and she was confused, not understanding. He saw the puzzled look on her face and stopped, spreading his hands wide, as if to encompass all the death surrounding them, the .45 he held seemingly forgotten.

"You still don't really understand me, Nancy. You never did. I don't care about the people who died from the China virus, or the ones here. They were just a means to an end. All people are like that to me. Just tools for me to use. I raised an army once and I can do it again. There's plenty more of my adoring fans out there. All I have to do is find them…or they find me. As for all the dead from Covid, I could care less. Over half a million? If it was two million I wouldn't care. Or three million. Those people were nothing but pawns for me to use as I saw fit to gain a second term in office. Nothing but a bunch of sheep. That's why they follow me, you know, always have and always will."

"You're despicable." Her voice dripped with venom.

He smirked. "Right back atcha, lady." He sighed. "I'm bored. It's time for you to join your people…in death." He chuckled. "I'm going to enjoy this."

The Republican and the Democrat stood alone on the hill, Trump's gun raised and poised to fire.

Apparently, even the end of the world wasn't enough to get the two sides working together.

But though Donald J. Trump hadn't changed since the apocalypse, Nancy Pelosi had. Since the world collapsed in on itself, she had learned to be a fighter, to do what had to be done and damn the rules.

Trump wasn't prepared when she turned slightly and her right hand, still hidden from view, snapped up holding a .38 revolver, her index finger already inside the trigger guard and squeezing the trigger.

Before Trump could shoot, she fired, but Trump, no slouch either, who had learned well from his training with Morrigan, was only a fraction of a millisecond behind her.

Standing only ten feet apart, both guns went off almost simultaneously.

Chapter 24

Donald J. Trump, the 45th President of the United States, opened his eyes.

Disoriented, he didn't know where he was, but then slowly, he shifted his gaze to the foot of the large, king-sized bed he was lying in.

He recognized the bed and his surroundings immediately.

He was in his own bed, in the White House.

He wasn't alone either. Surrounding his bed were a multitude of people, all with faces he recognized.

There was Vice President Mike Pence.

Secretary of Health Alex Azar and Trump's son-in-law Jared Kushner.

His Presidential aides, Hope Hicks and Steven Miller, were there.

And Mark Meadows, his Chief of Staff.

In the corner, separated slightly from the others, Peter Navarro stood talking softly with Rudy Giuliani.

"What the...?" Trump said, and as he came more awake, his hands went to his body, touching different parts.

First, he went to his hair, and was relieved to feel his long blonde locks there once more. Next he touched his abdomen, and had to admit he was disappointed when he felt his large belly and rolls of hip fat back where they'd been before waking.

None of this made sense. How could he be back in his bed in the White House? Washington was destroyed, zombies ruled the world. He was dueling with Nancy Pelosi. They'd both fired at the same time. Her aim was good. Her bullet was going to kill him.

But it didn't. But if that was true, how did he get here? And how were all the people he knew still alive?

When he raised his left hand he saw there was an IV hooked up to his arm. But then a pair of hands gently pressed his arm back onto the bed. He allowed it, not understanding. A man in a white coat, a doctor by his appearance, wearing a surgical mask, held Trump's wrist and checked his pulse, then said, "Pulse is strong. Looks like he's out of the woods." The man looked at Trump, who couldn't read the man's expression with just his eyes showing. "Just take it easy, Mr. President. You've been through a traumatic event, but it looks like you're going to pull through."

"Pull through from what?" Trump asked. "I don't understand any of this. A moment ago I was in Maryland, fighting with Nancy Pelosi. I had an army but I lost it, they were all killed. It was down to me and her and we were about to finish it, but then I woke up here." He shook his head angrily. "None of this makes sense. Mike! Mike Pence, get over here, now!"

Like a puppy bounding over to its owner, Pence shoved the others out of the way and moved up to Trump's right shoulder. Trump raised his right hand and touched Pence's arm. "Good old Mike. You'll tell me what's going on here."

Pence swallowed the knot in his throat and looked at first to the doctor, then the others in the room.

"It might be a shock to his system if you tell him straight out," the doctor suggested.

Giuliani walked over, pushing his way through, shoving Pence aside. "Bullshit. Donald can handle anything. He's as tough as they come." He turned and glared at Trump with eyes that looked like they would jump out of their sockets and roll away. "Donald, Mr. President, I have some bad news to tell you."

"Go on, Rudy, give it to me straight. I can take it."

"Well, Sir, it seems you were struck down with the China virus and it put you out of commission for a while. You were in the ICU for almost a week but then your vitals were better and they transferred you back here, where Doctor Simpson's been monitoring you day and night. He's your personal physician."

Trump turned his head to look at the doctor, who only nodded in acknowledgement. "But I'm okay now?"

Dr. Simpson spoke up. "It appears so, Mr. President. It looks like you'll make a full recovery. We were lucky we were able to get you that experimental antibody cocktail to beat Covid before the supply chain collapsed."

Trump was still fuzzy about everything, and he said so. "But I woke up from a coma in the hospital. There were zombies and everything was in chaos. Death was everywhere. It was all exactly what I said would happen at my rallies if Sleepy Joe Biden got elected in 2020."

"You must have had a fever dream, Mr. President. They can seem quite real when they're occurring," Dr. Simpson said.

"So you mean, I dreamed up the world being overrun by zombies?"

Mike Pence spoke up, "Ah, no, Sir, I'm afraid not. You may have dreamed about that but I'm afraid that part is terribly real."

Trump's eyebrows went up in curiosity, not fully understanding what Pence just said.

"Zombies are real, Sir, and they're taking over the world," Pence explained. "Covid-19, Sir, the novel coronavirus. It mutated, began turning people into zombies. It's been going on for weeks. The world is in chaos. Washington is in flames. In fact, Sir, it's time we all went down to the bunker; our families are already waiting for us. Secret Service said the White House is about to be breached, we need to go now."

"Help me up, goddammit," Trump insisted. "I want to go to the window."

No one argued with him, knowing better. With the help of Dr. Simpson and Pence, Trump rose on unsteady feet and hobbled over to the window, the two men the only reason he wasn't on his ass on the floor. The IV stand was moved along with him.

He was wearing a hospital gown, and his ass was hanging out yet again. A deep feeling of deja vu overcame him and he pushed the feeling away.

At the window, the curtains were drawn. Rudy jogged over and opened them. Trump stood tall before the window, on the second floor of the White House, looking down on the front grounds, and Washington beyond.

His jaw slid open to hang there, as he stared out at the chaos below and beyond.

In the darkness, a million fires burned brightly, banishing the night.

Shadowy figures were stumbling around, thousands of them. Soldiers and Secret Servicemen were seen shooting at the figures, more often than not becoming overwhelmed and taken down. One after another, Trump watched the perimeter of the White House being destroyed, the defenders attacked and eaten. In the backlight of a burning Hummer, a zombie tore off the arm of a soldier and held the trophy up in the air, the silhouette chilling to behold. Then the arm came down to the creature's mouth, where it began to feed.

A Blackhawk helicopter went down just outside the White House grounds. Trump thought he caught a struggle inside the cockpit and the strobing effect of gunshots going off within the aircraft. Then it struck the ground and became a roiling fireball.

Beyond the White House, in the plaza that had gone through too many name changes to list, buildings were burning.

St. Johns Church was a giant candle, the entire structure consumed with flames. Gunshots could be heard from all directions and what sounded like bombs going off, as well.

The world outside the White House window was absolute carnage. It was Hell on Earth come to pass.

"It's just like in my dream," Trump said under his breath, but Pence and the doctor heard him. "I've already lived through this."

Pence seemed to sigh in relief, for his loyalty to Trump was absolute. Pence made the hardest core sycophant seem like a barely interested observer next to him. He would die for Trump if given the opportunity. "That's wonderful, Sir. If you've experienced what's happening already, even if it was just in a dream, and you've already lived through a version of it all, you can lead us to the other side. You must have learned so much, made hard choices to survive."

Trump felt his strength returning, and he brushed off the doctor and Pence, both men moving a foot away from him, wanting to stay close in case Trump might fall.

Squaring his shoulders and jutting out his chin, as if he was in a photo-op, he appeared to be standing even taller before the window, only his bare ass hanging out detracting from the Presidential posture.

He shifted his gaze from what was going on outside to his reflection in the window pane, his face glaring back at him. "You'd think so, Mike, but you'd be wrong. I'm Donald J. Trump. I haven't learned a goddamn thing."

-FIN-

EVICTION NOTICE!

Disclaimer:
This short story pokes fun at Trump, so if you're a die hard supporter, skip this story. But if you have a sense of humor, no matter what you're political preference, Enjoy.

It was a crisp, clear morning on January 20th, 2021. At seven a.m., Donald J. Trump went golfing, like he'd done, and what seemed like, almost every day since being elected President.

It was his only hobby, you know.

He didn't read, he didn't build airplane models, and at his age if he masturbated, all that came out was a puff of smoke. He wasn't into gardening or going for long walks. The latter was because if he went for a walk, he'd need someone to go with him, and there was no one who wanted to spend time with him. Well, there was Melania, but he didn't want to go for a walk with her; he was afraid, much like a spirited dog, if he ever let her off the leash, she would bolt into the woods and be gone forever. So much like that same dog, he needed to keep her either on a leash or within a fence at all times.

Unknown to Trump, however, today was a little different when he returned to the White House that afternoon.

Today was eviction day for Number 45, whether he liked it or not. He'd been ignoring today, pretending it wasn't going to happen, that he was going to remain President for another term, and if he had his way, for life. Hey, Putin managed to do it, why couldn't he?

As he exited the black suburban that had taken him golfing, his clubs carried by an aide behind him, he found the doors were locked to the White House.

"What's this?" Turning to his aide, Trump said, "Some idiot locked the doors, I can't get in."

The aide said nothing, only looked down at his shoes.

"What's wrong with you, son, speak up. Do you know anything about this?" When the aide didn't reply, Trump walked around the White House, weaving through the Rose Garden until reaching another set of doors. He turned the knob but the door remained locked as well.

"What the hell…" Trump said, not understanding. He took out his cell phone. "I'll get to the bottom of this. I'll call Jared. He may have the personality of an overcooked potato but he'll help me." Dialing the number, using speed dial, Trump waited, but all the call did was ring. Finally, it picked up. "Oh, Good, Jared, I need your help…" But Trump stopped when he realized it was voicemail.

"Sorry to miss your call, but I'm not here right now. My wife has her shoe pressed onto my neck like always, and I'm capitulating to her every whim, which is why she married me, as I'm easy to control. *Beep*."

Trump lowered the cell phone from his ear and looked at it, as if it was a living thing. "That's a weird message. Sad."

The aide hadn't followed Trump; he was alone outside the White House. Not even a Marine guarded the door. The grounds seemed devoid of humanity—which was a lot like his heart. Where most people's hearts were filled with love, the only thing in Trump's heart was cholesterol.

If his heart could actually speak, it would have yelled out, "Is it time yet? Do I fail now?"

Which the reply would be, "No not yet, but don't worry, anytime now you can stop working."

"That's good. It's taking a lot out of me to keep this fat ass breathing, you know. It's like pushing a ten ton truck up a hill with a five ton car. It might work for a little while, but sooner or later you need to accept it just ain't gonna happen."

"Huh, that's what Melania says whenever they have sex," came the reply, to a quick drum beat.

But let's not digress.

Back to the tall Oompa-Loompa and his predicament.

Trump banged on the door for a full minute, and when no one came, he walked around the grounds some more, deciding he would go to the front of the White House, the grand doors visible from Pennsylvania Avenue.

But as he approached the set of double doors, he began to slow. It wasn't because he was tired, but yes, that was probably a factor. So far today, he'd walked more than he had in months.

With his blonde toupee blowing in the wind (what, you didn't know he was bald on top? You really believed a seventy-six year old man had the flowing locks of hair of a twenty year old?)

Sorry, got off track again, but as you know, when it comes to Trump, there's a lot to unpack there.

Trump paused at the doors, seeing a bunch of black suitcases piled outside them; some had fallen over. They looked familiar.

Walking closer, he saw the gold monograms on them. **DJT**. It was his luggage. There was a piece of paper tacked on the left door. It fluttered in the wind, catching his attention.

Forgetting about the luggage for a minute, he walked over to the letter and began to read; the words were simply printed in bold black letters on an 8x11 piece of white copy paper.

Well, it wasn't a letter, really, but a notice. The letterhead was from the *Office of the White House.*

The first words on the notice, in large bold characters even bigger than the rest, were the words: **EVICTION NOTICE!**

Trump began to read, "Must vacate White House, yadda, yadda, no longer President of the United States, yadda, yadda, fair election, yadda, the will of the American people," and on and on until he grew bored and tore the notice off the door and threw it away from him.

The crumpled paper went rolling onto the grounds, where a gardener darted out from hiding behind a bush, ran at the paper like a kid snatching a ball at a tennis match, and darted back into hiding.

Trump nodded. "Man, those guys are good." He banged on the doors, calling, "Mike, Mike Pence! Let me in! They can't do this to me. I'm the President of the United States. I'm Donald J. Trump. I don't want to leave, I like being President. People like me now. Mike!" But there was no answer.

Frowning, and looking around, expecting to see a horde of secret Servicemen running at him, he turned and went back to his luggage.

There was an envelope clipped to one of the larger suitcases.

To Donald was written in familiar script.

He ripped it open, letting the envelope fly away from his hand. This time he didn't acknowledge the gardener's mad dash to collect the litter. Trump was too busy reading, or at least sounding out the words like an immigrant child learning English for the first time.

The letter was short and sweet.

Donald,
It's over, you lost, so our agreement is finished.
I'm leaving you. You can have the kids, I never wanted them to begin with.
BE BEST
Melania
PS: I expect my fat check every month as agreed, which was the only reason I continued this charade for four long years.

"Shit!" Trump yelled. "No, it's not over, it'll never be over! It was all rigged! I'm still the President!"

Spinning around quickly, he took a moment to breathe, as that spin was much too fast for his out-of-shape body, then he stomped away, back onto the grounds. He went to a window and tried to open it, but it was locked.

"This isn't gonna end like this, I'm not leaving," he muttered.

Continuing around the White House, he tried another window, but that too, was locked. But then he slowed and ducked into a pair of bushes at the rear of the White House, the area where the movers would enter and exit with large furniture.

"Oooh, you no good..." Trump began but stopped, watching the tableaux before him.

Joe Biden, the 46th President of the United States and his wife, Jill, were standing to the side of a moving truck, directing the movers as they exited the truck and entered the White House. Of course, both were wearing masks to protect themselves and others from Covid-19, as were all the movers.

An idea came to Trump. He discarded his red MAGA hat, tossing it behind a bush, then sneakily crept over to the moving truck. When everyone was distracted, he tiptoed up the ramp allowing egress into the truck. Picking up a box the size of a microwave, he hefted it with difficulty and began walking to the open doors leading into the White House. There was a discarded mask sitting on a box at the edge of the truck, so he grabbed it and put it on, hiding his face from discovery. After everything that had happened, and over 305,000 dead from Covid at the time of this story, from a virus he'd simply ignored outright, and literally shunned masks in public, now was when he finally put on a mask.

Joe Biden saw Trump from the back and didn't recognize him, and said, "You there, my friend, put that in the kitchen in the residences." Then he turned to Jill and said, "You know, we're going to have to fumigate the entire place, right? I sure as hell don't want to be thinking about smelling that fat guy's old farts for the next four years. I mean, come on, man."

"Don't worry, Joe, the cleaners are doing everything but gutting the walls, which I have to be honest, I considered."

"Good, that's good. The inside of the White House must be like a Covid factory, the way that guy carried on."

Trump grimaced at hearing Biden's comments but kept walking. Once inside, he dropped the box without a care, smiling when he heard something made of glass break. He scooted off deeper into the White House.

But the place was much different than when he'd left to go golfing early that morning. There were people everywhere, cleaners and movers, each group engrossed in individual tasks. It would only be moments before someone stopped focusing on their task, looked up, and recognized him, even with the mask on. He needed to act fast, but not knowing where to go, he darted to the right, into the hallways that led to the residences. All the rooms were empty of his furniture brought from Mar-a-Lago, and only new boxes could be seen. The carpeting was being torn up as well, replaced with new fibers.

The room was empty when he entered it, but the only way in or out was at his back. Suddenly, he heard the voice of Joe and Jill Biden coming from behind him.

"I want you to see the color of the carpeting, Joe," Jill explained. "And how it goes well with the color for the walls I picked out. I'm adding a new wall closet as well."

"But, Jill, honey, I don't care about any of that stuff. I told you. I need to focus on saving the country after Trump practically destroyed it. The virus being my first priority."

There was an opening in the wall to his right, where the closet was being built. With nowhere else to go, he went to it and shimmied into the wall like a rat entering a house. The White House walls were wide enough to allow even his large and pear-shaped frame to fit; he went deeper into the substructure. He got stuck once or twice but sucked in his belly and got free.

"Try and get rid of me, will you," Trump whispered. Dust fell all around him and cobwebs were everywhere. "This is my house, dammit, and I'll be damned if I'll leave anytime soon."

Shuffling deeper into the walls, he began to explore his new environment.

Trump spent the next week crawling through the walls. For food, at night, he would sneak into the small kitchen in the residences, raiding the refrigerator for whatever he could find.

It was late one night, as he was shimmying across the ceiling, careful to only put his weight on the support beams, when he heard a television on, Fox News playing loudly.

"So far, more than a week has passed with no one having seen the former president. Rumor is he left the country in shame, after failing to concede the election. Viewers will remember at one of his rallies, the then-President Trump had warned of doing such a thing."

Trump scowled as he listened. "I didn't concede because I didn't lose. The entire election was fraudulent. Well, that is, only the states I lost in were fraudulent. Any state I won was okay with me. They all did a great job there. Only votes for Biden were fake." He shook his head. "Sad how fake it all was."

Joe and Jill Biden were in bed that night, as it was they who were watching Fox News. It wasn't that they were fans, but they tried to watch all the news channels, at least in snippets, to get a better idea of what the average American citizen was being exposed to.

EVICTION NOTICE!

"Oh, Joe, what do you think happened to him?"

"I don't really care, Jill. Truth be told, if we're ever going to heal this country and bring us all back together, it'll be without him. Think about it, one full week without one tweet from him. It's a miracle."

They heard a scratching sound from overhead and they both looked up, silent. Waiting, they heard it again.

Biden shook his head. "Must be rats or some other rodents. I'll tell my Chief of Staff to get an exterminator in here tomorrow ASAP. If the only thing Trump left behind were a few rats, I'll consider myself the luckiest man alive."

Jill shivered as she stared up at the ceiling. "I don't know if I can sleep thinking there are pests crawling around in the walls and ceiling, Joe."

He wrapped an arm around her. "It'll be fine, dear. By tomorrow the issue will be dealt with. I promise."

The exterminator arrived the next morning, after a call from the newly elected President's Chief of Staff, Ron Klain. The exterminator wore a white jumpsuit with the sign BUGS BEE GONE on the back of the jumpsuit, a mask with the company logo on his face. He was of Latin descent and had grown up in Virginia, before moving to Maryland where he started a family and his business.

At the moment, he was in a side room off the Lincoln room, a flashlight in his hands as he studied a few cracks in the ceiling. Following the cracks, they led him to a small closet. Upon opening the closet, he saw there was a man sized hole chewed through the plaster.

Behind the exterminator, a cloth-masked Ron Klain waited patiently after being called to join the man a while ago, after the exterminator had done a thorough investigation of the White House.

"Well, what is it?" Ron Klain asked.

The exterminator shook his head. "You got the worst thing a White House could have. You got a former president in your walls."

"A what?"

"You heard me. You got a Trump inside your walls." He went to the edge of the hole and touched something, removing his hand and showing his finger to the Chief of Staff. On the tips of the man's fingers, were the remnants of orange spray tan. "Everyone's wondered where he got off to. Looks like he never left the White House on January 20th. If you remember, people wondered if he would vacate the premises. Guess he decided not to."

"This is ridiculous," Ron Klain said. "You mean to tell me for over a week now, a grown man's been hiding inside the walls of the White House? What does he eat?"

"Follow me," the exterminator said and left the room, leading the Chief of Staff to the small kitchen that was for the sole use of the President and First Lady. Opening the pantry, he showed another hole hidden behind a shelf of dried goods. On the floor, was the residue of pieces of fried chicken, a few bones scattered near the edge of the hole. Ron Klain recalled fried chicken having been made a day ago and the leftovers had been put into the refrigerator for President Biden and his wife.

"He must come out at night and feed, then goes back inside when everyone wakes up," the exterminator explained.

"So how do we catch him? He could be anywhere within this huge building. This is an embarrassment to the presidency and the country. If word gets out that Trump is hiding inside the White House, we'll be the laughing stock of the entire world."

The exterminator nodded, understanding completely. He rubbed his chin with a hand in thought. "Well, the way I see it, you need to treat him like he was a rat or a mouse. If you think about it, he's about as smart as one, too." He gestured to the hole, then behind them to the actual kitchen where the small four-seater table was. "I think you need to coax him out. With a rat I'd use cheese or peanut butter. They love that stuff. So to get out Donald Trump, you need to use the kind of food he loves, then when he comes out, have some kind of trap set to capture him."

"That all sounds fine. You'll do it, right?" Ron Klain asked hopefully.

The exterminator shook his head. "No, sorry, above my pay grade. I catch rodents and bugs, not former presidents." He considered the situation for a moment and said, "You know, I was watching an interview with President Obama a few weeks ago on MSNBC. Lester Holt asked a hypothetical question. About what would happen if Trump refused to leave the White House on the twentieth. Obama laughingly suggested we could send in Seal Team Six to get him out. That's not a bad idea. Why don't you call 'em and have them come by. Surely they can figure out a way to capture Trump humanely."

The Chief of Staff weighed the idea and finally nodded. "You know what? That's not a bad idea. I'll run it by President Biden and then we'll see what we can do tonight." He paused before adding, "But do we really have to make it a *humane* capture?"

Later that night, just before nightfall, Ron Klain stood at the edge of the kitchen, by the entry, with the leader of Seal Team Six. The man's camo mask matched his outfit. The unit had been on a mission in Iraq, but once they were briefed on this new mission, they were flown directly back to the States via a supersonic jet.

Everyone agreed, getting President Trump out of the walls of the White House was a top priority.

When the new First Lady, Jill Biden had found out she was infested with Donald Trump, she demanded President Biden take her to a hotel until the infestation was dealt with.

"Nothing's worse than moving into a new place and the last tenants won't leave," she'd explained, Joe understanding completely.

The cleaning and administration staff had also been given the night off, in case Trump was difficult to remove. Trump was unpredictable if nothing else.

"Okay, Sir," the commander said to Ron Klain, "let me run down how this is going to go."

The Chief of Staff nodded his attention.

"So, on the table we have Trump's favorite foods. We have three cheeseburgers, extra cheese, a basket of French Fries cooked in lard and chicken nuggets, extra beaks, also cooked in the same. And a two liter of Diet Coke. Once he comes out to feed, we capture him and out he goes, coming with us. Problem solved."

"And you're sure it'll work?" Ron Klain asked.

The commander nodded. "My men are ready for anything. It'll work." He smiled. "If we can take down Bin Laden, we can get Donald Trump."

"Okay, everyone into position," the commander said into his radio as he ushered out the Chief of Staff. "We can watch in another room. The entire place is wired for sound and video, so we can watch it all go down in real time."

The kitchen lights were turned off and everyone stomped away, and soon, all was silent within the residences.

In the Blue Room, a table was filled with video equipment, monitors, and even heat sensitive imaging equipment, the relays in the kitchen, mounted to the walls and ceiling. The Chief of Staff thought that might have been overkill, but then again, they were going after Donald Trump, either the cleverest, or stupidest, man alive.

"Get comfortable," the commander said, "after all the noise we made and the bustle of activity, he's sure to be spooked. It'll probably be a while until he feels it's safe enough to venture out."

The Chief of Staff only nodded, but he did grab a chair and take it. The hours passed silently, the commander and Ron Klain becoming bored. The commander was reading a magazine, the Chief of Staff dozing off, the other men—all wearing masks similar to their commander's—in the unit sitting quietly and either nodding off or playing games on their cell phones. It was late into the night when there came the soft sound of scratching on the speakers on the table.

Instantly, the commander dropped the magazine and sat bolt upright. "I think we got something, Sir."

Ron Klain came fully awake instantly, his heart pumping in his chest quickly as a surge of adrenaline filled his system. This was it, here it comes, he thought.

On infrared, they saw something edging out of the pantry. Hunched over, it slowly exited and crawled into the kitchen.

"There he is," the commander said. "Your exterminator was right. You got Donald Trump in your walls, all right."

Donald Trump, hunched over slightly, walked out of the pantry and into the kitchen, his orange nose twitching as he smelled the fast food on the table. He was filthy, and even in the darkness of the kitchen his dishevelment was apparent.

He went right to the table. With his tiny, baby hands he reached out for a cheeseburger and began feeding.

"He's there, get him, get him already," the Chief of Staff said quickly, scared Trump would escape.

"Now hold on, Sir, let's make absolutely sure we got him. We only get one shot at this. We miss it, and he'll burrow so far into the White House we'll never get him out."

Pulling out a chair and sitting down, Trump grabbed a handful of nuggets in his small palm and shoved them into his mouth. He was fully adsorbed in the food, not paying attention to anything. Once, he did stop eating and perked up, his nose twitching as he listened, his head snapping back and forth, side to side, alert for danger, but then he went right back to feeding.

"Hungry little guy," the commander said as he watched Trump eating. "Okay, it's time." He picked up a small box the size of a remote control for a television and flipped open a plastic cover, beneath which was a red button. The device could be used to set off a hundred pounds of C-4, but today it was wired into a much more important apparatus.

"Come on, do it, damn it, he'll finish and get away," Ron Klain demanded.

The commander ignored the Chief of Staff. He knew his job; whether he was capturing terrorists or Donald Trump, it was all the same to him. "Wait for it," he mumbled, then said, "Wait for it," again. He watched Trump reach for the Diet Coke, and as the former president did so, he pressed the button.

The floor, which had been covered with a large carpet, so as to hide the net beneath, seemed to wrap around the table, encircling Trump as it came up to hang from the ceiling.

"Go! Go! Go!" the commander yelled into his two-way radio. Immediately, spotlights snapped on inside the kitchen and three more men came out of hiding, where they'd been secreted earlier. The Chief of Staff was amazed, he had no idea the Seals had been there.

Trump was screaming like a baby, bits of foodstuff flying from his mouth as he tried to escape his prison.

The commander's two-way radio squawked, and the matching image of one of the Seals talking into his own radio could be seen. "We got him, repeat, we got him! Fat man is down, repeat, Fat man is down!"

"Oh, thank God, it's over," Ron Klain said.

"Come, on, let's go see him." The commander stood up, grabbed his rifle, and led the Chief of Staff back to the kitchen.

Trump was being pulled from the net and put into a large cage on wheels.

"You can't do this to me!" Trump yelled. "This is my house! My house! I live here, I'm still the president! I order you to let me go and arrest Joe Biden. He's the criminal, not me. I'm the Law and Order guy! Better yet, go get Obama. He spied on my campaign, he's the bad guy, not me. You can't do this!"

A female medic moved up to the cage, a hypodermic connected to a six foot pole. Trump was too agitated to transport like this, so she gave him a tranquilizer to calm him down. Slowly, Trump deflated, calming down until he slumped to the floor of the crate and was mostly silent. Still, he mumbled continuously, slurring the words. "I gave myself a pardon, Russian probe, Fake news, Mueller report, rigged election," and on and on. His toupee was askew from a week inside the walls, and his pale, balding pate was visible.

Ron Klain shook his head as he looked down on the sorry sight that was Donald J. Trump. "If his supporters could see him now, I wonder what they'd think."

The commander snickered. "They'd think nothing at all about this. They're a cult, you know. It doesn't matter what he does, they love him. He's infallible in their eyes."

"And that's the most regretful thing about his entire presidency, I think," the Chief of Staff said sadly. He looked at the commander. "What will you do to him? You won't like, you know, ki…"

The commander stopped him instantly. "Whoa there, slow down. Don't even think of it. We caught him humanely and it'll stay that way. He might have been the worst President we ever had, but he was still a U.S. President. No, we'll do a catch and release."

"What's that exactly?" the Chief of Staff asked.

Trump was being wheeled out of the kitchen to a waiting Black Ops truck outside. "Well, we don't want him finding his way back here, and Trumps have a reputation for coming back when they're not wanted, so we need to take him far enough away that he can't find his way back."

Ron Klain didn't seem to fully understand.

"You see," the commander explained, "if you take a squirrel or even a mouse and you drive a few miles from your home and set it free in the woods, many times it'll find its way back to your house. They have an uncanny talent for doing this. It's quite amazing actually. I suspect all Trumps have the same ability, which is why we haven't been able to get rid of them completely for over four years." He patted Ron Klain on the shoulder. "Don't worry, Sir, we'll take him to a place that no one wants to either go to or call."

The Chief of Staff's eyebrows went up in curiosity.

"Better I don't tell you. Need to know and all that."

The activity in the kitchen wrapped up and the cleaning staff was brought in to begin the clean up. Everyone who came in to help was sworn to secrecy and had to sign NDA agreements. It could never be released to the general public that the White House had been infested with Donald Trump, well, at least for longer than the first four years he'd been elected to. The new administration would never live it down!

EVICTION NOTICE!

Joseph Biden, the 46th President of the United States, with his wife, returned in the morning, and finally, a sense of normalcy fell over the White House and the country at large. Soon, Covid-19 would be a thing of the past, thanks to the rollout of vaccines, and it would all be just one more terrible crisis the country and the world had survived, just like the presidency of Donald J. Trump.

As for Trump, he was taken to a place no one would ever find him again, a place no one ever called to invite the occupants to a party, or to be on TV, for the owner was so disliked in the Senate, he was a pariah in his own rights, even if he didn't know it or want to accept it. The perfect place to put Donald J. Trump for the foreseeable future.

Two days later, sitting on the couch, in a house in the state of Texas, Donald Trump looked up when Senator Ted Cruz walked into the room, carrying a plate of cookies and coffee. "I can't tell you how great it is to have company, Donald," Cruz said as he placed the tray on a small coffee table and sat down. "You can stay as long as you need to." Pouring a cup, he smiled at Trump, who only glared back at him.

"Now, Donald, it's not so bad here. Look on the bright side, at least they didn't send you to live with Mitch McConnell. One thing that's great is no one ever calls me. I guess they lost the number or something. But that just means I get more time to write my memoir. And wait till you try Tex-Mex, you're gonna love it. You'll see, it'll be fine." He held up the plate of cookies to Trump. "Cookie, Mr. Former-President?"

Trump crossed his arms like a petulant child while pouting deeply, and said, "This sucks."

NOW AVAILABLE WHEREVER BOOKS ARE SOLD!

FIRST THERE WAS NIGHT, THEN CAME DAWN, AND FINALLY, THERE WAS DAY, BUT WHEN DAY ENDS, SUNSET MUST FALL.

SUNSET OF THE DEAD
THE SEQUEL TO DAY OF THE DEAD

It has been years since the dead began to walk and civilization is now nothing but a memory. Cities are nothing but ruins, filled with the living dead, and where once small enclaves survived, now they are all gone.

One of the last holdouts, a group of soldiers and scientists hidden in an underground bunker in Florida, are also gone after being overrun by the undead.

But there were three survivors: Sarah, John and Bill McDermott.

Escaping in a helicopter, the group found refuge on an island off the coast of Florida, where they hope to begin life anew, away from the death and destruction that was once mankind.

But the island is far from uninhabited, and soon Sarah and the others find themselves embroiled in the struggles of a small camp of people that came to the island years ago at the beginning of the outbreak. Here, men of science as well as civilians have begun working on a cure for the undead plague.

But then Sarah finds out that she is the key to the cure, that she alone could be the one to save the remaining humans on the planet from a fate worse than death. Only there is one hitch. The key to the cure of the plague is buried in her notes back at the underground bunker, and the only way to reach Sarah's lab is through hundreds upon hundreds of walking dead that now fill the corridors.

With a small commando force joining in, Sarah, John and McDermott have no choice but return to the fateful bunker where Sarah and the others had only narrowly escaped with their lives weeks ago.

But unknown to them, the bunker harbors an evil far worse than the walking dead. An enemy they believe long dead has resurfaced with only one goal…vengeance and death.

Though at first there was the Day of the Dead, eventually night must fall. Then there is only the *Sunset of the Dead*.

www.ingramcontent.com/pod-product-compliance
Ingram Content Group UK Ltd.
Pitfield, Milton Keynes, MK11 3LW, UK
UKHW022228230426
12048UKWH00016BA/1129